Sweet, Sweet Spirit

One Woman's Spiritual Journey to the Asbury College Revival

ENDORSEMENTS

Rebecca Price Janney has provided a way for readers to experience the tumultuous times of the 1960s and then the beautiful outpouring of God's Spirit on a small Christian college campus in Wilmore, Kentucky. I have heard many stories about the Revival and the ripple of changes that took place. I love "seeing" it through Melanie McKnight's eyes – the curiousity, the apprehension, the fear, the freedom, and finally, her joy. While this revival happened 50 years ago, the impact of this visitation still affects us today. To God be the Glory.

—Lisa Falin Harper, Director of Alumni Relations, Asbury University

For those of us old enough to remember the actual events, Rebecca Price Janney's newest novel *Sweet Sweet Spirit* triggers a flood of memories. The assassinations of Martin Luther King and Robert Kennedy, coupled with Vietnam protests, Woodstock and the sexual revolution caused many of us to feel that the very foundations of civilization were being shaken. And then, an unexplainable revival at a small liberal arts college in rural Kentucky! *Sweet Sweet Spirit* brings the reality of those years back into sharp focus. Melanie McKnight's journey 50 years ago is far more than a nostalgic trip down memory lane. Her pilgrimage from despair to hope and from doubt to faith has the capacity to inspire and encourage you and me, as we seek to make sense out of the chaotic vanity of our modern world.

—Stan Key, The Francis Asbury Society, President

Sweet Sweet Spirit brought back many memories from fifty years ago. I recommend this book for anyone who needs to remember that the Lord has done great and mighty works, or anyone who needs Hope to believe for the future of revived hearts.

—Tim Philpot, family court judge, trial lawyer, former state senator, author, and president of CBMC International

In remarkably true-to-life fashion, Rebecca Price Janney tells the story of Melanie McKnight, an aspiring young journalist with an ambivalent attitude toward religion. In the early chapters, we learn Melanie adores Bobby Kennedy and yearns for a closer relationship with her father. In that beginning, she may be a fictional character, but as the momentum builds toward the closing chapters, she could be any one of us who was there and had the very real and personal experience of coming face-to-face with the Holy Spirit. *Sweet, Sweet Spirit* is an inspiring rendition of the Gospel of Jesus Christ.

—**Homer Pointer**, 1970 Asbury Collegian editor; retired Navy JAG , assistant general FBI counsel, counsel to the President's Foreign Intelligence Advisory Board, part-time law professor

Fifty years ago, the campus of Asbury College (now University) and the lives of an entire community were changed when God showed up in a chapel service. The ripple effect traveled across the nation and even today is spoken of as a pivot point in many lives. Rebecca Price Janney has done an excellent job of telling the story in a fresh way by helping us to understand the current events the students in America were facing in the late 1960's and early 1970's.

—**Carolyn Ridley**, Asbury University Advancement Team, former Alumni Director

Rebecca Price Janney does a fabulous job making history come alive once again. In this story her heroine becomes enthralled with presidential candidate Robert Kennedy and sees him as the only hope for the nation. She is disillusioned by his unexpected assassination, but she finds hope in a movement that's sweeping the nation. Highly recommended.

—**Cynthia L Simmons**, author, speaker, coach, *Heart of the Matter* radio host

This story was a beautiful stroll into the past, through the intrigue of Bobby Kennedy's presidential run and the horror of his assassination, with nostalgic songs, Beetle cars and Beatles music, culminating in the breath-taking awe of God's presence at Asbury College and the revival that happened there. I love how Janney brings history to life and makes readers feel as if they, too, are living the pages of history and experiencing God's work through real and fictional characters. I'm so glad I had the opportunity to walk with Melanie, the main character, through the events of the late '60's and early '70s in America and see that world through her eyes, and so see God a little clearer.

—**Marlo Schalesky**, award-winning author of *Women of the Bible Speak Out*

Out of the tragic brokenness and racial tension that symbolizes America in the 1960s, the unlikely "Sweet Spirit" of renewal transforms lives. Dr. Janney has delivered a captivating romantic tale of Melanie and Jack, two souls caught in the crossfire and upheaval of the times—two souls forever touched by the loving hand of Almighty God!

—**Rick Steele**, publishing house editor, owner, Rick Steele Editorial Services

When revival broke out at Asbury College fifty years ago, the impact traveled throughout the nation and even abroad. Experience the event through Melanie McKnight, leading character in *Sweet, Sweet Spirit*, a captivating, fact-based fiction work by Rebecca Price Janney. Budding journalist Melanie, seventeen, struggles with the loss of her cherished mother and feels distanced from her father (an acclaimed journalist). Coupled with national crises (tragic deaths of Martin Luther King Jr. and Robert F. Kennedy), a weight of hopelessness settles on her young shoulders. Invited to the Asbury campus by a student (her special friend, Jack), perhaps she'll find healing and direction. A sweet spirit flavors this story!

—**Dianne Barker**, speaker, radio host, and author *I Don't Chase the Garbage Truck Down the Street in My Bathrobe Anymore!*

Sweet, Sweet Spirit

One Woman's Spiritual Journey to the Asbury College Revival

Rebecca Price Janney

PUBLISHING THE POSITIVE

ELK LAKE PUBLISHING INC.
Plymouth, Massachusetts

Cover and Interior Design: Derinda Babcock

Editor(s): Deb Haggerty

Author Represented By: WordWise Media Services

PUBLISHED BY: Elk Lake Publishing, Inc., 35 Dogwood Drive, Plymouth, MA 02360, 2020

Library Cataloging Data

Names: Janney, Rebecca Price (Rebecca Price Janney)

Sweet, Sweet Spirit: One Woman's Spiritual Journey to the Asbury College Revival / Rebecca Price Janney

216 p. 23cm × 15cm (9in × 6 in.)

Description: Melanie, depressed by the deaths of Dr. Martin Luther King and Robert F. Kennedy, finds answers at the Asbury College Revival.

Identifiers: ISBN-13: 978-1-951080-82-2 (trade) | 978-1-951080 83-9 (POD) | 978-1-951080 84-6 (e-book)

Key Words: Revival, Awakening, Religion, Christianity, 1960s, Assassinations, RFK, Spirituality

LCCN: 2020930924 Nonfiction

Do not put your trust in princes,
in mortal men, who cannot save.
When their spirit departs, they return to the ground;
on that very day their plans come to nothing.

Blessed is he whose help is the God of Jacob,
whose hope is in the Lord his God,
the Maker of heaven and earth,
the sea, and everything in them—
the Lord, who remains faithful forever.

He upholds the cause of the oppressed
and gives food to the hungry.
The Lord sets prisoners free,
the Lord gives sight to the blind,
the Lord lifts up those who are bowed down,
the Lord loves the righteous.

The Lord watches over the alien
and sustains the fatherless and the widow,
but he frustrates the ways of the wicked.

The Lord reigns forever,
your God, O Zion, for all generations.

Praise the Lord.
—Psalm 146:3-10 (NIV)

For Bert and Barbara Freeston, Debra Kinsley, Chip Price,
and Mary Burchfield Bohan

"The righteous live with integrity; happy are their children
who come after them."

—Proverbs 20:7 (CEB)

CHAPTER ONE

Melanie gazed at her cousin Mac's photo nestled among other family portraits, biting her lip to staunch her tears. Her cousin looked handsome and rugged in his olive green fatigues and crew cut, which he'd worn with great pride at his farewell party back in November, the one she'd missed. Shadows from her grandmother's votive candles leaped over the picture like a *danse macabre*, the church-like atmosphere in strong contrast to the dining room down the hall where her grandfather's portable TV blared. The only McKnight not to have been raised Roman Catholic, still she found a measure of peace in her grandmother's do-it-yourself shrine marking feasts and saints' days. They seemed to her a portal to knowing God. Even with her Sunday school upbringing, Melanie hadn't a clue how a person could actually know God. Maybe a person had to be a saint or, at least, really upstanding. Certainly not herself. None of her own prayers had done a bit of good to save Mac's life. *What if God doesn't care about us? What if he made the world and stepped aside, and we're on our own here?* She shuddered.

"There you are." Her father's famous baritone startled her. He flipped on a light switch muttering, "It's so depressing in here. Why are you avoiding your family?"

Melanie's eyes took a moment to adjust to the sudden brightness and intrusion. *And why does he keep forgetting I'm seventeen, not seven?* "I just don't feel like talking to anyone." She inclined her head toward Mac's photo, hoping her father would pick up her cue.

His tone softened. A little. "You were thinking about him."

She couldn't tell if his words were a question or an accusation. She proceeded with caution. "I'm just missing him, Dad. Don't you think it's weird nobody talks about him?"

The same thing had happened when her mother died.

Cliff McKnight moved a step closer to the picture, winced, and backed away as if he'd found himself at the edge of a sheer drop. Melanie took in her father's expression, then looked back at the photo of his wedding portrait next to Mac's picture.

"Dwelling on what happened doesn't bring back the dead."

"I'd just like to say his name or something."

"Don't." A muscle twitched over his right eye.

"Aunt Eileen and Uncle Al just act like nothing ever happened to their son. That can't be right."

"You would only cause hurt feelings."

And what about my feelings? This whole visit was turning out badly; surrendering might result in a truce. "I won't say anything."

He sighed, then smiled—a sight not often seen. "Now let's go back to the dining room. Mother has dessert ready."

She groaned. "Oh, Dad, if I put one more ounce in my stomach, I'll burst!"

"I guess you'll just have to burst then."

When he touched her right shoulder, warmth from his fingers radiated straight to her heart. She smiled up at him, and he quickly removed his hand and motioned toward the dining room.

Her Uncle Al sprawled in a corner, smoking a vile-smelling cigar and watching Ed Sullivan with the volume cranked up to accommodate Patrick McKnight's hearing loss. The latter, a man of few words, nodded to his granddaughter as she passed by.

"Sit down, sit down." Her grandmother motioned Melanie to a seat at the dining room table where she and her father sat across from his sister Eileen. All the other McKnights had come and already left the obligatory Sunday after-church visit featuring overcooked corned beef and the usual bickering.

Maureen McKnight went out of her way to make Melanie comfortable in the home smelling of candles, boiled cabbage, and Guinness, and although she appreciated the effort, Melanie always came away feeling as if she were in the family but not of it. She reluctantly accepted a slab of apple pie roughly the size of a recliner and set out to get at least a couple bites down, so she didn't insult her grandmother. An added bonus was the prolonged time she got to be with her father. A renowned ABC News anchorman, Cliff McKnight had been on the road since January with aspiring presidential candidates, and Melanie had only seen him twice. She'd been living in the interim with her maternal grandmother in Princeton.

Her Aunt Eileen poked her left shoulder. "Eat up, you're far too thin!"

Melanie smiled and took another bite, chewing slowly, listening as her grandfather and uncle discussed the weather, spring training, and the presidential primaries. Not a word about Vietnam or Mac. Out of the blue, she felt her chair begin to vibrate. Pictures on the walls rattled in time with the piercing guitar riffs of a Jimi Hendrix song detonating from the neighbor's adjoining duplex home.

"I don't know what the young people in this country are comin' to," her grandfather said above the racket. "Donald O'Shay does nothin' but listen to riotous music."

"And he never bathes or cuts his hair." Eileen leaned into Cliff as if this were worthy enough news for his nightly broadcast. "He came into the store the other day with stringy hair and bare feet. I felt like kicking him right out. No one respectable will shop there if they see riff-raff like him in the store."

Melanie couldn't help but think her maternal cousin Sandy might get along pretty well with this O'Shay fellow.

Uncle Al turned the TV's volume all the way up, the syncopated noises warring against each other.

All at once, Al started yelling, "Shh, everybody! The President's comin' on, and I want to hear him."

Heavy dark bands encroached on the screen at the top and bottom, a sure sign this *I-Love-Lucy*-era TV had seen better days. The neighbor's "riotous music," coupled with the TV's volume, nearly deafened Melanie.

Her grandmother paused in the doorway to the kitchen, leaning toward the set. "He's lookin' awful."

President Johnson bore a striking resemblance to a bassett hound about to lie down for a nap as he spoke for several minutes about de-escalating the war in Vietnam. Toward the end of the speech, he dropped his own bomb.

"This country's ultimate strength lies in the unity of our people. There is divisiveness among us all tonight. ... With America's sons in the fields far away, with America's future under challenge right here at home ... I do not believe that I should devote an hour or a day of my time to any personal partisan causes. … Accordingly, I shall not seek, and will not accept, the nomination of my party for another term as your president."

Cliff stood up so fast he nearly knocked over his chair. "I have to get to the station. Melanie, get your jacket."

His mother shouted above the din. "Ya haven't been here but two hours, Clifford. We don't hardly get to be seein' ya anymore, and now Melanie's with her other relations."

Melanie went to the living room to retrieve her navy blue pea coat and purse—the one holding a key to their New York apartment. One of these days, she'd get back there.

"C'mon Mel. Hurry up."

Her grandmother nipped at her dad's heels all the way down the front hallway. "How sorry I am you have to be leavin', Melly." She crushed the teenager to her breast.

"Uh, yuh, me too."

"Drive careful, Clifford. Don't be racin' the devil to get back to work in your showy car."

He muttered a distracted "Goodbye, Mother" as he and Melanie climbed into the Caddy. Cliff clicked on the radio to an all-news station and focused on the feverish commentary surrounding the president's decision as they pulled away from the Trenton neighborhood, leaving behind television eyes flickering inside the row homes.

A sinking sensation filled Melanie's stomach, not just because she was stuffed or because her father was lighting another Viceroy, but because she hated the very thought of going back to her Grandmother Markley's house. Although she wasn't entirely comfortable with the McKnights, she would rather have stayed with them while her father gallivanted around the country—at least they showed some affection.

She slumped into the leather seat. A few weeks earlier, she had told her dad how tough the adjustment to Princeton was, and he had basically told her to suck it up. "You have no other choice. You'll just have to make the most of the situation." A swell of loneliness broke over her. Her mother was gone. Jackie McKnight and Melanie's beloved Grandfather Markley had died within a year of each other five years ago. Their housekeeper and friend, Harriet Lemunyon, was in Ohio nursing a daughter with a shattered ankle.

Her father threw a life preserver to his drowning daughter. "Sorry to pull you out of there, Mel, but I need to get back to New York right away. I can just imagine the uproar everyone's in at the studio." His mind was already in the newsroom. "I don't think any of us saw this one coming. Imagine! Johnson resigning!"

Melanie tried to climb aboard his train of thought. "What does this mean to the Democrats?"

He took a drag from his cigarette, blowing the smoke away from her. "I'd say Gene McCarthy and Bob Kennedy have a decent shot at the presidency now."

"Who are you supporting?"

He frowned. "You know better than to ask such a question. I'm a newsman."

"Yes, I know, but I'm talking off the record, Dad, just for me."

"I could be a Republican for all you know."

"I don't think so." She hoped her attempt at a joke would relieve the sudden tension. "Grandmother Markley says you're as Democrat as you are Irish."

He looked like he'd just burned his finger on the cigarette lighter. "She does?"

Claire, the middle child of her mother's two sisters, once told her Cliff McKnight had always felt ill-at-ease around his mother-in-law despite his being one of America's top television journalists. To Edith Markley, he was still a Catholic from the "wrong side of the tracks."

Melanie rushed to appease him. "Oh, don't worry, Dad. She's just such a staunch Republican. She really likes you a lot."

"Well, I'm glad to hear that."

"Who do you think has the best chance of becoming president?"

"A month ago, I thought McCarthy was foolish to take on Johnson. You just don't run against an incumbent president. Then, I couldn't believe Kennedy had the gall to enter the race after the New Hampshire primary." He shook his head. "It's like Kennedy wanted McCarthy to test the waters because he was too cowardly to go first himself."

Although Robert Kennedy was her state's senator, Melanie didn't know much about him. She was, of course, aware her McKnight family idolized the Irish-Catholic Kennedys. Her grandmother even kept a photograph of the slain president in a frame in the dining room.

"Do you think RFK could be as good as his brother was as president?" Her father turned toward Princeton on Route One.

"Melanie, President Kennedy's the one who sent troops to Vietnam in the first place."

She sighed and turned to look out the window feeling so … inadequate.

They stood in the foyer of her other grandmother's home on Stockton Street where a recording of a Haydn concerto provided a deceptively soothing ambience. Melanie's sixty-three year-old grandmother stood before them in a gold lamé dressing gown with matching leather slippers—the housekeepers had the night off or Edith Ward Markley would not have stooped to answer the door. Melanie noticed her father shift from one foot to the other, a man completely poised around presidents, senators, and foreign dignitaries, but who was reduced to one of "those Trenton McKnights" around his mother-in-law.

Melanie broke the awkward silence. "Did you hear President Johnson announced he isn't going to run for re-election?"

"I did not. I have been reading." She turned to her son-in-law. "Well, Clifford, I guess you must be getting back to New York then. I was not expecting you this early."

"I'm afraid so, Mother Markley. I'd like to use your phone before I go."

"Help yourself." She waved him into the parlor.

Melanie caught a whiff of Chanel Number Five as her grandmother turned on a light for him. Edith Markley had known Coco Chanel in Paris long ago while tracing the outlines of a short-lived literary career, one resulting in the publication of a briefly best-selling historical novel, *Promise of Versailles*. With the book's royalties and her father's bequest—mostly the latter—Edith had built Ward House. After she married, she insisted upon staying put.

Melanie heard her father speaking as she wandered into the parlor. "Okay, Ralph, I should be there in about an hour, maybe less. Sure." He hung up and stood by the chintz-covered settee. "I hope she's not giving you a hard time," he said to Edith with the makings of a grin.

"I hardly know she's here."

Isn't that the truth!

Cliff gave his mother-in-law's cheek a requisite kiss, then did the same with his daughter.

"Thanks for today, Dad. I hope I see you again soon." She tried to sound casual, despite a mighty urge she felt to throw herself at him and demand he take her back to New York where she belonged.

Cliff made for the door. "Bye, Melanie."

He made no promises, offered no hope.

CHAPTER TWO

Melanie wasn't hungry after her father left, but she followed her grandmother to the kitchen for a cup of tea. Although the house boasted six sizeable bedrooms upstairs, Edith insisted on installing Melanie in what had once been maids' quarters to the left of the main entrance. She always believed her grandmother's coldness toward her was probably a result of her mother's marrying beneath the Ward-Markley social class.

"And what do you think of your father's running off on you again?" the woman asked, pouring Earl Grey.

The sharp words found their mark, but Melanie fended off the flaming dart. "Sometimes he has to leave at a moment's notice. Can you believe President Johnson dropped out of the race?"

Edith waved a hand. "That does not concern me. Politics is a dirty business."

"Well, I do think it's important to try to keep up with current events."

"Child …"

Oh brother.

"… in a few years you will be old enough to vote. When you do, I hope you will follow the Markley tradition and be a Republican. Until then, do not fill your mind with drivel."

As usual there was no room for anyone else's opinion, least of all hers, so Melanie rose wordlessly and rinsed her cup and saucer in the sink, careful to wipe off the pink crescent her lip gloss had left behind.

"I have homework." She moved toward her room. Although she had completed her assignments on Friday afternoon, she would find something to do. "Goodnight, Grandmother."

"Good night, child."

The "child" retreated to her room and turned on WIBG at the lowest possible volume, risking her grandmother's ire because music provided a necessary outlet for her. She decided to start an editorial for the school paper on President Johnson's withdrawal from the primaries and settled in at the mahogany desk to think and write. After she ended the rough draft an hour later, Melanie added, *Maybe now there can be a legitimate chance for peace in Vietnam.*

She snapped the last page out of the typewriter and leaned against the machine with her chin in her hands, staring at the silver frame on her desk containing the last family photo of her parents and her from Christmas 1962. Not quite a year later, Jacqueline Markley McKnight had died from breast cancer at thirty-three.

Unlike Edith Markley, Jackie had been kind-hearted and generous, a woman who had managed both her family and a part time career hosting a weekend cooking show on ABC in New York. Melanie smiled as she remembered how her mother permitted her to hang around the set after school while the show was being taped and how much fun she'd had eating the results of her mom's on-camera cuisine.

Melanie's gaze came to rest on her dad's face in the picture. He was smiling, but his expression betrayed the tension of being the husband of a seriously ill wife. If only her mother were still alive.

"Will you please turn off that annoying radio?" Edith thrust the door open, nearly scaring Melanie to death.

She dropped the picture, which clattered to the desk. Once she recovered her wits, she snapped off the music. "I honestly didn't think the volume would bother you."

"Believe me, it did. Goodnight, then." She closed the door and swished away.

"Oooohh!" Melanie got up and stomped into her bathroom to brush her teeth, sneering at the avocado linen towels in regimental formation on the rack. Edith insisted her housekeeper, Bea Gaylord, hang them precisely. If Melanie forgot to arrange them just-so on her way to school, she always found them "corrected" upon her return. She wiped her mouth hard on one now, leaving a streak of toothpaste behind, and threw the towel to the floor.

"For goodness' sake, wake up, Melanie!" Edith stood in the doorway at six o'clock the next morning. "You will be late for school if you continue this dallying."

Melanie willed her crusty eyes open and tried to fire back at the accusations, but she could only muster a croak.

Edith wagged her well-coifed head. "What did you say? I have told you countless times a young lady does not mumble. Is that really too much to ask?"

"I-can't-talk."

"Well, what about school?"

"I-don't-think-I-should-go." She tried to sit up, but her entire body ached.

"You have been sick a lot lately, Melanie." Edith prided herself on robust health and peered at the girl over her eyeglasses as if she were a rare and contagious specimen.

Melanie watched her grandmother stride into the bathroom where she produced a thermometer from the medicine cabinet. She sighed as Edith made an elaborate show of dusting off and rehanging the crumpled face towel, then shook the thermometer down until the mercury retreated past the numbers and plunged the slim glass tube under Melanie's tongue.

"I will return in five minutes."

"I will return in five minutes," she mimicked after her grandmother left.

Edith reappeared and checked the reading. "So, you do have a temperature, after all. Just like a McKnight. I suppose you will have to stay home, although I find this very inconvenient. My garden club meets here today, and I will be giving a talk. I cannot look after you."

As if you ever do.

"Do you think you can keep from getting underfoot?"

Melanie frowned, but Edith appeared not to notice.

"Bea will bring a tray for you. If you come to breakfast in your condition, I might catch whatever you have." Edith turned to leave. "I have always carried on no matter how sick I was."

CHAPTER THREE

She woke up following a long nap and went to the second floor library where she always felt closer to her mother and grandfather.

Melanie leafed through a family album she found on the end table after wrapping herself in the Black Watch stadium blanket her grandfather had always taken with him to Princeton football games. She lingered over photos of her mother, passing quickly a section devoted to her Aunt Clair, preferring to focus next on her Aunt Jane, who lived in Richmond, Virginia, with her husband, an OB/GYN.

After she finished, she was ready to start researching President Johnson and Robert Kennedy when a different book caught her eye—one she'd barely noticed before: *A Brief Genealogy of the Sharp Family*. She knew her grandfather's middle name had been Sharp, and there was a coat of arms behind his desk bearing the inscription "Scharfenstein." She decided to look into some of her family's past, discovering in the initial pages how the Scharfenstein's had come to America in the early 1720s and quickly changed their name to "Sharp." They'd established a farm and blacksmithing operation in Warminster, Bucks County.

"This is interesting." Melanie spoke aloud as she read, 'The Reverend Henry Sharp was educated at the nearby Log College by William Tennent, a prominent Presbyterian minister during the First Great Awakening. Henry, and later his wife, Catherine, became traveling companions of the renowned revivalist George Whitefield and later ministered to Presbyterian congregations in Bucks and Northampton Counties."

I didn't realize there were any ministers in our family. Mom never said anything to me, although she was pretty involved with the Presbyterian Church. My grandmother certainly doesn't talk about them, but then they were Grandfather's family, not hers. She wished she could somehow sit down with this Henry and his wife to ask them why God wouldn't cure a mother's cancer or save a young man's life in the heat of battle. She wasn't exactly angry at God, reasoning he had an entire world to look after so surely he dropped a ball now and then. What would it take, however, to get him to notice—to save the day?

After researching her family history, Melanie was ready to find some books about President Johnson so she could comment intelligently on his withdrawal from the race, then say something in her newspaper editorial about Robert Kennedy's and Eugene McCarthy's chances of winning. Her search proved disappointingly fruitless. She found plenty of copies of her grandmother's *Promise of Versailles*, but the only remotely pertinent title was *Profiles in Courage* by John F. Kennedy, published in 1956 before he'd been president. She opened the volume, doubtful there would be anything inside about JFK's younger brother. When there wasn't, she replaced the book. This was, after all, a Republican household.

By dinner time, Melanie's throat still resembled burning sand, and while she would have preferred to go to bed with a bowl of chicken noodle soup, her grandmother insisted she come to the dining room "like a normal person." She didn't bother to ask how Melanie was feeling.

A gilded chandelier shone softly above the dining room's exquisite cherry furniture, which flaunted a mirror-like finish thanks to Bea's scrupulous housekeeping. Chintz curtains harmonized with the table linens, and an enormous arrangement of white tulips and some sort of moss dominated the table, having been much-exclaimed over during the garden party. Edith was in an especially good mood, prattling about this and that aspect of the gathering, glowing over the governor's wife's presence.

Trying to look like she cared, Melanie nodded sporadically and muttered obligatory "uh huh's" while allowing the coarse salt on her roast chicken to bathe her throat. After finishing a bowl of blueberry cobbler with vanilla ice cream for dessert, Melanie asked if she could watch the evening news, the only format in which her father became accessible to her every week night.

Edith sipped coffee from a porcelain cup, as contemplative as if Melanie had just sought her consent to enter a convent.

"You may." Her permission sounded like a decree.

Melanie left the table, carefully putting the napkin next to her plate. Surprisingly Edith rose too. "I think I'll join you."

They left the dining room as Bea slipped in to clear the table. The TV was in the library since Edith had a general distaste for "the idiot box" and wanted the set as far removed from the main living area as possible.

Edith sat as if at attention on a wingback chair while Melanie turned on the TV and curled up on the couch with her grandfather's blanket. ABC's lead-in music began playing and vaporous images on the color TV chased each other before they clearly revealed Ralph Brody's craggy visage. He'd gotten his big chance at the anchor's chair when Cliff McKnight had requested a temporary leave from those duties to cover the primaries.

> Good evening. A political earthquake shook the nation's Capital last night when, in a televised address to the nation on Vietnam, President Lyndon Baines Johnson announced he would not seek or accept the Democratic nomination for the presidency. Our correspondent in Washington, Kent Armstrong, files this report.

Melanie listened as the field reporter spoke of tremors shaking the Washington establishment, wondering whether her father would follow with his own story. The anchorman reappeared three minutes later.

> The President's declaration has deeply affected the candidacies of Eugene McCarthy, now considered by many pundits to be the Democratic front-runner, and his arch-rival, New York Senator Robert Kennedy. First we have this report from the McCarthy campaign in Wisconsin.

As Brody went on, lively images of RFK burst on the screen behind him—people clutching his hands and coat sleeves while he passed through a huge crowd.

> Less than one month ago, Senator Robert F. Kennedy grappled with the decision whether to challenge President Johnson for their party's nomination. Some Kennedy associates urged him not to run, predicting his candidacy would split the party, while others told him he had to run because of his strong

anti-war convictions and his perceived ability to reconcile the nation's racial divide. However, not even the Senator could have anticipated last night's White House bombshell. Bringing this report from the Kennedy camp in Boston is our chief political correspondent, Cliff McKnight.

"There he is."

Every time Melanie's father came on TV, Edith said the same thing. In spite of her severe indictment of television and her personal distaste for Cliff's humble origins, she relished hearing her friends exclaim over his success. Melanie found this irritating and not a little amusing.

This is Cliff McKnight reporting live from Boston where Senator Robert Kennedy is in a brand new race for the Democratic presidential nomination.

She leaned closer to catch the interviews with key people in Kennedy's circle, including campaign manager Steve Smith and press secretary Frank Mankiewicz.

"Now there's a real chance the war in Vietnam will end," Smith said.

Melanie wondered what made him so confident his candidate could stop the fighting but thrilled at the hope he offered.

"We also talked to the candidate himself earlier today," Cliff said.

She raised her eyebrows when forty-two-year-old Kennedy appeared, taken aback by his youthfulness and Pepsodent smile. *This is a politician?* She leaned forward for a better look.

On his right stood his wife Ethel in a Lilly Pulitzer mini-dress, along with five children of various ages, all sporting their parents' toothy smiles. In the background, dozens of people in their teens and twenties held "RFK for President" signs and chanted, "RFK! RFK! RFK!" Melanie was reminded of the time the Beatles first appeared on the Ed Sullivan Show.

"What a big family! How many kids does he have, Grandmother?"

"Kids are the offspring of goats, Melanie, and I assure you, where Senator Kennedy is concerned, there are more children than meet our eyes."

"More?"

"At last count, ten."

"Ten ki--uh, children?"

"Yes." Edith sniffed. "Just like an Irish-Catholic."

Melanie rolled her eyes and focused instead on the TV, wondering how the older, less glamorous Eugene McCarthy hoped to stand a chance against this youthful exuberance.

Her father shouted into his microphone.

> Senator Kennedy, do you believe, as some assert, that your candidacy, announced just two weeks ago, caused the President to withdraw from the race?

Cliff tipped the microphone in Kennedy's direction.

> I'm certainly as surprised as anyone else.

She was finding him completely compelling.

> President Johnson made a thoughtful decision based on what he believes is in the best interests of the country, Kennedy said. He has served the American people faithfully.

> How does this affect your own chances for the nomination? Cliff asked.

> I think they've always been good. Kennedy seemed to be joking. Of course, this definitely improves them, but we mustn't forget Senator McCarthy is a formidable opponent.

> How much of an edge do you think Eugene McCarthy has, considering his campaign machine has been functioning longer than yours?

> I think the playing field is more level since the President's announcement.

Suddenly a child jerked the lower part of Kennedy's suit jacket, and the cameraman panned for the shot. RFK leaned over to listen, Cliff McKnight grinning at the scene.

He'd have a coronary if I ever interrupted him like that.

The senator touched his child's cheek, then took her hand.

> You'll have to excuse me, Cliff, but there's a family crisis. It seems one of our dogs has defected, perhaps to the McCarthy camp, and I need to help find him.

Melanie's mouth fell open when her father laughed.

> Thank you for your time, Senator, and good luck finding the dog.

Cliff spoke into the camera as the candidate and his family departed.

> As you can see, Kennedy is confident the President's announcement will mean more support for his own campaign. The senator will have an uphill struggle in Tuesday's primary, however, in Eugene McCarthy's home state of Wisconsin where polls give the native son at least a twenty-percent lead. Kennedy will have to wait until the Pennsylvania and Indiana contests to see how far he can ride on the crest of President Johnson's remarkable withdrawal from the race. It also remains to be seen whether Vice-President Humphrey will now enter the race. This is Cliff McKnight reporting for ABC News with the Kennedy campaign in Boston."

Edith Markley pursed her lips. "I think that is terrible."

"What's terrible?"

"The way Robert Kennedy permitted his daughter to disturb him in the middle of an important interview." She rose from her chair. "If he wants to be President of the United States, he had better get his own house in order."

Long after she'd gone to bed, Melanie carried the image of Bobby Kennedy and his daughter in her heart.

❧

"Now, then, what other ideas are there for the next few issues?" The editor's Faye Dunaway-style hair swung with intended precision as she looked from one person to the next.

Melanie spoke up. "I think we should do something on the presidential elections."

"We never covered politics before. They're such a crashing bore."

Wendy Jarvis was beside herself. "You're out of touch with what's going on in this country."

"I hardly consider myself out of touch." As Terry Mayfield flipped her hair again, Melanie could almost read the senior's thoughts: *Two weeks ago Vidal Sassoon cut my hair in London. I am a jet-setter who skis with Jean-Claude Killy, knows Julie Andrews on a first-name basis, and has preferred accounts at Sak's and Bonwit's.*

As she preened, Bill Hoffnagle passed gas loudly, and the situation completely broke down, leaving even Wendy shrieking with laughter. Terry's face went white, and she slapped the desk top with the palm of her hand. "I don't know why I put up with you Neanderthals. You might as well be in a public school!" She turned on Melanie. "It never used to be like this, McKnight."

The hilarity dissolved into a series of low "Oooh's."

Jack Clyde spoke up. "You're right, Terry, things are different since Melanie joined the staff, and in my opinion, they're a whole lot better. I think we should profile each candidate and his positions on important issues. The articles could be a great way to help students understand the political process."

Wendy was practically bouncing up and down. "Hey, wait a minute! Your dad knows all the candidates, right, Melanie?"

She nodded, not wanting to appear stuck up because of her father's position, unlike Terry.

The editor's voice dripped. "How about using your father's considerable influence to get those stories, Melanie? Isn't that why the headmaster made me put you on the newspaper?"

"You should know all about coattails, Terry," Wendy said. "Your mother has pulled you along on enough of them."

"The Pennsylvania primary's coming up soon," Jack said, turning his green eyes on her. "I'd love to help you with the stories, if that's okay."

Melanie wondered how she'd be able to get in touch with the candidates, let alone her dad. Contacting him when he was on the road was always challenging.

Wendy squealed. "Oh, this could be so exciting, you two! Just think, Melanie, you could talk to Eugene McCarthy, Hubert Humphrey, and Richard Nixon!"

"Don't forget Bobby Kennedy. He's young, and a lot of young people follow him," Melanie said.

She fell into a daydream about meeting the senator, being close to his idealism and energy, having him turn his smile on her. This was something she could get excited about during the bleak months trapped in her grandmother's house. She'd grown up around newsmakers, watched them come into her home and greet her parents on the sidewalks of New York. How hard could getting an interview with him be?

"I'll get the Bobby Kennedy story," she said. "I can't promise about anyone else, but I will definitely interview Kennedy."

CHAPTER FOUR

Jack smiled as Melanie, sagging under the weight of a pile of books yet looking completely unburdened, approached his table in the school's library.

She sat across from him and said, "Most of these are about President Kennedy, but there should be stuff about Bobby in them too, don't you think?" She paused. "What did you come up with?"

"I'm researching Richard Nixon. Did you know he was a war hero like JFK?"

"No."

"And they're about the same age—or ... *were*, I guess I should say"

She chewed on her number two pencil, running her tongue over the smoothness of the yellow paint. "Somehow Nixon always seemed so much older."

Jack tapped the notebook with the back of his fingers. "Maybe so, but from what I've read, Nixon is a man of much greater substance than President Kennedy was."

Melanie was about to protest when Jack uttered, "Uh-oh."

The librarian hovered over them. "I would sincerely appreciate it if you took your conversation outside."

Jack smiled up at her. "I'm sorry, Mrs. Cline. We're just discussing an article for *The Monitor*, and I guess we got carried away."

Melanie watched as the woman thawed right before her eyes.

"All right, you may stay. Just don't talk so much—or so loudly."

"How did you do that?" Melanie whispered.

"I've got the knack." He blew on his fingernails and rubbed them against his blazer lapel.

Melanie started reading again, pausing over haunting images of President Kennedy's assassination—the moments just before the fatal shot, Jackie Kennedy lunging over the rear of the car ... people weeping outside

Parkland Hospital. When she'd had enough of that dark event, she focused on information about the thousand other days of his administration, about RFK's role as attorney general and his campaign against organized crime. After filling eight pages of a notebook with information, Melanie put down her pen.

"Looks like you hit pay dirt," Jack said. "I've been thinking, it'll probably be a while before we can actually interview any candidates, but based on our research, we could at least profile candidates over the next few weeks."

Melanie didn't mind the way Jack inserted himself into her plan, as long as he didn't try to horn in on Bobby Kennedy.

"I like your idea."

"We can get all the information we need right here, then when the Pennsylvania primary comes, we can try to interview some of the candidates since we're close by."

"I hate to put a damper on this, Jack, but I'm nervous they won't take time for a couple of high school reporters." Melanie leaned her head against her palm.

"Normally they wouldn't, but your dad can help, right?"

"Well, I don't know. He's constantly moving around. Even I don't always know where he is." She couldn't bring herself to look at him. "Maybe he could help us get at least one interview." She knew just which one.

❖

They left the building, a late afternoon sun splashing against their faces while a clipping March wind blew open Melanie's pea coat. Checking her watch, she realized the last bus had gone.

"I have my car, Melanie. I'll be glad to drive you home."

She smiled into Jack's face, framed by wind-blown wisps of light brown, slightly curly hair. Although they didn't agree on politics, she liked him.

"Thanks, Jack."

"No problem!" He paused and scanned the parking lot, scratching his chin. "Now, let's see. I think he's in the student lot behind Main."

"He?"

"Sam. My car."

"Why in the world did you name your car 'Sam'?"

"I'm not really sure. Guess I just liked the name."

They walked past guys returning from baseball practice.

"Hey, Jack!" A stocky guy nudged Jack's arm and winked as he passed by, his voice low and suggestive. "How's it *goin'* for you?"

Jack blew off the comment, chattering as they passed daffodils waving along the parking lot's banks. "There's Sam."

She clapped her hands. "Oh, I love Beetles!"

"John, Paul, George, or Ringo?"

"This kind, silly, but just for the record, Paul."

Jack opened the passenger door for her with great ceremony.

"My mother had a Beetle." Sweet memories filled Melanie as she climbed in and felt the familiar contour of the vinyl seat and gazed at the recognizable dashboard.

"Want me to put the top down?"

"Sure. May I help?"

"Nah. No help needed—just pop two levers, and push it back."

"What year is Sam?" she asked as he went to work.

"A '63. I bought him when I got my license in October."

Finally, Jack plopped into the driver's seat. "What's your address?" he asked when the engine kicked in, and he turned on the AM radio. "Ferry Cross the Mersey" was on.

"I love this song. Oh, I'm at 242 Stockton Street."

"That's not far at all."

She blushed. "Like I said, I could walk."

"And waste the opportunity for a nice drive?" He paused. "Do you have time for a nice drive?"

"Sure." She was in no hurry to return to her grandmother's.

"Do you mind the radio?" Jack steered onto Mercer Street in the direction of the Princeton Battlefield, the engine's hum like the sound of a thousand rubber bands against as many bike spokes.

"Not at all. I listen to this station all the time."

"Me, too! I like Hy Lit at night when I'm doing my homework. He's a blast."

"Do you mean 'Hyski O'Roonie McVoutie O'Zoot?'" Melanie giggled.

"The very one."

She smoothed her hair back, feeling a little like Grace Kelly riding next to Cary Grant in *To Catch a Thief.*

"Some people don't like Top 40s music," she said. "My cousin Sandy thinks only Janis Joplin and Jimi Hendrix have anything meaningful to say, but their style gives me the creeps."

"The drug part? Uh, excuse me," he said, reaching across the seat where he located a pair of aviator sunglasses in the glove compartment. When he brushed against Melanie's knee, she shivered.

"I don't like the whole drug scene." She paused. "Promise you won't tell if I let you know what singer I really like?"

Jack crossed his heart like a child would, then leaned closer, Melanie smelling a clean, powdery scent clinging to his hair and clothes. "Promise."

"Andy Williams."

He gave a laugh. "We may not agree on politics, Melanie, but with Andy Williams, we are as one. I always watch his TV show, and 'Moon River' is my favorite song."

"You're kidding!"

Spontaneously, they broke into an off-key rendition of the soulful ballad.

"*Breakfast at Tiffany's* is my favorite movie," Melanie said. "You know how Holly Golightly liked Tiffany's so much because she felt nothing bad could ever happen to her there?" Jack nodded. "I'd love to find such a place."

Jack regarded her curiously as "The Ballad of Bonnie and Clyde" came on. "Have you seen this movie?" he asked.

Melanie was puzzled. "What movie?"

"*Bonnie and Clyde?*"

She assumed a dignified accent. "My grandmother doesn't think the film is 'suitable.'" Using her own voice she added, "Can you imagine, at my age forbidding me to see a movie?"

"Does your grandmother live with you?"

"The other way around, actually."

"Oh. I guess you pretty much have to do what she says then. Actually, she may have a point. My parents don't like a lot of the current music and movies."

Melanie thought she should say something about her situation. "I've been living with my grandmother since the Christmas break because of my dad's work."

"Where's home?"

"New York."

"City?"

"Uh-huh." She pictured her parents' elegant apartment over-looking Central Park, just a few blocks from Jackie Kennedy's. Occasionally, Melanie would see the former First Lady on her walks, and once, Mrs. Kennedy stopped to talk when Melanie was with her father.

"I guess your dad's pretty busy traveling with the Kennedy campaign, then?"

"He's constantly on the road. At first, we thought our housekeeper could just stay with me—she's been part of our family since I was a baby— but then her daughter broke a leg and arm skiing, so Mrs. Lemunyon is looking after her in Ohio. Mine is strictly a temporary situation." She added, "My mother died a little over four years ago."

"I'm sorry."

She was pleased he didn't say anything stupid or ask for all the gory details the way some people did. Rather, he simply seemed to observe a respectful silence.

"Where do you live, Jack?" she asked above a radio car commercial.

"In Lawrenceville, on your road, actually. I guess you know Stockton Street becomes Route 206."

She nodded. "Where does your dad work?"

"My parents own a medical text book company."

"Like for schools?"

"And medical organizations." After turning around in the battlefield lot, Jack headed back toward town.

"Sounds interesting. So what do you want to do after school?"

"The truth is, I'm sensing a call to be a television journalist. I feel pretty weird telling his daughter this, but ... Cliff McKnight is sort of my hero. I mean, you might get the wrong impression and think I'm trying to brown-nose you or something."

Melanie actually had known some kids over the years who wanted to be friends because her parents were celebrities, but Jack didn't strike her as that type at all, especially because of his honest confession. "He is the best in the business, but then I'm biased." She paused. "What do you mean by sensing a call?"

"I believe God created each of us for a purpose, and the work he wants us to do is part of that—so a calling."

She chewed on his words for a long moment. "Do you really think God cares what we do with our lives?"

"Of course. I want to honor him with the skills he's given me. Don't you?"

"I never really thought about life that way."

"What work do you want to do?"

She was grateful for the shift away from God talk. "I'm thinking of journalism too—print journalism. I love to write."

"I'm not surprised. You'd make an excellent journalist. You have a strong drive, and you aren't afraid to work hard to get a good story."

Melanie gestured to point out her grandmother's impressive residence as they drew near. "There's a circular driveway, so you can pull in and drop me off."

As Jack drove onto the private roadway, she groaned at the sight of a Studebaker covered with flowers and peace signs. "That's my cousin Sandy's car. She's an artist."

She didn't tell him her cousin had been kicked out of Miss Porter's for smoking marijuana with a Negro boy who'd spent the night in her room, or that at twenty-one, Sandy had just earned her GED and opened a funky shop in New Hope, Pennsylvania, where she sold art and, Melanie strongly suspected, drugs. She toyed with the idea of asking Jack to come in, but she wasn't sure what the climate would be like. Of course, if Sandy had just come to visit their grandmother, then all would be warmth and friendliness—surprisingly the two of them got along well. If Claire was also there, bitter winds would howl. Melanie decided not to.

"Thanks for letting me drive you around," Jack said.

"Thank *you*."

As the car idled, he became animated. "I have an idea, Melanie. Let's go to Firestone Library at the university after school tomorrow and research the candidates there. They have a great collection of newspapers and magazines."

"I especially want to learn more about Bobby Kennedy."

"You're pretty determined to interview him, aren't you?"

"Yes. I'm going to try to talk to my dad tonight."

He got out of the car and opened the door for her. She was hoping he'd drive away before she had to ring the doorbell and wait for someone to let her in, because her grandmother hadn't given her a key.

"See you tomorrow!" she called over her shoulder as he pulled away and Joe Gaylord opened the door.

Following dinner and the evening news, Melanie phoned the network, identified herself, and asked where she might reach her father on the campaign trail. The man gave Melanie the name and number of a hotel in Madison, Wisconsin, but when she dialed, her dad wasn't in his room. She left a message at the front desk for him to call her as soon as possible, then began a vigil near the phone while she did her homework. By the time her grandmother ordered Melanie to bed at eleven o'clock, Cliff had not returned the call.

CHAPTER FIVE

Jack raised his voice above the din as the mass exodus began at the end of the school day. "Are we still on for Firestone Library?"

"You bet."

"Hey, what's this about the Princeton libes?" Bill Hoffnagle came up behind them with ever-present Cindy alongside. His unbuttoned school blazer revealed a Rolling Stones tee shirt, and Melanie wondered why he never got caught breaking the rules.

"We're going after school to get information about our candidates," Jack said.

"Not a bad idea. Maybe we should all go so we can get that stupid history assignment out of the way. There's a lot I'd rather be doing tonight than writing an essay about a presidential candidate." He winked at his girlfriend. "Do you have your car today, Jack?"

"Yes."

"Then how's about we all squeeze into Sam and go together since it's raining sheep and goats?" Bill playfully punched Jack, who was considerably shorter than his friend.

"All right." He gave Bill a mock left hook.

"I need to check with my mom first, but I'm pretty sure I can go," Cindy said.

Bill pointed to her like a drill sergeant. "You must come. Otherwise, no fun for me."

"Come with me while I make the call."

Melanie sat in the car with Jack, discussing the campaign, when Cindy and Bill came bouncing toward them and piled into the VW. Jack drove to Firestone Library, Cindy chattering nonstop.

"I wonder if sardines ever come in navy blue uniforms," Bill said.

"You sure look like one with your legs running up the back of the seat like that!" Cindy howled as she thumped Bill's arm and he gave her playful shove, making the little car rock.

Jack glanced back at his friends through the rearview mirror. "Hey, could you guys save the gymnastics for PE?"

"Sure thing, buddy. Hear that, Twiggy? We have to behave."

They folded their hands in their laps and plastered prim expressions on their faces—collapsing in frenzied laughter seconds later.

"Maybe you should have sat up front, Bill," Jack said. "Your legs are a lot longer than Melanie's."

"How would *you* know?"

Melanie blushed to the very roots of her hair. A side-long look at Jack informed her the comment had affected him similarly.

Bill's multi-track mind quickly shifted to another subject, which Melanie considered a blessing. Had Cindy been given the last word, no doubt she would have made another embarrassing aside about Melanie and Jack's growing friendship.

"Hey, turn on the radio, will you, J?" Bill asked. "I need some music."

"What do you want, B?"

"How about Hyski O`Roonie McVoudie O`Zoot?" Cindy asked. "He's always good for laughs."

"Hy Lit doesn't come on until six, but I'll put on WIBG anyway." When he did, a Rolling Stones song filled the car with its sassy lyrics.

"My mother thinks this song is decadent," Cindy said.

Mimicking a TV reporter, Bill held an imaginary microphone to her. "What do you think, young lady?"

"I like the song. Now ask my friend Melanie."

Squirming in her seat she muttered, "The song is suggestive." She hoped Cindy's interest would be mollified so they could move to the next, hopefully less volatile, matter on Bill's cluttered mind.

"I heard Ed Sullivan made the Rolling Stones change the words before he would let them sing the tune on his show," Bill said. He started playing an air guitar, his gyrations prompting Jack to ask him once again to stop rocking the car.

"Mick Jagger wasn't too happy. Every time he sang the different words, he made a face." Cindy swooned. "He is so groovy."

"He has hippopotamus lips." Bill squooshed up his own lips to make them look bigger.

"The song's about free love," Cindy said. "Do you believe in free love, Bill?"

Melanie's ears turned scarlet.

"My parents don't approve, and neither does my church. Personally, I don't see what the fuss is about. I mean if consenting adults want to get it on, it's nobody else's business, right, Jack?"

"Which church do you go to?" he asked.

"Hopewell Episcopal. Can you believe my parents still drag me to Sunday School?" He banged out the song's beat on his thighs.

"How about you, Mel? Where do you stand—or lay—on the issue?" Cindy laughed at her own joke.

Melanie shot a "Will-you-please-shut-up" look over her left shoulder. "I'd rather not say." The truth was, she thought the church she'd been raised in would teach a more traditional approach to morality which, for some reason, remained important to her. She didn't feel like casting her thought pearls to these swine, however.

Jack came to her rescue. "Let's discuss something else, you guys."

Melanie couldn't help but wonder what he would have said about "free love." Since he was such a religious guy, she figured she already knew the answer. At least she hoped she did. There was just something about the freewheeling morality of the times she found unsettling.

When the foursome emerged from Firestone Library at dusk, old-fashioned lampposts flickered, attempting to illuminate a drizzling cheerlessness. Melanie, however, was glowing from within. Her further research into Robert Kennedy's life had kindled her spirit, and she was bursting to tell Jack—alone—what she'd discovered, knowing the others could never understand her passion. Maybe there was some way to shake them, like dropping them off, then going somewhere with Jack for a Coke or another drive around town. At the library entrance, Melanie asked what time they all had to get home.

"Oh, not for a while," Cindy said. "We don't eat until seven most of the time."

Bill nodded his head. "Same here."

"I don't have to leave right away either. Do you want to do something else?" Jack looked at Melanie in what she thought was a hopeful manner.

"Hey, guys, I'm getting just a little too damp out here." Cindy pulled her school blazer more tightly around herself. "The hair you know. How about going to Mimi's?"

"Count me in," Bill said. "I scream, you scream, we all scream for ice cream!"

Melanie felt like screaming all right.

"Hey, Mel, I looked up your Bobby Kennedy." Bill spoke around a large mouthful of fudge ripple ice cream with banana sauce, a large drop clinging to his chin. "That guy has more kids than the old lady who lived in the shoe. Doesn't Ethel ever get tired?" He nudged Cindy.

Melanie noticed Jack sigh and raise his eyes to the ceiling.

"I don't know how Ethel stays so skinny," Cindy said.

"I could tell you." Bill made Groucho Marx eyes at her, and Melanie felt heat rise into her face, wanting very much to shut them up.

"How many kids do they have?" Jack asked, seeming sincere.

Melanie leaped into the conversation heart-first—RFK was her territory, and she was going to put her friends on higher ground. "Ten. He's great father, too. Just look at these."

Handing her cone to Cindy, Melanie dug into her book bag and produced a volume about the Kennedys filled with photos of the senator and his family. In some, he played with his and Jackie Kennedy's children, rollicking in pools, gliding down ski slopes, paddling canoes, romping on the front lawn with colossal dogs. Other photos gripped her imagination—Bobby visiting migrant farm workers in upstate New York who lived in a broken down bus, the children lying on a mattress covered with flies. In one picture, the senator held a child smudged with dirt.

Particularly poignant for her were the snapshots of him with Martin Luther King Jr, leading her to recall the time she'd met Dr. King when her father introduced her to him at the studio. She smiled at the memory of the sweet way he'd touched the back of her head and smiled.

Her friends regarded the pictures with mild interest, but she was on a roll as she commentated. "The other night on the news my dad was interviewing Bobby, and one of his little girls interrupted. Can you believe the senator cut the interview short to help her find a stray dog?"

"Imagine, being moony-eyed over a politician." Bill elbowed Cindy again, and she giggled. Melanie felt as if she'd been stung by a hornet.

An ill wind suddenly blew through the door.

Cindy muttered behind her right hand. "Here comes the May Fiend with her entourage."

The editor and two other seniors strutted over to their booth like models on a Paris runway. "Hi, guys, what's up?"

"Melanie has a crush on Robert Kennedy," Bill said. "She's going to get you an exclusive, you know."

Melanie wondered whether murdering him would result in a first degree charge, or if, under the circumstances, the state of New Jersey might consider her action to be justifiable homicide.

"Oh, my, didn't I tell you?" Terry put her leather-gloved hand to her mouth.

Jack eyed her. "Tell us what?"

"I've canceled those articles on the candidates. I asked around, and there just wasn't enough interest." She yawned.

"You can't do that, Terry. We made those decisions at a meeting," Jack said.

"Yes, darling, I know." She leaned close enough to caress his shoulder, but he pulled away. "Still, as *The Monitor's* editor-in-chief, I have to do what's in the paper's best interests. Don't worry, though, I'll give *you* a better assignment." She kissed two of her fingers and touched the top of his head. "Ciao!"

She and her friends slinked away, and Cindy fumed. "I can't believe she did that to you, Melanie. She's really out to get you."

"Well, you guys certainly didn't help. Why did you have to say that, Bill? You just blurt whatever's on your mind."

"Sorry, Melly." He squeezed her arm, but she jerked away. "I was just trying to have a little fun."

"Sometimes you need to think first, Bill," Jack said. "Now Terry's pulled the plug on Melanie's project." He pushed his ice cream soda away.

"I'm not giving up." Melanie gathered her courage and sat up straighter, noticing Terry's smirk as she waited in line.

"What can you do?" Cindy asked. "As far as she's concerned, Terry's like God on the newspaper."

Melanie clenched her hands. "I'm not sure how just yet, but I will interview Bobby Kennedy and have my story published."

Bill's eyes narrowed. "Why's it so important to you? He's just a sneaky politician."

"What do you mean?"

"Would he really have gotten this far if he weren't riding on his brother's coattails? I mean, think about it—he's a senator from New York, but he's not even from New York."

She bristled, refusing to believe this was in any way underhanded. While studying at Firestone, her heart had been even more strangely warmed by Bobby Kennedy, touched by the way he'd grieved so deeply after JFK's assassination, how the sorrow had seasoned him. Melanie was intrigued. At roughly the same time her mother had died, Bobby had been struggling through the loss of his brother, a man of sorrows, also acquainted with grief—someone who could understand her own suffering. To meet him would provide a connection with someone who could relate to everything she felt, and inspire her to become better.

Bill interrupted her thoughts. "Even if you do meet Kennedy, who's going to publish your story?"

She suddenly found herself in the midst of a Tasmanian Devil-variety inspiration, but Terry broke in again.

"Tootles, kids!" she called, sauntering out the door with a hot fudge sundae.

Cindy sneered after her. "I hope she gets as fat as Mama Cass."

Bill and Jack laughed. Melanie was a thousand miles away.

"What on earth is going on in there?" Bill pretended to lift the top of her head and look underneath the "hood."

She shook him off. "Forget *The Mercer Monitor*. We can do our series on the candidates for the local paper, Jack."

"Right." Bill stretched the word into several syllables. "Why would *The Princeton Packet* publish stories from a couple of teenagers?"

"That's exactly why they would." Melanie turned her animated face on Bill. "Jack and I could give *Packet* readers a young adult perspective on the candidates."

"I doubt many people in Princeton would be interested in a Democrat like Bobby Kennedy," Cindy said.

"The paper needs to cover both parties." Melanie wasn't about to forfeit any ground.

Jack nodded. "I think it's worth a try. The worst the editor can say is 'no.'"

"Will you go with me to *The Packet's* office tomorrow after school, Jack? I'd like to get started on this right away."

He held out his hand for her to shake. "We have a deal, partner."

At dinner, she poked at her food while her grandmother complained about her lack of gratitude. As quickly as possible, Melanie excused herself to watch the news, thankful Edith had a meeting of the hospital board of trustees.

The first political report of the telecast dealt with the Wisconsin primary, with ABC projecting Eugene McCarthy winning handily. Melanie was disappointed but reminded herself Bobby's name hadn't even appeared on the ballot, and, her father had explained—very much to her liking— Kennedy wasn't overly concerned about the loss because of his late entry.

Next on the report was footage of Kennedy's visit to an Indiana ghetto in preparation for the state's May 7 contest. Melanie couldn't believe how cut up the candidate's hands were from people grabbing and shaking them. She'd read in one of the papers at the library RFK had begun using a personal bodyguard to prevent admirers from pulling him out of his open touring car. She needed to reach him as well, and that meant calling her dad while her grandmother was away. The only problem was Edith would find out about the furtive call once she got the next month's phone bill, and then she'd probably go ballistic, maybe even put the phone off limits entirely. Melanie huffed in frustration. There had to be a better way.

There was. After all, the Gaylords had their own phone.

She dialed the number at ABC News and asked where her father was staying, her initial excitement dissolving into humiliation at the questioning tone of the worker's voice. She hated chasing after a father who either was too busy or too uncaring to call, wondering what the guy on the other end must think as he brought her up to date about her dad's latest whereabouts. Melanie wrote the information on a notepad, then called her father's hotel. He wasn't there.

"He has checked in, hasn't he?" she asked the desk clerk.

"Yes, but at present he's not answering his phone," the woman said.

"Would you please tell him his daughter called, and I'd like him to get back to me tonight? This is very important."

Apparently, her father didn't think so.

"How may I help you?" The woman's voice was as crisp as her appearance.

"We, uh, we'd like to sp—uh, talk to the editor." Melanie regretted not letting Jack go first.

"I am she."

Melanie dared continue. "We're interested in the presidential primaries, and since young people are so politically aware now, we would like to write a series of articles about the candidates from a younger perspective."

After a long moment, the editor swung open a creaky gate at the side of the counter. "Enter," she said, just like one of those vampires on the late night movies.

Melanie and Jack followed the editor to her office in the back of the room, a male and female staffer watching them with raised eyebrows. After they took seats across from the woman's desk, the editor asked for their names.

"I'm Jack Clyde, and this is Melanie McKnight."

"Ellen Harper." She looked straight at Melanie, who tried not to squirm.

"Nice to meet you, Mrs. Harper," Jack said.

"Miss." She corrected him. "What makes you think you're ready for *The Packet*?"

"We brought samples of our work." Jack produced a small leather portfolio containing five of each of their best clippings, and to their surprise, Ellen Harper took her time reading each one. Finally the editor handed the articles back to them.

"You both show considerable promise." Then, as if to herself, "I've been wanting to do something different for the election year."

Melanie gave Jack a "way-to-go" glance.

"I can't pay you much, say ten dollars an article—whether one or both of you write it—but if you're willing to try, I'll give you the opportunity." She pulled out a slip of paper from a folder on her desk. "I happen to have a lead for your first story, a fund-raising cocktail party in town for Richard Nixon on Friday the twentieth." The editor rose, and she escorted them to the door. "Melanie, are you by chance related to Cliff McKnight?"

"He's my father."

"I look forward to seeing what his daughter can do."

After the evening news, Melanie lingered in her grandfather's library, looking up information about Richard Nixon, surprised to find herself more interested in the native Californian than she initially expected. Like John F. Kennedy, Nixon had served in the Navy during World War II—hadn't Jack told her that earlier? He also had a beautiful wife and two girls, but his beginnings were far humbler than JFK's, and he definitely lacked the Kennedy charisma. Melanie jotted down some questions she hoped to ask him about Vietnam and the youth vote.

At seven-fifteen, the phone rang, but she was too engrossed to answer. Besides, her grandmother preferred to have her house help take calls when they were around.

"It's for you, Melanie." Bea's voice called over the intercom.

Melanie pushed her book aside and went over to the desk. "Hello?"

"Hi, Melanie, it's Jack." Something in his voice wasn't quite right.

"Are you okay? You sound upset."

"Martin Luther King was just shot."

CHAPTER SIX

Melanie sank into her grandfather's chair trying to wrap her mind around what Jack had just said. "Dr. King's been hurt? When?"

"The news flash came twenty minutes ago. The announcer said Dr. King had been shot."

"Where?"

"I'm not sure, but I think in the head."

She suppressed an unholy urge to laugh. "I meant what city, what place?"

"Somewhere in Tennessee, I think. He was mediating a garbage strike or something, and while he was standing on his motel balcony, somebody shot him."

She couldn't speak.

"Melanie?"

She swallowed the tennis ball in her throat. "Is he alive?"

"Yes, they're about to begin surgery, but he's in critical condition."

"You said he was shot in the head?" The words tasted vile.

"I'm afraid so."

"Then the prognosis must be pretty bad."

"Yeah."

She got up and turned on the television, straining the phone cord. A few seconds later, she saw Ralph Brody's ashen face.

"Are you all right?" Jack's voice was mellow.

"I'm okay." She sniffed back tears. She could just hear her grandmother— "For heaven's sake, Melanie, Markley women do not cry."

"Would you like me to come over?"

There wasn't anything she would like more, but she never invited anyone to Ward House. If only her father would call to console her, but she knew the chances of getting hit by a flying elephant were greater.

"I'll ask my grandmother."

"Take your time."

Placing the phone on the ink blotter, Melanie hastened downstairs where she found Edith in the family room placidly working on a floral needlepoint pillow, Debussy on the stereo.

The woman looked up, frowned. "Melanie, you are pale as a sheet. Don't tell me you're sick again."

She swallowed anger, which burned all the way down. "Jack Clyde from school is on the phone. He told me Martin Luther King was just shot."

Edith dropped the needlework. "Good heavens! What is this country coming to?"

"May he come over and watch the TV reports with me?"

She gazed at Melanie over the top of her reading glasses. "This is the boy who's working at *The Packet* with you?"

"Yes, Grandmother."

"Is he of the medical text book Clydes?"

She shifted her stance. "Yes."

"Then I suppose I should meet him."

Like Madame DeFarge, Edith returned to her knitting.

❧

Jack arrived fifteen minutes later, his face pale, hair uncombed and apparently as much in need of Melanie's company as she was of his. Edith received him with courtly politeness, then they retreated to the library, settling a few feet apart on the sofa, the TV playing.

"I'll bet your dad has met Dr. King.

"Yes." She paused. "I have, too."

His eyes sparked. "Really? When?"

She liked how he didn't appear overly impressed as she briefly described the meeting.

"I'd love to see your picture," he said when she finished the story.

"Unfortunately, it's at home in New York."

Following a commercial break, Ralph Brody reappeared on camera.

> We are interrupting our regularly scheduled programming this
> evening to bring you on-going coverage of the Martin Luther

40

King Jr. shooting. To recap, Dr. King was gunned down more than an hour ago on his motel balcony in Memphis, Tennessee. Although his assailant has not been apprehended, eye witnesses say a middle-aged white man was seen fleeing the area seconds after the attack.

The report jumped back and forth from ABC's correspondent at the hospital to Brody, the cadences reminding Melanie of another assassination five years ago, which inevitably led to thoughts about her mother. Then her cousin Mac. And her Grandfather Markley. All of them gone. Fresh tears sprang to her eyes, but she quickly doused them.

Jack flexed his fingers. "I don't know why some people have to express their opinions by shooting people. I just hope Dr. King makes it. I'm praying he will."

Melanie bit back a response, not wanting to hurt her friend, the only friend she seemed to have in this season of her life. If God hadn't prevented the shooting, why would he heal Dr. King?

The wall clock read eight-ten when Ralph Brody's voice caught on his latest announcement.

Thirty-nine year-old Dr. Martin Luther King, Jr., the great civil rights champion, has just died.

Melanie's shoulders drooped. Jack put his hand over hers, and she desired to indulge in a good cry, but she bit her stiff lower lip like a good Markley woman.

Bea Gaylord appeared bearing a tray of tea and cookies. "I thought you could use these." She placed the food before them on the coffee table, looking Jack over but seemingly trying to appear as if she weren't.

"Thank you, Bea. I'd like you to meet my friend, Jack Clyde." After they greeted one another Melanie said, "Dr. King just died."

Bea clapped her hand over her mouth. "Oh, dear God." She watched the TV reports for a few minutes, wiping at her eyes with a handkerchief she kept in her apron. Then she excused herself.

Jack rose. "Thank you, Mrs. Gaylord. It was nice to meet you."

"Nice to meet you as well."

Melanie poured two cups of Darjeeling, but neither she nor Jack ate anything. The cookies sat there, a memorial to their grief.

Reports came into the newsroom of riots exploding in American cities, and around nine o'clock, Brody said,

> We have a report from Cliff McKnight, our special correspondent with the Kennedy campaign.

Melanie's father stood against the backdrop of a gathering of African Americans, speaking quietly into his microphone.

> I'm here in Indianapolis, where the most extraordinary thing is taking place. Senator Kennedy was on his way to a campaign rally in this city's worst ghetto when he received news of the King assassination. His aides urged the candidate to cancel his appearance and the city's chief of police warned Kennedy he could not be responsible for the senator's safety. Kennedy has sent his wife back to their hotel and is about to address this crowd, minus a police escort.

Melanie's breath caught in her throat— *If Bobby is at risk, so is my father.*

> This group has been waiting eagerly for Kennedy's arrival for hours and, as you can see, the mood is upbeat because they don't know yet about Dr. King.

"Oh, Jack, what will happen when they do find out? They might start rioting!"

He held her trembling hand as the candidate climbed onto a flatbed truck. Oak trees swayed softly above and just behind him, his expression as somber as his black overcoat. No band played a high-stepping Sousa march; he wasn't announced as "the next president of the United States."

The senator got straight to the point.

> I have bad news for you, for all of our fellow citizens, and people who love peace all over the world, and that is that Martin Luther King was shot and killed tonight.

A collective gasp echoed through the throng. Some wept openly, others stood immobilized by horror. She felt the pressure of Jack's hand on hers, and she squeezed back.

> Martin Luther King dedicated his life to love and to justice for his fellow human beings, and he died because of that effort. In this difficult day, in this difficult time for the United States, it is perhaps well to ask what kind of a nation we are and what direction we want to move in. For those of you who are black--considering the evidence there evidently is that there were white people who were responsible—you can be filled with bitterness, with hatred, and a desire for revenge. We can move in that direction as a country, in great polarization—black people amongst black, white people amongst white, filled with hatred toward one another.

> Or we can make an effort, as Martin Luther King did, to understand and to comprehend, and to replace that violence, that stain of bloodshed that has spread across our land, with an effort to understand with compassion and love.

Robert Kennedy had his finger on the pulse of Melanie's emotions.

> For those of you who are black and are tempted to be filled with hatred and distrust at the injustice of such an act against all white people. I can only say that I feel in my own heart the same kind of feeling. I had a member of my family killed, but he was killed by a white man. But we have to make an effort in the United States, we have to make an effort to understand, to go beyond these rather difficult times ...

> We've had difficult times in the past. We will have difficult times in the future. It is not the end of violence; it is not the end of lawlessness; it is not the end of disorder.

> But the vast majority of white people and the vast majority of black people in this country want to live together, want to improve the quality of our life, and want justice for all human beings who abide in our land.

He seemed to be winding down the speech.

> Let us dedicate ourselves to what the Greeks wrote so many years ago: to tame the savageness of man and to make gentle the life of

this world. Let us dedicate ourselves to that, and say a prayer for our country and for our people.

Melanie hung on his every word, her last hope.

She stared at the screen, wishing Jack were with her and not in Florida with his family for spring break. A pair of mules bore Rev. King's unpretentious casket through Atlanta's sweltering heat for five miles from King's Ebenezer Baptist Church to his alma mater, Morehouse College. Cliff McKnight and Ralph Brody provided solemn commentary. Melanie chafed at the irony. *My father is comforting millions of Americans, but he hasn't even bothered to call me.*

She scanned the crowd, catching a glimpse of Jacqueline and Bobby Kennedy walking in the procession. The senator had removed his suit jacket and flung it over his shoulder, his white shirtsleeves rolled up in signature fashion.

> There is Senator Robert Kennedy. He's walking with his sister-in-law, Jacqueline, as you can see. How sad to watch history repeat itself.

He noticed too.

Brody continued the subject.

> From the looks of things, I'd say that if this crowd were to elect the next president, they would choose Senator Kennedy, who's been consistently applauded and offered drinks all along the route. Although Eugene McCarthy, Hubert Humphrey, and Richard Nixon are also here, they've been largely ignored. He paused. Cliff, do you find it odd President Johnson didn't come?

> Not necessarily. He does have his hands full with the urban riots.

> I understand you saw some up close.

Melanie's ears perked up. Something had happened to her father, which she was only to discover along with the rest of the world.

> Last night, I accompanied Senator Kennedy to Washington, DC's black district, a very dangerous place just now. It reminded

me of those days we read about during the French Revolution when the poor wreaked vengeance on the authorities. I saw smoke pouring from so many buildings I lost count, and National Guardsmen were posted on every corner. When the residents realized Kennedy was there, a crowd formed around us.

Some soldiers got nervous about the size of our group, and I could see them put on their gas masks and ready their guns as our entourage approached—they thought we were a mob. Fortunately they spotted Senator Kennedy.

Melanie shivered even as anger rushed through her temples. *He could've been killed too! Why doesn't God do something?* At least she could count on Robert Kennedy.

CHAPTER SEVEN

A white Lincoln idled at the front entrance, Jack gesturing toward the vehicle. "There's my dad, and the Kennedy campaign coordinator is in the passenger seat. He's been hanging out at my house a lot, and Mom and I do our best to be civil to him." He winked.

"I can just imagine the fireworks!"

"We respect each other's opinions." He grinned. "Well, most of the time!"

Melanie wondered whether the campaign guy had met Bobby Kennedy, how much access he had to the senator, and whether he could help her get an interview. As they piled into the spacious back seat, she heard a far-too-perky elevator music rendition of a Sinatra standard on the car radio. Jack introduced her to his father, a handsome middle-aged man with abundant brown hair, which Melanie knew her dad would practically kill for—his receding hairline was a daily vexation.

"I'm very glad to meet you, Melanie."

"Same here, Mr. Clyde." The incredible resemblance between him and his son made her wonder if Jack would look the same when he was older.

Michael Clyde pointed to the man beside him. "Melanie, this is Roger Roberts from the Kennedy staff in New York. He's come down here to help in the Pennsylvania primary. Roger, this is Jack's friend from Mercer Academy, Melanie McKnight."

Roberts turned around in his seat and shook her hand. "Nice to meet you."

Melanie liked his New England accent, and his coal-black eyes reminded her of a sleep-deprived raccoon. "I'm glad to meet you, too," she said. "Do you actually work directly for Bobby Kennedy?"

Roberts shook his head as Mr. Clyde drove toward the main road.

"Do you know him at all?"

"I've met the senator a few times."

"What's Bobby, uh, Senator Kennedy, like?"

He spoke over his shoulder. "He's a great man."

Mr. Clyde spoke up. "Melanie's father actually works with him."

"Is that right?" His eyes converged with hers in the rearview mirror.

"He's a newsman covering the Kennedy campaign."

"What's his name?"

"Cliff McKnight."

Roberts looked at her more closely, seeming a little more impressed with her now. "I've met him. In fact," he lowered his voice, "Mrs. Kennedy is particularly fond of him."

"Really?"

"Mrs. Kennedy's as loyal to her husband as a tigress, and reporters know not to cross her. She's been known to banish journalists who say something unfavorable about him."

Melanie didn't consider such behavior particularly admirable, but then again she might act the same way if she were married and had media scrutinizing her husband's every move.

"Melanie and Jack have landed a job with *The Princeton Packet*," Mr. Clyde said as he began negotiating Business Route One's plethora of traffic lights. "They'll be writing feature stories about the candidates from a teenager's perspective. In fact, their first interview is with Richard Nixon this Saturday night at a fundraiser."

Roberts snorted. "I'll bet you're happy about that, Jack."

He grinned, his chest expanding. "I am, actually."

"We don't have an interview scheduled yet with Senator Kennedy," Melanie said, "but he's next on our list. Can you … do you think you can help us, Mr. Roberts?"

"There are always opportunities for such things."

They dropped Roger Roberts off at his hotel, then covered the brief distance to Jack's house, an attractive white colonial in Lawrenceville where his mother appeared on the front steps in black slacks and an off-white sweater.

"How are my campaigners?" As her husband kissed her, her eyes fell upon Melanie. "Well, hello there."

"Mom, this is Melanie McKnight. Melanie, my mother, Ann Clyde."

"Hello, Mrs. Clyde." She extended her hand.

"Melanie got locked out of her house," Michael Clyde said. "She's going to stay here until her grandmother gets home."

His mother's soft green eyes reminded her of Jack's.

"That was fortunate for us, then."

A wonderful scent trickled in from the kitchen as they entered the house, and Melanie removed and handed her coat to Jack.

"I've been baking cookies for school lunches," Ann Clyde said. "Do come into the kitchen. They're just about ready."

The house was typically Princeton—early American, understatedly elegant. A spirit of hospitality bathed the rooms and for a brief, shining moment, Melanie felt like she'd found her own Tiffany's.

"Please, have a seat," Ann Clyde said. "Tell me all about your adventures while I get the last batch of cookies into the oven."

Her husband began to recount their stories, leaving everyone in stitches. "Jack, tell your mom about the woman who thought you and Melanie were mailmen."

Jack and Melanie took turns telling the story until a little girl in a yellow chenille robe wandered into the kitchen, her eyes hooded from sleep.

"Hey, Meggums," Jack said.

The girl slipped into an easy embrace with her father.

"This is our daughter, Meg. Meg, this is Jack's friend, Melanie," Michael Clyde said.

"Hi."

"Hi, there." Melanie smiled, intrigued by the same quality in her eyes which seemed to run rampant in this family, something she couldn't put her finger on but which made them compelling in a way deeper than physical beauty. She couldn't say the same for the little girl's fingernails, which flaunted the garish red remains of an old, hasty manicure.

"Would you like to visit the 'space exhibit' in my room, Melanie?"

She tried not to gape. How many ten-year-olds had "space exhibits" in their bedrooms?

"She may not be interested in space, Meg," her mother said.

Meg demurred. "I know. All of us like different things."

"Do you mind, Melanie?" Jack asked.

"Not at all. I've never seen a space exhibit before, at least not one like Meg's."

"Hurry back," Ann Clyde said. "I'll have your snack ready in a few minutes."

Her little face beaming, The little girl led her brother and Melanie through the hallway and up the stairs where Melanie gazed at portraits of tranquil-looking family members. Even the ferns on the landing looked smugly contented.

Meg's room was to the left of Jack's, and as they passed, Melanie stole a quick peek at his pleasantly messy student desk, a Volkswagen poster above his headboard, and a pair of downhill skis propped in a corner. She blushed when she glanced at his bed and quickly looked away, hoping he hadn't noticed.

"Here we are!" Meg waved toward her room.

Melanie gaped at a display of scale model Gemini and Apollo spacecraft suspended from the ceiling against a backdrop of ruffled, yellow curtains, dainty wallpaper, and a matching comforter. On one wall, Mr. Spock gave the Vulcan salute on a poster—on another, a giant picture of the solar system stretched across the entire wall. An aquarium with two small turtles resting under plastic umbrellas sat atop a white dressing table. She sniffed at a slight fragrance of lemons.

Meg pointed toward the ceiling. "I made each of those models."

"Those are really impressive. I'm amazed by the intricate details."

The girl repeated the names of each model and space flight since 1961, along with the names and missions of their crews.

"You know, Meg, I've never been interested in space travel, but if I hung around you long enough, I would be."

"Thank you. That is high praise indeed."

Melanie heard Jack suppress a laugh as he lowered his chin to his chest.

"I plan to become an astronaut one day."

If any other little girl had said such a thing, Melanie might have laughed too. Coming from Meg, the prospect struck her as perfectly credible.

"Melanie, tell me what you think of extraterrestrials," she said out of the blue.

Jack, who was sitting on the side of his sister's desk, covered another laugh with a lame cough into the back of his hand. Meg shot him a glance. "Do you have any theories?"

"Extraterrestrials? Do you mean like *Star Trek* and *My Favorite Martian*?"

"They are highly exaggerated representations."

"I'm afraid I'm out of my element. I suppose there could be people from other planets because the universe is so huge, but I'm not sure."

"I'm having difficulty with the concept." Meg sat on her bed and rested her chin on her hand, a miniature *Thinker*. "I believe God made the world, and humans are very important to him. There could, however, be other people on other planets whom he loves just as much."

Meg's question led her down the path of her recent musings about God. If he loved the world so much, why was there so much chaos? Why didn't he do something to end the pain? "I'm afraid I haven't figured that out."

"Neither has Jack. Have you?"

"No, Meggums, I haven't, but God has, and for now, I'm satisfied knowing he has all this under control."

Melanie wanted to believe him, but she didn't know how.

As they put the finishing touches on their plans to cover the Nixon event in Princeton, Jack told her, "I can't stay too awfully long there since I have church the next morning."

"Oh." Her grandmother always took her to Nassau Presbyterian, but she didn't look forward to services the way Jack seemed to. "Where do you go?"

"Lawrenceville Methodist."

"I don't know much about Methodists." She could've kicked herself for sounding so lame.

"What are you?"

"Well, my mother's side of the family is Presbyterian, and my father was raised Catholic, but he doesn't go to church." She shrugged her shoulders. "I guess that makes me a Presbyterian. I'm not sure how different Presbyterians are from Methodists."

Jack spread his hands. "Really, we're not that far apart on important issues."

"Like what?" She leaned on her open right palm.

"Salvation, the Virgin Birth, the resurrection of Jesus, the existence of heaven and hell, the second coming of Jesus." Jack recited them like a catechism, but seemed to relate personally to each one. He paused, gazing at her. "Do you believe those things?"

Melanie searched his face and when their eyes met, her arms tingled. "Um … I guess. I, uh, have a lot of questions. I've never been able to understand why God doesn't do something to stop all the pain in the world. He strikes me as disinterested." She started twisting a lock of hair around a finger. "I just don't think he cares."

She released a soft sigh when rather than take offense, Jack nodded. "I think everyone feels that way sometimes."

Her ears perked up. "Do you?"

"Not too much, but under any doubts I may have is a strong belief God is in control of my life and the world. I think he has a purpose for everything, even the bad stuff." He paused. "I guess I have faith enough to at least give God the benefit of my doubts."

His eyes locked onto hers, and she didn't look away for a long moment.

CHAPTER EIGHT

Jack swung his Volkswagen into the circular driveway at Ward House where light spilled outside from the living room as well as the Gaylords' third floor apartment. "What a night!" He rested his hands on the steering wheel and turned to Melanie. "It was cool being so close to Nixon."

"Maybe, but I am disappointed we didn't get one-on-one with him." She pushed a stray bobby pin back into place.

"I think we can do a decent enough story using his responses to the questions we asked about teenagers."

"Uh, okay. Sounds good." Melanie eyed the door, unsure what to do next. She'd been on dates before, but nothing quite like this evening.

Jack wore his enthusiasm wide open. "So … what did you think of him, Melanie?"

She jabbed her finger at the air. "Oh, I liked him well enough, but don't you get any ideas about converting me, Jack Clyde."

"Not to Richard Nixon anyway."

His eyes twinkled, and she smiled. Was he trying to "convert her" to his faith? If so, did she mind? She knew she wasn't any kind of Christian like he was, and although she admired his convictions and the peace they seemed to produce in him, she didn't know if she wanted to be religious.

He became reflective. "You know, I liked how he mentioned Martin Luther King. Sometimes at school, I get the impression no one really cares, like they're hardly aware he even died."

"I know what you mean." After a brief silence she asked, "So, when do you want to work on the story? We only have until four o'clock Monday afternoon."

"I know. Tomorrow's Easter Sunday, so I have church in the morning, but we really should try to get together afterward unless your family has plans."

She yawned, covering her mouth. "I nearly forgot about Easter. I'll have to go to church, too."

"How about the evening? I could come over here, or you could come to my house, whatever works best for you."

She jumped at the opportunity to go to the Clydes' again but put brakes on sounding as eager as she felt. "How about if I come to your house?"

"Sure."

Jack smiled at her again, a glint in his eye. "I want to make this story so good Miss Harper will be thrilled she took us on and decide to keep us around permanently."

"That would be nice." Melanie opened her door, and when Jack started to get out, she held up her hand. "Don't bother. I'll see you tomorrow."

She missed the droop of his mouth as he called after her, "Happy Easter!"

❁

Edith Markley burst into Melanie's room like the Gestapo. "Get up, young lady. You have overslept, and we must leave for church in twenty minutes."

She took refuge under her pillow, moaning.

"Very well." Edith crossed her arms and tapped a foot. "If you fail to get up, you will stay in this room all day."

The words were ice water—there was no way she'd miss going to the Clydes'. She hopped out of bed, retrieved the outfit she'd worn to see Nixon and took a quick shower, skipping breakfast. Joe Gaylord drove them to Nassau Presbyterian, and during the service, Melanie fended off a continual onslaught of yawns, fully aware of her grandmother's scathing glances. Her problem wasn't merely sleep deprivation but the sermon, the minister droning on about nature's annual regeneration and the symbolism of resurrection. Melanie escaped into a day dream, finding herself having a great interview with Bobby Kennedy.

She startled when her grandmother hissed in her ear. "Stand up!"

Melanie slammed back to reality, mechanically bolting to her feet for the final hymn, "Come, Ye Faithful, Raise the Strain."

Back at Ward House, her cousin Sandy and Aunt Claire were waiting, having skipped church altogether. They belonged to Nassau Pres but never went, not even at Christmas or Easter. They certainly didn't act like Christians, especially not Claire who barked at the housekeeper over brunch. "This ham is undercooked. We could all die of trichinosis."

Sandy passed the platter to Melanie as if she were handling snakes. "Ham is full of carcinogens. I've gone strictly vegetarian."

Edith put her two cents in. "Bea, these cloth napkins aren't properly starched. I've told you a dozen times how I like them."

Claire whined about her former husband. "That rat thinks I should be paying *him* alimony, Mother. Can you imagine!" She stabbed a beet as if it were the man's heart.

Melanie moved her food around the plate, finding difficulty putting anything in her mouth, remembering a proverb about a morsel of bread in an attic being better than a banquet with a contentious woman. *Solomon must have known Aunt Claire.*

Edith slammed her napkin onto the table and made a beeline toward martyrdom. "I do not know why I even bother to feed you people. No one appreciates the effort."

Melanie glared at her. Bea was the one who'd slaved for hours. How the warmhearted housekeeper put up with such a woman was a complete mystery.

After dinner, they retreated to the travesty of a family room, and Claire prattled on about how no one worked or suffered as much as she did. Edith sat in her Queen Anne chair, a monarch holding court while Sandy and Melanie played five hundred rummy, the latter yearning for Jack to call. When the phone rang at one-fifteen, she pounced on the receiver.

"She must think it's her father," Edith said.

A man on the other end of the line asked, "Is this Melanie McKnight?"

"Yes?"

"You don't recognize your own cousin's voice?"

"Jeff!" she shouted, and everyone turned in her direction. "How are you?"

"Fine."

"Where are you?"

"Between you and me, I'm in Erie, Pennsylvania, campaigning for Gene McCarthy, but Mom and Grams think I'm at school. Got it?"

She smirked, happy to be getting the best of them for a change. "College is going well, then?"

"Except for your twerpy friend, yes."

Her back stiffened. "What twerpy friend?"

"Kennedy is wreaking havoc with my man's campaign."

She opened her mouth to defend her "friend," but Claire ripped the phone out of her hand, scratching Melanie with her scalpel-like nails. "Let a mother talk to her own son, for Pete's sake."

Melanie stood frozen with fury, then rushed across the room and pushed open a French door to the patio. If the entire neighborhood wouldn't have been able to hear her, she would have roared to dispel her pent-up rage.

Sandy approached her in the garden a few minutes later and put her hand on Melanie's shoulder. "You okay?" She nodded, wordless. "My mom's too much. I wonder how you stand living here."

Melanie turned on her cousin. "I don't have a choice."

She took the front porch steps two at a time and used the brass knocker as Joe drove away. Jack opened the door immediately, as if he'd been waiting for her. She began thawing.

"Happy Easter!"

"Happy Easter to you!" She entered into the mood.

"Come in." He ushered her into the hallway. "Let me take your jacket."

She breathed deeply of cloves and baked bread, the scents soothing her, splices of animated conversation flowing out to meet her. The spirit of Easter was alive here.

"I'm so glad you came early," Jack said, hanging her jacket on a coat rack.

A voice came from upstairs. "Me, too!"

Melanie looked up to see Jack's bespectacled sister peering over the railing.

"Hi, Meg!"

The girl bounded down the stairs with thuds too loud for words, Melanie amazed such a small person could make so much noise.

"I've been waiting for you." Meg looked like she wanted to hug Melanie but held back.

"Really?" She hadn't felt this good since the last time she was here.

"Uh-huh."

She looked from Jack to his sister. "So, what's going on? You seem like you're up to something."

"Come to the family room. Roger Roberts has something to tell you."

Hope sprang eternal. "Is it about Bobby?"

Jack just grinned.

Jack led Melanie and his sister down the hall to the family room where the Clydes, Roger Roberts, and a pink-cheeked blond were talking. The men stood when she entered. "Melanie, I'd like you to meet my Aunt Carol," Jack said.

"Hello, Melanie."

"I'm glad to meet you."

"What would you like to drink?" Ann Clyde rose from her rocking chair. "A soda maybe? Some iced tea?"

"I'll have a Coke, please."

Michael Clyde invited Melanie to sit on the couch, Meg sat alongside her, Jack plunked to the floor at their feet.

"So," Melanie said, "something's going on, right?"

"Do want to tell her, Roger?" Jack asked.

"Everybody who's anybody in the party thinks Hubert Humphrey will announce his candidacy soon, and if he does, the state big-wigs will have all kinds of pressure to endorse him. New Jersey doesn't have many delegates, and Senator Kennedy's name won't even be on the ballot, but we don't want to completely ignore the state."

Is this the big news? His message was like biting into a chocolate Easter rabbit you thought was solid but ended up being hollow inside.

Roberts continued. "My main job is to work in Pennsylvania, plus go behind the scenes in New Jersey to secure political support whenever possible." He smiled at her. "This Friday there's going to be a party fundraising dinner at the Bellevue-Stratford Hotel in Philly, and Senator Kennedy's planning to be there."

She clapped her hands together. "Oh, that's wonderful!"

Jack smiled up at her. "This could be your big chance to meet him, Melanie."

"There's just one potential problem."

Melanie didn't want to know, but he told her anyway.

"The dinner is five hundred bucks a plate."

Michael Clyde asked, "Couldn't they get in with press credentials?"

Roberts pressed his lips together and shook his head before saying, "The guy in charge is only giving passes to major market reporters." He gazed at Melanie. "There's still one other possibility."

She caught on quickly. "Maybe my dad could get us in if he pulled some strings. He'll probably be there since he travels with Bo—uh, the Senator."

Michael Clyde's eyebrows raised. "Do you think he could?"

"I … could … ask." She had spoken in haste and now repented, knowing how much difficulty she had contacting him.

Roberts scooted to the edge of his seat. "Call him now, why don't you?"

"I, uh, I guess."

"You can use the phone in the kitchen," Jack said.

She rose to carry out the assignment, stomach clenching. This was her big chance, what she'd been waking up for every morning, perhaps her only chance to meet Bobby Kennedy, yet when was the last time her father had come through for her? He'd been as distant as God himself. She dialed the numbers slowly, waited, then heard an unfamiliar voice on the other end of the line.

"ABC News, Tim Emmons speaking."

"Hello, Mr. Emmons, this is Cliff McKnight's daughter, Melanie."

"Yes, hello, Melanie. What can I do for you?"

"I need to speak with my father—it's very important. Do you know what hotel he's at?"

After a pause he said, "I'll check his schedule." She heard the riffle of pages in the background. "Yes, but his crew hasn't checked in yet."

"I'm at a friend's house, and I'm not sure how long I'll be here. I'll give you a different number for later this evening."

"Okay, either he or I will get back to you."

"Thanks so much."

Jack poked his head in the doorway. "How'd it go?"

"Pretty good." She stepped away from the phone and explained the situation.

"If you can only get one press pass, or one ticket, don't worry about me, okay?"

"That's really sweet, Jack, but if I faint when I meet Bobby, I'll need you to pick me up." She grinned.

Jack put his hand on his forehead and faked a swoon.

They were concluding the article on the Nixon campaign stop when the phone jangled. Melanie's heart popped into her throat.

Jack answered on the third ring. "Hello? Yes, she's here." He cupped a hand over the mouthpiece. "Melanie, I think it's your father."

Her hand trembled as she took the receiver. "Hello, Dad? Oh, hi, Mr. Emmons. Really? Wonderful! Yes, we can, thank you. Thank you so much!" She hung up, beaming.

"What? Tell me!" Jack spread his hands.

"Tim Emmons works with my dad."

"And?"

"He reached my father a few minutes ago on some kind of remote hook-up and told him about the Philadelphia dinner. Dad said he'll either pick us up himself or send a driver around four o'clock on Friday. We're in!"

Maybe God cared after all.

CHAPTER NINE

"This is nice work, very nice work," Ellen Harper said. In the background, typewriters provided crisp harmonies.

Melanie basked in the praise. "When will the story run?"

"This Wednesday." The editor tapped a pencil against her desk. "So, tell me about this dinner."

Melanie spoke. "It's this Friday in Philadelphia, and my dad's going to help us interview Bobby Kennedy."

Ellen Harper frowned. "Is this a dinner solely for Kennedy?"

"It's actually a Democratic Party fundraiser," Jack said.

"Maybe you'll see McCarthy, too, and there's always a chance Humphrey will show up." Melanie didn't care who else showed up. Her single-minded goal was meeting Kennedy around whom her world turned. Jack could interview everyone else.

She barely slept, too excited about the day ahead, and when the alarm finally rang, she hopped out of bed and showered, carefully hanging her best dress in the bathroom to ward off wrinkles, although Bea had ironed the garment to perfection. At breakfast, Melanie reminded Edith about the dinner and how her dad, or a network driver, would be picking her and Jack up.

"Melanie, you have told me about this several times. Are you incapable of talking about anything but Robert Kennedy?"

She smiled. "Not right now, I'm afraid."

"I will not be spoken to in that manner, young lady."

No one was going to get to her today, not her grandmother, Terry Mayfield, nor even her aunt, should she rear her ugly head. After school,

Jack drove Melanie to Ward House where they changed their clothes and waited in the living room for their ride.

"I'm looking forward to meeting your father."

Melanie nodded politely. Usually she'd be over the top about seeing him, but today he was a means to a greater end. She picked at her cuticles, careful not to disturb her fresh coat of nail polish. "Maybe we should go over our questions one more time." She reached into her purse and pulled out a note pad. After ten minutes, though, Melanie grew concerned. Ten minutes later, she was ready to pull out her hair.

"Maybe he or the driver got delayed," Jack said. "You know how traffic gets around here."

At four-forty-five, he suggested they take his car to Philadelphia. "Maybe we should just meet him there. I don't think we should wait any longer."

"You're right. I wish we'd done this sooner."

Melanie bolted for the door, and soon they were racing toward Philadelphia, weaving through rush-hour traffic. When at last they arrived at the Bellevue-Stratford, they had difficulty finding a parking spot, so Jack took advantage of the hotel's costly valet service. They finally got inside the hotel at six-thirty to find well-heeled Democrats moving toward the ballroom in a glittering, smoke-and-perfume-induced haze. When they arrived at the press table, a staff woman shook her head.

"I'm sorry, but there aren't any for Melanie McKnight or Jack Clyde."

"Do you have one for Cliff McKnight of ABC News?"

She narrowed her eyes at Melanie. "Yes."

"He must not be here yet," Jack said.

Melanie wanted to jump out of her skin. "Can't you call our editor or something?"

"Sorry, but I can't." She was clearly done with them.

As they wandered back to the area leading into the ballroom, Jack grabbed her elbow. "There's Eugene McCarthy."

"Let's just try to sneak into the dinner." She glanced around to make sure no one could hear her. "All we have to do is act like we belong, and we should be able to fade right into the crowd."

"I guess we're not being dishonest. We really are supposed to be here."

The plan failed when a man at the ballroom door asked to see their tickets.

"We're with the press," Melanie said.

He held out his hand. "Your credentials?"

"We don't have them." She hurried to say, "My father, Cliff McKnight, was going to bring them, but he's not here yet." Although she detested name-dropping, she was desperate to see Bobby.

"She's telling the truth," Jack said.

"Nice try." He gestured for the next—paying—customers to come through.

Anxiety flamed through Melanie as she and Jack retreated back toward the twin escalators, but she wasn't ready to succumb. She spotted an ABC camera crew coming up to their floor with Hamilton Sutton, who sometimes substituted for her dad. "Mr. Sutton!"

He looked up in her direction as the escalator reached the floor level, and waved.

"Have you seen my dad? Where is he?" She had to walk rapidly to keep pace with him.

"Out in the Midwest somewhere. I got called to cover this dinner for him tonight."

Her heart sank. "He was supposed to leave press credentials for me and my friend." The din was so intense she had to shout. She was desperate, a pauper. "Do you have any extra tickets?"

"I did, but I gave them to some friends here in town. I'm sorry, Melanie." He disappeared with the fast-moving crew into the ballroom.

"I don't believe this!" she shouted as Jack came up beside her. "My dad's assignment changed!"

He put his hand to his ear as the babble intensified. "What?" When she explained, he said, "Let's just stay out here. Maybe we can at least catch a glimpse of Kennedy when he arrives. I have a feeling he's getting closer, judging from the noise."

No sooner were the words out of his mouth than she saw the senator step off the escalator not more than ten feet away, sandwiched between members of his campaign staff and the press.

She glimpsed his familiar smile, more vivid close-up. He began shaking people's hands, his presence electrifying sophisticated men and women acting like teenage girls at a Monkees' concert. Melanie pitched herself into the mob so she could touch the hem of his garment. "Senator Kennedy! Over here! Please!"

Kennedy met her eyes and smiled at her, his arm hovering within two feet of hers. She strained to reach him. A big man stepped on her foot, but she felt no pain. If she could just get an inch closer … Kennedy was about to take her hand when a woman built like a Sumo wrestler thrust Melanie beyond his reach and seized his arm. An instant later, he disappeared into the ballroom.

❊

When they arrived at Ward House, she said good-night and waved to Jack as he sped off, ready to drop from exhaustion. She was grateful to discover her grandmother had gone to bed because the last thing Melanie wanted was to tell Edith her dad hadn't shown up, nor had she met Bobby Kennedy. She wandered into the kitchen for a glass of milk and found Joe Gaylord changing a washer on the kitchen faucet.

He looked up from his work as she put a glass on the counter and went to the refrigerator for the milk. "So, how was your Bobby?"

Melanie told him everything.

"That's an awful shame, Missy." He looked as if he wanted to say a good deal more.

She reached for the cookie jar and pulled out a Lorna Doone. "You know how busy Dad is. He can hardly keep track of himself. Jack and I are going to try other ways to meet Senator Kennedy one-on-one."

Joe grinned. "You have spunk, that's for sure. You don't let things get you down."

"Nope," she said, flipping her hair off her shoulder.

When he cleaned up his tools and left, Melanie went to the phone and called ABC's news department where she learned, to her surprise, her father was in Washington, DC, not the Midwest. With a slightly unsteady hand, she dialed the number given to her. Cliff answered on the fifth ring.

"Dad!" The word contained one-part accusation, one-part gladness.

"Melanie."

She took off. "You didn't come for us, and Jack and I went to the dinner in Philadelphia, but you weren't there, and I didn't get to meet Bobby Kennedy."

"Whoa, girl. My schedule got changed at the last minute."

"I counted on you."

"Melanie, I thought you were mature enough to understand how unpredictable my work is. I shouldn't have made any promises in the first place, but you kept pestering me. Why is it so confounded important for you to meet him?"

She didn't feel safe telling him RFK was the hope of an America falling apart, as well as her source of hope. She wouldn't dare explain the kindred-spirit connection she felt with Kennedy, or how pursuing a meeting with him gave her a reason to go on when her life was so hard just now.

"I want to be a great journalist, like you, Dad. Getting a story with Bobby Kennedy will help me get a good start." This wasn't the whole truth, not by a mile.

"I'll do what I can, but I cannot and will not promise anything. Even when I do have a lead—like I did with this dinner—I can't guarantee things will work out. I should've made that clear in the first place." He sighed. "If you're going to be a good reporter, you can't just get there on my coattails. I have to go now."

"When will you—"

He had hung up.

Before English class Monday morning, Terry Mayfield bumped into Melanie hard enough to knock her three-ring binder to the floor, where it slid into a wall like Brooks Robinson stealing second base. Melanie scowled as she picked up the notebook and shook gray dust off.

"How clumsy I am!" Terry said. "I'm just so excited today I'm not quite myself."

Melanie refused to take the bait, but Terry continued. "I guess you didn't hear, then?"

"No, I didn't hear, then."

"Well then, darling, let me tell you. I met your precious Bobby Kennedy." She had invented the word "smug."

"You what?"

Terry grinned. "I met Bobby Kennedy on Friday night. Can you believe it? I went to dinner at the Bellevue-Stratford with my parents, where there was this fundraising thing, the one you and Jack were going to. Funny, though, I didn't see you there."

Melanie gasped. "How did you get in?"

"My father's friend knows the senator and introduced us privately. He thought I might like to meet Kennedy, in spite of our whole family being Republican."

She could barely get the words out. "And you met him?"

"Why, of course." She jabbed again. "Didn't you?"

"No."

"Oh, Melanie dear, whatever happened?" She was a lousy actress.

She wanted to be anywhere but there. Even Ward House. Words failed.

"Well, darling, the man just reeks of money, which is the only good thing I can say about him. That and he's cute."

"What did you say to him?" Melanie was repulsed and fascinated at the same time.

"He was terribly busy, but I managed to ask him a few questions for the paper so I could write an exclusive. Bobby told me the most innocuous things, like"—she started imitating Kennedy's Massachusetts accent—"'the future of our country is its youth,' then he went on about the immoral Vietnam War. I honestly don't know why he has such a hold on you, Mel, unless it's that dazzling grin or his gorgeous bod." She paused. "So, whatever happened to you and Jack? I thought with your father's connections, you'd practically be at the head table next to Ethel."

Melanie turned on her heel and walked away.

Terry's voice dogged her steps. "Too bad your father didn't help you."

CHAPTER TEN

On the evening newscast Cliff McKnight spoke with his characteristic, cool objectivity, but Melanie went numb.

> I was in the Kennedy campaign plane when the pilot had to abort our take-off. We nearly skidded off the run-way. I assure you, Ralph, there were some anxious moments.

> How did Senator Kennedy respond?

> As a matter of fact, he made a rather amusing remark about how if the plane went down, the names of reporters would have been in small print in the next day's newspapers.

Brody laughed for a perfect measure of TV time.

> We're glad to hear everyone is all right, Cliff. Stay safe out there.

The thought of losing her father or Kennedy was unimaginable. Ever since her mother had died, Melanie had harbored a secret dread about what would happen to her if her dad passed away as well. She considered how some people, like Jack, would find strength in their faith, but she didn't understand how a distant God could get close enough to help a lost and grieving person. As if he cared to begin with.

On Saturday night Melanie's cousin Jeff surprised her with another phone call. Fortunately, her grandmother had gone to a play at McCarter Theater and wasn't around to invade her privacy.

"Hey, Melanie."

"Jeff! What's going on?"

"You sound surprised."

"I am." She sat on the edge of the couch and waited for an explanation.

"I hear you're writing for a newspaper, a young person's guide to the primaries."

"My friend and I have only done one story so far—on Richard Nixon. We were supposed to meet Bobby Kennedy at a fundraising dinner, but things didn't work out." She recalled the bitterness and gall of the aborted attempt.

"Gene McCarthy is going to be at Princeton University next Friday, the seventeenth. If you can get the go-ahead from your editor, I'll guarantee a private meeting with him."

Why can't this ever happen with Bobby?

❦

Melanie wanted to tell Jack about the McCarthy opportunity, but she felt weird about calling a guy, even though she'd done so once before and he was, after all, just a friend. Instead, she went to her room to reread parts of her library books describing the anguish Bobby Kennedy had experienced after his brother's death. One account stood out to her in particular, about how the senator sometimes used to stare for hours out of his office window, neither speaking nor moving because he was in such deep pain. *He's a devout Catholic. I'm guessing he found comfort in his religion. I wish I knew how that worked.*

She closed the book and decided to go for a walk to clear her mind, which meant she needed to retrieve her Tretorns from the family room where she'd left them the night before. Claire had come for a visit, and she and Edith were discussing their upcoming trip to Jeff's graduation.

She gave Melanie an acid once-over. "I suppose you'll want to come along, too."

"Actually, I already have plans." She enjoyed having the upper hand for a change.

"A date maybe?" Her aunt snickered.

"Something more important." She faced her grandmother. "I have an assignment for the newspaper that Friday night and would prefer to stay here."

"Then I shall instruct the Gaylords to attend to your needs."

For once she actually felt like hugging her grandmother. The phone rang, and she answered. "Oh hi, Jack." She smiled.

"Are you busy?"

Not really. I was just about to go for a walk. Actually, I have something to tell you." She spoke softly about the opportunity to meet Eugene McCarthy.

"That's terrific! Maybe we could work on the interview questions this afternoon. I'll be glad to pick you up if you can come over."

"I'd love to."

"When's good for you?"

"Any time." As far as she was concerned, Jack couldn't get there soon enough.

"Great! I'll pick you up in a half-hour. What? Excuse me a minute, Melanie." She heard him consulting with someone in the background. "Oh, my mom asked if you'd like to stay for dinner—nothing fancy, just soup and sandwiches since we have our main meal after church."

Better to have soup and sandwiches at the Clydes' than lobster thermidor with two quarrelsome women at Ward House. She agreed.

They spent most of the afternoon discussing the McCarthy interview and Kennedy's chances in the Nebraska primary that coming Tuesday. Before dinner, they went for a sun-splashed walk through Lawrenceville with Meg, who couldn't stop talking about a book she was reading on the original seven astronauts. She hated to leave when the time grew late.

"We like having you around," Jack said as he drove her home. "My parents like you. My sister adores you." He turned to her. "I'm pretty fond of you myself."

"Thanks, Jack." She was glad he couldn't see her blushing in the semi-darkness.

"I'll bet it's tough being apart from your dad." Jack covered her hand with his. "When do you think you'll be going back to New York?"

Melanie wasn't expecting the physical contact, feeling heat rise to her cheeks. "I ... I'm not entirely sure."

"Well, I'm glad you're here now." He removed his hand so he could downshift, and they said little more to each other until they reached her grandmother's house. Jack cut the engine, and she wondered what was on his mind as he ran his right hand over the steering wheel, appearing in deep thought. "Uh, Melanie, this year, the junior prom's going to be on June first, and I was wondering if you'd like to go with me, unless you've already made plans."

"The prom?" In her single-minded pursuit of meeting Robert Kennedy, she'd barely noticed the rhythms of the school's social calendar. "June first. Isn't that the night of the California debate?" Jack pinched his lips together, and she tried to cover her remarks. "Oh, never mind. Sure, I'll be happy to go with you. Thanks."

CHAPTER ELEVEN

She felt like shouting from the housetops when the radio announcer gave the Nebraska primary results: "New York Senator Robert F. Kennedy has scored a major victory over his colleague, Eugene McCarthy. Early projections show Kennedy may end up with as much as a twenty-point lead."

In Melanie's state of exaltation, she even dared to call her father at his Omaha hotel. His voice conveyed a "Let's-cut-to-the-chase" tone.

"McKnight here."

"Hi, Dad!"

"Melanie. What can I do for you?"

One moment sky high—the next, digging a hole to China. "I was excited about the election and just wanted to talk to you for a few minutes. I certainly didn't mean to bother you."

Her sarcasm seemed to have missed its mark. "No bother." He paused. "I got that letter you sent."

A tiny shot, like heavy full bore coffee, perked her up. "You did? I was afraid—"

"I'm not so sure about giving it to Bob Kennedy."

"Why?"

"It's not exactly professional."

She wasn't sure what part of not professional he meant. "But I need to interview him, Dad."

He made a puffing sound. "Well, I guess I could tell him what you're doing for the paper, but I think the best thing is to try to hook you two up when he's near Princeton."

"Oh, would you, Dad?" Her emotional roller coaster began another ascent.

"It's the least I can do after that Philadelphia fiasco. Just don't get your hopes up. Campaigns are crazy things—anything can happen."

"Oh, Dad, I just know this will work out."

"I need to get going. Someone's at the door."

She grasped for just another minute. "Is Bobby Kennedy close by?"

"He's on the next floor."

She wondered how he could be so blasé about someone who was making her world turn. She would've given anything to be there.

The Princeton University gym was overly warm, and Melanie felt like removing her pale green jacket but decided not to because she feared looking young and unprofessional. By six forty-five, her stomach started imitating the way her old dog's used to growl, low and rumbling, and she regretted Jack hadn't let his mother make sandwiches when she'd offered. Not until seven-ten did McCarthy climb the side stairs to the stage, telling his audience, "I apologize for being so late. Our plane was delayed. Ethel Kennedy seemed to have let all the air out of the tires."

He spoke for twenty minutes about the war, poverty, and racism, then took questions while Melanie and Jack went backstage where an aide directed them to a room. The sight of a platter full of sandwiches made Melanie's mouth water. Several minutes later, McCarthy appeared and as he shook her hand, Melanie registered surprise over how small he was up close. He politely answered each of their questions while several aides bustled around. Melanie didn't realize she was staring at his glass of water until McCarthy asked, "Young lady, would you like a drink?"

"Uh, yes, thank you." She felt a tickle coming on.

"Barry." The candidate nodded toward his advance man as he waved first at the metal pitcher, then Melanie and Jack. Her friend's composure as he asked a question about Vietnam impressed her—he seemed born to be a journalist. As for herself, she felt no jitters. By the time she met Bobby, she figured she'd be a seasoned pro.

Twenty minutes later, a McCarthy handler pointed at the clock, and the candidate stood. "I've enjoyed meeting you." He shook their hands. "I'm glad to see young journalists."

"Thank you for seeing us privately, Senator," Melanie said.

"Jeff's been working hard for me."

Her mouth fell open, and he smiled, then winked. "I keep track of my best people."

She watched him leave the room, shaking hands as he went. *What a nice man. I can understand why Jeff is so passionate about him. He's no Bobby Kennedy though.*

Melanie met Bill and Cindy at the Clydes' the next day so they and Jack could work on a school project. They were just finishing the final drafts when Roger Roberts dropped by to talk to Jack's father about a voter registration drive, but especially with news for Melanie and Jack.

"I talked to some people who coordinate Senator Kennedy's media outreach, and they put you on a special list to get press passes to whatever appearances the senator makes near here."

Melanie didn't try to hold back—she leaped from her chair and hugged Roberts, who gave a small hop like a Mexican jumping bean. "When is he coming?"

Roberts wore a self-satisfied grin. "There's nothing official, but … the Senator may be making a stop in Princeton this weekend."

She screamed. "You're kidding!"

Bill and Cindy put their fingers in their ears, and Jack broke out laughing while his parents and sister stood in the doorway to the family room smiling.

"A lot depends on how the tracking polls are going in California. That's the key state right now, and the race is close." He paused. "Just in case he doesn't come, I have other people looking into a telephone interview."

"Oh, thank you, Roger!"

"Glad to help."

Melanie noticed Bill eyeing her and suddenly realized he wasn't making any jokes about her affection for her candidate. He just smiled and said, "Congratulations, Mel. I hope you get to meet him this time."

Melanie didn't relish the news report that came in later in the evening. Based on Oregon exit polls, ABC projected McCarthy as the winner.

Roberts took the update hard. "How could those idiots have let this happen?"

Cliff McKnight reported the Kennedy camp's reaction. Melanie didn't recognize the charcoal suit her dad wore, and she noticed he'd also had his hair cut—changes contributing to her feeling of a relentlessly growing distance between them.

> With me is the senator's campaign manager, Steven Smith. Steven, the results of both the Indiana and Nebraska primaries led many to conclude Robert Kennedy was well on his way to the nomination, but now it appears the McCarthy campaign has not derailed after all. How do you explain that?

He tipped the mic toward Smith.

> As you know, Cliff, Oregon has been a different state than the others from the first. It's prosperous and mostly middle class, with virtually no ghettos. It's also somewhat conservative, so the anti-war movement isn't nearly as strong as in other primary states."

> In light of this upset, do you foresee a change in strategy for California?

> We're pleased with the Senator's performance.

He turned and left.

Cliff addressed his anchorman back in the studio.

> I don't get a sense of panic from the Kennedy people, Ralph, but they're going to be analyzing this loss carefully. One defeat doesn't have to be damaging, but another one in California, where the polls show a horse race between Kennedy and McCarthy, could have disastrous consequences for the senator from New York. They also need to factor in Vice-President Humphrey's growing influence.

Roberts's eyes flashed. "We could've had Oregon. I saw this coming."

"How?" Melanie asked.

When a commercial came on the air, Michael Clyde got up and lowered the volume.

"A month ago, when the campaign should've been at full throttle, there were only three people out there." Roberts shook his head. "Those idiots should've been kicking McCarthy's butt."

"Maybe you should go, Roger," Jack's dad said. "We may not be the best company for you tonight."

Bea brought her the mail a couple days later, a letter from her Aunt Jane and a flat manila envelope. She jumped up and down, squealing when she read the return address, "Senate Office Building, Washington, DC." Edith inched closer to see what this official-looking object could be, but Melanie held the envelope close to her chest and went to her room, unwilling to share something possibly from Bobby with the likes of her acerbic grandmother. She ran her fingernail under the sealed flap with a suddenly sinking feeling. Maybe Jeff was having campaign material sent to her for *The Packet* article or to try to convince her to support his candidate.

But no, she pulled out a mass-produced color photo of Robert Kennedy and smiled at his warm expression before reaching back into the envelope for the personal letter she knew would be inside. Or so she thought. There was none. She studied the picture again, realizing this was the same pose from campaign brochures she'd once handed out, one in which he looked particularly reflective, focused on something beyond the camera. In the background was an American flag, and his heavy black signature appeared across the bottom—"Best wishes, Robert F. Kennedy." Not, "To Melanie with best wishes," just the standard message everyone else got. She doubted he'd even signed the thing. Was this to be the only answer she'd be getting from her letter? Before her spirit plummeted to the basement, she did her best to take heart. She was, after all, going to meet him face-to-face next Saturday. *He must not have seen my letter. Probably some aide just sent this to me. Bobby Kennedy wouldn't let me down.*

CHAPTER TWELVE

Stepping into the warm embrace of a spring evening, Melanie tottered in her heels, then abruptly paused. Before her stood the Clydes' white Cadillac, polished to blinding perfection. "Where's Sam?"

Jack winked at her. "You can't take a beautiful girl to the prom in a Volkswagen now, can you? I thought Dad's car would be more special."

They paid a quick visit to the Clydes' where Jack's dad took home movies, and Meg exclaimed repeatedly over Melanie's shimmering blue dress. Just before they headed back out the door, Roger Roberts bounded up the porch steps without so much as a nod to their gussied up condition, his cheeks flushed. "You're not going to believe this! I was talking with some guy at national headquarters this morning. Senator Kennedy's not coming to Princeton this weekend, but he will be here next Saturday, the eighth, to meet with East Coast strategists and supporters."

He talked in such a rapid fire manner Melanie leaned closer to catch every word, an apple of gold in a setting of silver. Her heart pounded. "Can I, uh we, meet him?"

Roberts leaned against one of the pillars, grinning. "The guy said he'll make sure you and Jack interview Senator Kennedy—privately."

She rushed through supper and flew upstairs to the library to watch news reports about the last day of campaigning in the California primary, a political horserace in which Kennedy held a slight lead in the polls over his nearest opponent. McCarthy had focused his energies on college campuses, where he'd been received heroically for standing up early against the Vietnam War, while RFK hit the ghettoes where bodyguards protected him from fervent supporters. When the candidates had debated each other on television, analysts declared a draw. After losing in Oregon, Kennedy needed California. Although the New Jersey primary was being held concurrently, Melanie recalled Roger Roberts saying although Bobby's name wouldn't be on the ballot, voters would be able support him by electing delegates identifying themselves as the "Regular Democratic Organization." He said, "Those people will then vote at the Chicago convention for the frontrunner. Of course, we know who that will be."

Her father, standing before the famous "Hollywood" sign, penetrated her reflections.

> The Senator's chances are improving for a victory tomorrow, however, there have been some anxious moments in this manic campaign.

A scene played behind him of Kennedy and his entourage riding in a sort of parade. Melanie pulled her grandfather's blanket over her regardless of the room's warmth.

> During an event in Chinatown today, Kennedy's entourage had a scare at the sound of something like gun shots. Fortunately, they only turned out to be Chinese firecrackers. In addition, Kennedy has not been up to par physically, worn out from the punishing demands of this most necessary of campaigns if he is to secure his party's nomination. Up before dawn this morning, the Senator has traveled the length and breadth of California. Tomorrow he and his staff will know whether the efforts paid off. This is Cliff McKnight reporting from Los Angeles with the Kennedy campaign.

Her father's image disappeared, leaving an imprint in her mind of what might have happened to Bobby Kennedy if those firecrackers had been bullets—what must not ever happen to him. She took comfort in recalling an old saying, "Lightning never strikes twice in the same place."

Wanting to shake the nightmarish thoughts, Melanie called out to Joe Gaylord when he passed by the door. "Who are you going to vote for in the primary tomorrow?"

He winked. "I'm with your man, but don't let your grandmother know."

She loved how Joe referred to Bobby as "her man."

"Don't worry, I won't!"

Jack called after the news broadcast to discuss their upcoming meeting with Kennedy, but Melanie couldn't seem to think past an elephant in the room. Her body tingled as she remembered what had taken place as the prom wound down the previous Saturday night.

"Are you sure you won't come with us?" Bill Hoffnagle had just invited Melanie and Jack to accompany him and Cindy to New York "to watch the sun rise." At first, Melanie's spirit had leapt at the opportunity to go home until she remembered she hadn't put the key to her apartment in the small clutch she carried. She might have invited her friends to see where she normally lived, but then again, the thought of Bill and Cindy in an unchaperoned apartment gave her a sense of relief about forgetting her key.

"I told my grandmother I'd be home by two," Melanie said, glancing at Jack.

"And my parents are expecting me to be home tonight as well."

Cindy stuck out her tongue and wagged her head. "Party poopers!"

They left the prom shortly afterward, Jack taking his time, opting to drive around Princeton with the radio on. The topic at the top of her mental list was Bobby Kennedy's visit to Princeton in just a few days.

"I can't believe he's finally coming, and we're going to meet him! What a dream come true this is."

Jack had given her a sweet smile, but his eyes told a different story. When they finally reached Ward House their song, "Moon River," floated over the airwaves.

His eyes had sparkled as he turned off the motor, climbed out of the car, and opened her door. Leading her to the porch, he held her hand. An alarm seemed to go off inside her at his touch, though not the jangling kind to get you out of bed when you'd rather stay under the covers. This was more of a church chime marking the advancing, expectant hours.

She hadn't been able just then to look into his eyes. "Thanks, Jack. I had a really nice time."

"I was with the prettiest girl at the prom." He'd brushed a stray hair off her cheek, the gesture sending a shiver through her. Then he leaned over and kissed her for several, long seconds, a kiss she could still feel on her lips as she sat on the leather couch under the Black Watch blanket in her grandfather's library.

On Tuesday night, no amount of her grandmother's whining or shaming sufficed to extract Melanie from the television where she watched California election returns trickle in.

Edith huffed. "I do not understand why this is so important. You can read the results in tomorrow's paper like a normal person."

There was no use trying to explain, so Melanie kept quiet as she gazed at the TV. Her grandmother discharged a parting shot. "Don't sit so close. You'll get radiation poisoning."

Melanie was wise enough to keep her mouth shut.

Finally, Ralph Brody gave an update, saving her from wearing her fingernails to a nub.

> According to exit polls, the New York Senator appears to be running five to six points head of McCarthy.

She found herself breathing more normally. Melanie reached for a pack of bubble gum in her book bag to help relieve the overall suspense.

Another skirmish broke out as the polls closed in California at eleven eastern time, her grandmother insisting she go to bed. Releasing a sigh loud enough to be heard to the Princeton Battlefield, Melanie turned off the TV in the knowledge Bobby Kennedy was ahead and had, so far, managed to capture more delegates than McCarthy, even in New Jersey.

What's that stupid woodpecker doing in my room? She moaned and rolled over, trying to shut out the noise by shoving her pillow over her head. The sound persisted, louder, and she realized through brain fog she wasn't dreaming. Someone was at her door. Surely not Edith, who would've just barged in. "Melanie! Wake up. Wake up Melanie."

Bea.

She slid out of bed, squinting at the faintly illuminated numbers of her alarm clock in the dawn's early light. Five-thirty. *What in the world ...?* She grabbed her bathrobe from the edge of the bed and pulled the cloak around her as she opened the door to the housekeeper, who was red-faced, her eyes puffy pillows.

Her kaleidoscopic thoughts swirled. "What's wrong?"

Bea sobbed into her hands. "It's terrible. I hardly know how to tell you."

Melanie pulled the door open wide. "What's terrible? What's wrong?" Her body trembled. *Something must have happened to Dad.*

"Oh, Melanie … Robert Kennedy's been shot."

She blinked, her mouth agape. *What did she say? Something about Bobby Kennedy being shot. This must be a dream, a very bad dream.* She shook her head to make herself wake up, but this was the coldest reality she'd ever faced this side of her own mother's grave.

"What are you talking about, Bea?" Her teeth chattered.

"Your Bobby Kennedy's been shot, Melanie. Oh lord, I'm so sorry, sweetheart!" She moved to embrace her, but Melanie couldn't return the hug and quickly broke away.

"Are you saying he's d-dead?" She was by this time rudely awake.

"No, but he's real bad." She dabbed at her eyes with a well-used handkerchief. "They shot him in the kitchen."

The kitchen? What in the world was he doing in a kitchen, and why would he be shot there? He was on his way to winning the primary last night. What in the heck is Bea rambling about?

She dashed out of the room and vaulted up the stairs two at a time to where the library reposed in the gentle first light of a late spring morning, the fragrance of lilacs pouring in through a slightly open window. All at once, she despised the smell of lilacs. Melanie hastened to turn on the television. Bea entered the room and stood next to her.

"C'mon, c'mon." Melanie willed the blank screen to life with its usual snaps, crackles, and pops. Had the picture tube ever taken so long to warm up?

A glowering Edith appeared in the doorway. "Just what do you think you're doing, young lady? You know very well I don't allow the television on at this unholy hour."

Melanie turned on her, venting all the frustration of the past five months. "Just go away, Grandmother!"

Edith took a step toward the impudent girl, but was intercepted by Bea, who took her by the arm and whispered something. Melanie hardly noticed the mini-drama unfold as she waited in an agony of impatience for the TV to come on. Finally there was Ralph Brody, haggard, five o'clock shadow across his jaw, his dark hair flat, the tie askew. The cadence of his voice was doing a mean impersonation of the robot's on *Lost in Space*.

It's now the top of the hour, and if you're just tuning in, Senator Robert F. Kennedy won California's Democratic Primary last night by a narrow four-point margin over his closest opponent, Wisconsin Senator Eugene McCarthy.

Somehow victory had never tasted so flat.

Just around midnight, Kennedy left his room at the Ambassador Hotel in Los Angeles to address supporters in the Embassy Ballroom downstairs.

Melanie watched a smiling Bobby making a V-for-victory sign as he guided Ethel through the animated crowd. Her eyes searched the screen for her father.

Then Senator Kennedy gave his victory speech in a packed ballroom filled with joyous supporters.

The pro-Kennedy crowd cheered and screamed, including young women in straw boater hats with "Kennedy" printed on red, white, and blue ribbons. There was a mocking air about this whole replay. She kept waiting for the other shoe to drop.

Then the Senator finished thanking everyone.

The tape rolled of RFK.

Mayor Yorty has sent the message we've been here too long already. And so my thanks to all of you, and it's on to Chicago, and let's win there!

He flashed another *V* and smoothed back his chronically unruly bangs. Waves, cheers, whistles, and yells filled the Embassy Room as Kennedy and his wife stepped down from the platform and disappeared around a corner. Ralph Brody picked up the story.

Following the speech, Senator Kennedy was scheduled to meet with members of the print media in a room near the hotel's lobby. He instructed aides to find a short cut through the dense crowd, however, and they chose a direct route through the kitchen. ABC News correspondent, Cliff McKnight, was there.

Melanie's pulse roared in her ears. Someone was putting her hand on her shoulder—she didn't want to look away from the television to find the source. The camera angle followed Kennedy disappearing into the kitchen, and Cliff McKnight was speaking casually just off screen about the implications of the narrow California victory and Kennedy's chances to win the party's nomination in Chicago. The throng of happy campaign warriors chanted, "We want Bobby! We want Bobby! We want Bobby!" Then a sound like the splitting of dry wood. The hand tightened on Melanie's shoulder.

A muscle on her father's jaw twitched. He turned away from the camera.

I believe there's been a disturbance, Ralph.

Shouting. Screams. Panic emptying its vials.

Something has happened in the kitchen. Someone just said there's been a shooting, but I don't know if it's true, or who's been shot.]

A man burst onto the scene.

Is there a doctor? Senator Kennedy's been shot!

Oh, my God!

Dozens of people took up the lament.

No, God, no!

A teenager pounded on Cliff's arm and cried out, until someone pulled him away. Her father's face morphed into a strange shade of gray. Several women buried their heads against the chests of boyfriends and husbands.

Not again. This cannot be happening again.

Edith lowered herself onto the sofa. Melanie stood rigid before the TV listening to her dad's stout voice wobble.

I understand Senator Kennedy has been shot, Ralph.

The camera followed him as he began walking.

I'm going to try to get to the scene of the shooting.

Melanie screamed. "No! Don't go there Dad!" She swayed, and Joe Gaylord moved quickly to catch her.

"Steady, Missy. Steady." Joe held her with both arms, and she clung to the human life preserver.

The camera shook when Cliff stopped in the crowded portal of what looked like a wall-to-wall, stainless steel vault. A young man stood on a counter, pointing his hand toward his head as if it were a gun, mouthing "pow, pow, pow."

Get the gun! Get the gun!

Several people, including football star Rosey Grier, had wrestled the assailant to the ground and were trying to seize the weapon.

Break his fingers if you have to! We don't want another Oswald!

The ground beneath Melanie quaked.

Her father called out.

> I can't get a good view of who fired the shots, but it appears to be a young man. I can see Senator Kennedy now, Ralph. He's … he's lying on the floor with blood around his head. I'm not sure where Ethel is. They seem to have been separated after he left the podium, but I assume she's nearby. I'm not sure if anyone else has been shot, but Senator Kennedy is down and bleeding from his right temple. I think the shooting has stopped now, and it seems there was just one gunman.

When Melanie caught a glimpse of Bobby Kennedy lying on the floor, Joe's hold was the only thing keeping her upright. A young Hispanic-looking man was holding the senator's bleeding head, Kennedy's lips were moving slowly. She willed the image away, to no avail.

"If he doesn't look like President Kennedy laying there," Bea said from behind her.

EMTs rushed the slain candidate to an ambulance and off to the hospital while Melanie's father continued his running commentary.

> We'll keep you up-to-date as we receive further bulletins.

His voice actually faltered, along with Melanie's heart.

> This is Cliff McKnight … with the Kennedy campaign in Los Angeles.

Ralph Brody reappeared onscreen, and Melanie realized that, of course, what she'd just seen had occurred while she was sleeping. What had happened in the aftermath?

Brody continued the report.

Five other people were injured in the shooting last night, but to our knowledge, none of them seriously. Senator Kennedy was taken to the Los Angeles Receiving Hospital, comatose and in shock from bullet wounds to the head and chest. An hour later he was transferred to Good Samaritan for surgery, and we understand the operation was to have begun by now.

Brody glanced at a clock on the wall, then put a hand to his ear.

I'm just getting news the surgery has not yet started. Although the gunman is in police custody, his identity remains a mystery. He is a slightly-built man in his twenties, and police think he may be Hispanic or an Arab. We will provide additional information as it becomes available.

ABC paused for a commercial break—soap powder had to be sold. The Gaylords and Edith started talking to each other, Melanie kept staring at the screen. She did something unusual for her, something she would only attempt in a moment of desperation. She prayed. *Dear God, please listen to me if you can possibly hear me. You must save him. If this is the only prayer of mine you ever answer, the only time I get one in my life, let it be this. I'll never ask for another thing.* A sob wrenched her body. She had managed to live without her mother, her Grandfather Markely, and her cousin Mac. She'd even adjusted to her dad's absence, but she didn't think she could manage without Bobby Kennedy in the world. Without him, all was lost.

CHAPTER THIRTEEN

Following surgery, Kennedy was in stable condition, but the prognosis was not good for his survival. Even if he did wake up, news people speculated, he would never be the same. The day dragged for Melanie, who had refused outright to go to school, planting herself in front of the TV despite her grandmother's caustic comments. She endured mindless game shows and soap operas just for a bit of news, learning that Los Angeles police had traced the gunman through his pistol's registration, and at the man's apartment, officers had found several notebooks containing venomous remarks against Kennedy.

Ralph Brody reported.

> Initially it would seem, he's an Arab from the Middle East who was upset about the senator's pro-Israel stance. Police sources have revealed the suspect in the shooting, whose last name is Sirhan, wrote obsessively in the notebooks, "RFK must die."

Melanie recoiled. How, she wondered, could someone have hated Bobby Kennedy that much? Disagreed with him, yes, but abhorred to the point of murder? She was glad ABC had assigned other reporters to cover the assailant, leaving her father to keep watch at the hospital. *If only he would call me. What a lifeline he could be to me just now.* She sighed, knowing she was hoping against hope.

At four o'clock Bea entered the library, wearing a soothing smile. "There's someone here to see you."

Melanie turned away from the television and caught her breath upon seeing Jack in the doorway, looking at her with such tenderness she broke down. Seconds later, he was beside her on the couch with his arms around her, imparting warmth and strength as he might have soothed his little sister. "It's okay, go ahead and cry."

She pulled back, staring at him. "It's okay?"

"Why shouldn't it be?"

She blurted in as proud a manner as she could muster, "Markley women do not cry."

"Well, they should." When the flood began to recede, he told her, "I was worried when you weren't at school."

"I couldn't come. I had to be here."

He wiped a stray tear from her cheek with a finger, glancing at the TV set. "So, how's Bobby doing?"

"About the same. There hasn't been any news since the surgery ended. Oh, Jack." Her voice caught as if on a thorn bush. "He just has to live!"

"Hello, Jack." Edith stood at the door, arms crossed.

He rose. "Hello, Mrs. Markley."

"Were you in school today, may I ask?"

"Yes, ma'am."

She spoke as if Melanie were not present. "Imagine taking this Kennedy affair so personally she wouldn't go to school."

"Mrs. Markley, I'd like to take her to my house for a while. Would that be all right?"

The prospect kindled Melanie's soul. Yes, she could get through this if she were with the Clydes.

Edith waved her hand. "Take her away."

Melanie sprang up. "Let's go, Jack. I just need to get my purse." Wordlessly, she brushed past her grandmother.

Ann Clyde hugged Melanie for a long moment, followed by Meg, whose tear-streaked face bore witness to her own sadness. Michael Clyde was in the family room in front of the TV when they came in, and he also embraced Melanie. When Jack's parents set up trays filled with chicken noodle soup and egg salad sandwiches, Melanie discovered she could eat after her day's unintentional fast.

"I wonder if your father's slept at all," Ann said.

"I doubt it. He stayed up for three days in a row during the Cuban Missile Crisis." At least no one asked whether he'd been in touch since the shooting—they probably knew better by now.

Melanie grew weary of Ralph Brody's repetitious, old news, but the lack of fresh tidings wasn't entirely his fault. Since the senator's surgery had ended hours earlier, there'd been no significant change in his condition, and regular programming resumed punctuated by news bulletins, each one slicing through Melanie's spirit. By nine-thirty, there was still no change, and Meg had gone to bed. She reappeared after some time in her pajamas.

Her mother frowned, but compassion drew deeper lines in her expression. "Why aren't you in bed?"

"I want Melanie to hear something. You, too, Jack." Meg motioned for them to come upstairs, and they followed her to her room where music was playing. "I couldn't sleep, so I turned on the radio. When Hy Lit asked for requests, I called and asked him to play something for Melanie. It's coming up next." She pointed to the transistor on her bureau.

"You're a sweetheart, Meg." Melanie hugged the little girl and sat with her on the twin bed while Jack leaned against the doorway.

Hy Lit began talking. "I just had a conversation with a dear little girl from Lawrenceville, New Jersey. Meg Clyde asked me to play a special song for a good friend of hers who loves Bobby Kennedy. Melanie, this song's for you from Meg, and me, Hyski. Don't give up hope, my friend. Let's all keep praying."

"To Dream the Impossible Dream" came over the airwaves. Melanie immediately recognized the tune as one of Bobby Kennedy's favorites, information she'd gleaned from a magazine article. She covered her eyes, bowing her head in deep sorrow, Meg and Jack holding her in a circle of love. When the song ended, Meg made another request, this time of her father who'd come upstairs. "Could Melanie stay here tonight? In my room?"

"That's up to her, and even if she does, you still need to hit the hay." He turned to Melanie. "Would you like to stay? You're certainly welcome."

She didn't have to think twice, unable to imagine returning to Ward House tonight. There was, however, the problem of her grandmother's consent, as well as not having her school uniform on hand. Even she realized she had to return to school in the morning.

"Frankly, I do not understand this," Edith told her over the phone, "but if the Clydes want you, go ahead."

Ann took the receiver and began talking. "Yes, Mrs. Markley, she's more than welcome. No trouble at all. Yes, we're all quite sad. If it's all right with you, I'll come over to pick up Melanie's school outfit and night clothes."

"That is kind of you but not necessary. I'll send Joe Gaylord over with them."

Melanie smiled at Ann Clyde. "You'll never know how much this means to me."

"I think I do."

The vigil continued before the television, which remained stingy in its output of information. At eleven-thirty, Cliff McKnight reported in a strained voice.

> The senator's electroencephalogram is registering a straight line.
> The prognosis at this time is grave.

Mr. Clyde rose from the couch. "I think I'll go to bed now." Sadness tinged his voice.

"Me, too," Jack said, yawning. "If you don't mind, Melanie."

"I don't mind." She wasn't ready for sleep. She also wanted to talk to Ann Clyde alone, feeling drawn to the woman, needing to confide in someone as motherlike and sympathetic as her own had been.

Not ten minutes later, she dared to plumb the depths of the situation— and her soul. She was sitting on the floor, Jack's mother on the couch behind her. "Bobby can still make it, can't he, Mrs. Clyde?"

She let out a sigh. "Oh, Melanie, I don't think so, dear."

"Doesn't God care?" Her voice quivered.

"More than we can possibly know."

She blurted, "Then why doesn't he do something to stop things like this?" She immediately hung her head. "I'm sorry. I'm not angry with you."

"You're frightened, and I understand. The world isn't anything like the way God originally intended. He never meant for people to get sick or die. Earth was a perfect place, can you imagine?"

Melanie smiled, a little.

"Unfortunately, the first humans rebelled against him because they thought they knew better how to live, and as a result, our world is fallen. Now everyone must die sooner or later. Some people are fortunate enough to live a long time, others …"

She nodded, the message making a certain amount of sense.

"I am convinced Bobby Kennedy won't die until God's plan for his life has been fulfilled."

Her eyes sparked. "So, God could make him better, right?"

"He could," Ann said slowly, "but from what I've seen, it doesn't seem like he's going to, for reasons we can't begin to understand because, well, we're not God. We don't see the big picture."

Melanie's shoulders slumped.

"How about if we say a prayer together before we go to bed?"

"I … I guess so. If you think he's listening."

"Believe me, he is."

Somehow, she did. Besides, the last time anyone had prayed with her was her mother, at a long ago bedtime, and she needed the maternal reminder.

Her friend's mother reached out for Melanie's hands and prayed from her heart for the senator, the nation, and Melanie, just as if she were talking to a God who really listened, who was somehow present. When the prayer ended, she felt sleepy enough to go to bed after Ann Clyde gave her a heartfelt hug. Careful not to waken her young friend as she undressed, Melanie climbed into a sleeping bag on a cot, closed her eyes, and was overtaken by exhaustion.

Melanie awakened at quarter to six and hurried downstairs to the family room to find Michael and Ann Clyde standing with their arms around each other. She knew without asking.

"Melanie."

She blinked. The TV was on in the background.

"Melanie, we're so sorry. We know how you felt about him."

He was dead.

Michael shook his head. "First Dr. King, now RFK."

How could Bobby be dead? She was supposed to meet him on Saturday. She and Jack were going to interview him.

Ralph Brody's voice droned against the backdrop of a photo of Bobby.

Senator Robert F. Kennedy, dead at forty-two.

❦

Melanie moved through the school day in a zombie-like haze, classes changing with their relentless precision. Students laughed and flirted in the hallways as if this were just an ordinary day at the end of the school year. She found the experience surreal, in complete contrast to the nation's somber mood as seen on TV. When she asked Terry Mayfield to cancel the regular school paper meeting, the editor refused. "It's not like he was the president or anything."

Her current events teacher talked about the assassination, but most of the kids sat there yawning, sleepy from filling their stomachs in the cafeteria.

Jack had driven her home and was sitting in the kitchen drinking iced tea when Ellen Harper called from the paper asking if he and Melanie would cover the funeral in New York.

She put her hand over the receiver and repeated the request.

"I'll be there."

"Yes, of course," Melanie said.

"I'll see about getting credentials for you to get inside for the service, and, of course, *The Packet* will cover your expenses. Make sure Jack takes lots of pictures. I want you to write your impressions of the event." Ellen Harper mellowed. "Weren't you and Jack supposed to interview Kennedy in Princeton this Saturday?"

"Yes."

"I'm sorry."

She didn't ask her grandmother's permission—she wouldn't have listened if Edith had said "no" anyway. Melanie wondered whether she'd see her father there. Twin pangs of anger and longing tore through her. She needed him, but he didn't care. All he cared about was his work. How she would have managed without the Clydes was too bleak to consider.

On Friday evening, the day before the funeral, Jack asked Melanie if she'd like to go with his family to a memorial service at their church. They'd also invited Roger Roberts, but the campaign coordinator had already left town for the funeral.

At first, Melanie was confused. "Did your church support Bobby Kennedy?"

"Our pastor shies away from politics, but he believes America's going through a really bad time and needs healing. Prayer and worship are a good way to begin. Personally, I think he's right." He paused, looked down at his feet. "What a terrible year—the Tet Offensive. Martin Luther King's assassination. The riots. Now this."

Had she ever told Jack about her cousin's death in Vietnam? She couldn't remember. "I'll go with you tonight, Jack, although I think you should know I'm none too pleased with God."

Jack just squeezed her hand.

The church was packed and sweltering, and after scouting around, Jack's parents found a few metal folding chairs still available in the balcony. Mrs. Clyde went into the makeshift row first, followed by her husband, Meg, Melanie, and Jack. In that close proximity, Melanie could smell something of Jack's scent, a blend of Ivory soap and some unidentifiable aroma all his own. He took her right hand, and she managed a brief smile.

The Reverend George Bennely was a middle-aged man who wore a suit in the pulpit instead of a Geneva gown, unlike the Presbyterian style she was accustomed to. He opened the evening service with a simple prayer, followed by a heart-breaking congregational singing of "America, the Beautiful." Melanie's voice kept catching. Meg cried softly, and even Nixon-supporting Jack faltered. When they sat down, he placed the hymnal they'd shared under his chair, and Meg took Melanie's left hand. Michael Clyde's arm went around his wife's shoulders. Melanie hadn't been in church with a mother and father since the months before her mom's death when Jackie had to stop going. Her father never went back. Maybe he had reached the same conclusion as Melanie—why bother when God didn't listen anyway?

The pastor began his sermon after another prayer and the anthem, "Eternal Father, Strong to Save." Melanie fanned herself with the bulletin in the hot balcony, listening as he spoke about the need of Americans to draw together, to pray for the healing of their embattled land, a nice enough message which she found rather banal. As he came to the end ... what was this? The minister stepped out of the pulpit and continued speaking, something she'd never seen a pastor do before.

"In our nation's recent, difficult times, many people have looked to men to solve our problems," he said. "Both Martin Luther King Jr. and Robert Kennedy offered hope to many."

A baby near the Clydes began crying, and Melanie strained beyond the noise to catch the message.

"After Dr. King's death two months ago, many black people expected Senator Kennedy to carry their fallen leader's banner, but what are they to do now? What are all of us who put our hope in those men to do now?"

So I'm not the only person who's wondering this. She breathed a sigh of relief when the mother with the shrieking baby got up and left the balcony.

"I understand what it's like to put one's hopes in that proverbial knight in shining armor, riding into the sunset on a white steed. Years ago, when I was studying for the ministry, I deeply admired one of my seminary professors, clinging to every golden word from his silver tongue. He seemed to have all the answers to my questions about life and faith." He paused, his face pinched. "Then came the terrible day when I discovered my teacher had been involved in a scandal. He resigned from the seminary and the ministry in disgrace, and I thought I could never trust anyone again. I became disillusioned, as well as afraid. If that great man could fall, what hope was there for someone like me to follow God's ways? Why hadn't God stopped my hero from doing what he'd done?"

Melanie had never heard a minister speak so vulnerably before. She forgot how uncomfortably warm she'd been.

"Friends, one day God showed me how unwise any of us is to expect more of people than they are meant to give."

Bennely spoke softly, but his words hit hard.

"He taught me that all people, even great people, are fallible. We all sin. We betray ourselves and our deepest convictions, and even when we don't fail each other morally, we'll still end up disappointing each other because everyone gets sick, and eventually, we all die. In fact, had Robert Kennedy lived, had he been elected president, he would have disappointed those who followed him sooner or later because, like everyone else, he was a flawed human being."

She flinched. *Bobby could never have disappointed me. Could he?* The pastor's statement smacked of truth. Melanie suddenly felt embarrassed. Maybe, she thought, her all-out admiration for Kennedy had been blind, even immature.

"In seminary, God showed me he's the only one who will never disappoint me, the only one who will never leave me or forsake me, the only one the grave cannot contain, the only one who will never change even if the earth shakes and the mountains fall into the sea."

The pastor walked back to the pulpit, leaned over the edge, and looked straight into their faces. "A terrible tragedy has once again shaken our country, even as our brothers and sons fight and die on distant shores, but you can still hope, and you can still dream, not because there is a human leader who has the answers and solutions, but because the God of the universe, the Father of our Lord Jesus Christ who raised him from death itself, is still in control. For those of you who may be in doubt—I promise you, God is in control. He has a plan and a purpose for this world. He has a plan and a purpose for you. He will never let you down. He will never go away. I urge you to put your life and trust in His capable hands."

Melanie sucked in her breath. Tears streamed down her face as a glimmer of light began flushing some despair from the dark corners of her spirit. He sounded so sure of himself. She wasn't certain of what he'd said, but he was. *Only one of us can be wrong. I hope it's me.*

CHAPTER FOURTEEN

Melanie leaned against Jack, who wrapped his arm around her while Edward Kennedy struggled through his eulogy at St. Patrick's Cathedral. They stood on the steps, too late to be admitted inside. Would she ever get to see Bobby? She had no one else to support her. The thought of her father's neglect had become a low-grade fever in her spirit. She hadn't heard a word from him since the shooting even though he knew how much she adored Robert Kennedy.

"My brother need not be idealized, or enlarged in death beyond what he was in life, to be remembered simply as a good and decent man, who saw wrong and tried to right it, saw suffering and tried to heal it, saw war and tried to stop it."

He faltered, pushed on, each word choking Melanie up as well.

"Those of us who loved him, and take him to his rest today, pray that what he was to us, and what he wished for others will someday come to pass for all the world. As he said many times, and in many places, to those he touched and who sought to touch him, 'Some men see things as they are and say, 'Why'? I dream things that never were and say, 'Why not'?"

The service ended on a literal high note, the "Hallelujah Chorus" filling the vast church with far more hopeful words echoing the message Jack's pastor had given the previous night. Melanie couldn't recall if the word was "chariots" or "princes," but the gist was "Some trust in those things which do not prevail against the Lord Almighty's purposes."

Maybe God does care about his creation. Maybe he does have a plan for it, maybe even for me. She was at least willing to consider the possibility.

❧

Jack put the radio news on, and the steady rhythm of the broadcast along with the heat, as premature as her hero's death, lulled her toward sleep and dreams. A collage of images and voices, hopes and fears. Pieces of Bobby's speeches. Attempts to interview him for the paper. Other campaign dinners. Arguments with her grandmother. The Clydes. Mercer Academy. Sirhan Sirhan.

"Melanie. Melanie."

She opened her eyes and slowly sat up. "Where are we?" Her cotton dress clung to her back and legs.

"Trenton Station. We're in time for the funeral train." He snapped off the radio. "The place is packed."

A cop waved them toward an embankment where Jack parked, and she began peeling her clothes away from her skin as discreetly as possible.

"It's nearly three-thirty. Traffic was heavy, but the train is way overdue."

The station wasn't in the best part of town, and there'd been an almost continual string of riots in Trenton since Martin Luther King's assassination. Nevertheless, Melanie felt safe. Those who came today would be there to pay their last respects, their mood likely to be more somber than angry—at least she hoped so. Clutching her purse and notebook, she accepted his outstretched hand as they hurried through suppurating humidity, tar bubbles squishing under their footsteps. The United States flag hung limply at half-staff. In the dense crowd, Melanie winced, the stench from hundreds of sweating bodies storming her senses. Jack led her into the throng, pulling his press card from a pocket and holding it up as they ploughed through.

On their side of the tracks, African-Americans had gathered while on the opposite side, hundreds more lined the funeral train's route—all of them white. On the rails themselves, dozens of helmeted police presided between the two groups, all but two of them white. Almost no one was talking, as if they were at a funeral.

Suddenly a man jolted the silence. "Hey, you—reporters!"

Melanie and Jack turned toward the voice which belonged to a thirty-something black man in soggy-looking khakis and a white button-down shirt. He pointed at them. "Who you with?"

Melanie eyed the police a few yards away.

Jack angled himself in front of her. "We're with *The Princeton Packet*."

"A honky paper." He spat on the ground. "Well, write this down for whitey. This country is going straight to hell. This is the white man's fault. He did this."

His anger riveted her.

Someone called out. "Hey buddy, it isn't her fault."

"No, it ain't," said an older woman behind Melanie. "You better remove yourself before those police do it for you! And if they don't, I most certainly will!"

The over-heated man paid no heed, and the woman's prophecy came true when three officers intervened. The man commenced with yelling obscenities at the "honky pigs," who muscled him away. More officers moved to the scene, saying little but standing guard in case anyone else got out of line.

Jack rubbed the back of Melanie's damp neck. "Are you okay?"

She nodded, her knees quivering.

The older woman was addressing her. "The likes of him don't talk for me. He just angry. Anger don't get nobody nowhere. As for me, I'm just plain sad today. No anger, no hatred, just sad." Tears streaked down her face. "Bobby Kennedy, he understood all people, blacks, whites, Hispanics. We just come to pay our respects. Ain't no place for that hooligan."

Above the woman's voice Melanie caught a distant, mournful whistle. Then again, closer, a bit louder. Someone shouted, "It's the train!" A crush of bodies moved resolutely toward the tracks, Melanie caught in the grinding humanity, Jack propelling her to the front. They managed to get to within the second row when a police officer raised his arms sideways to form a human barrier. "No further."

Melanie craned to see the first glimpse of the train against the sun's harsh glare. People ceased to jostle and shove, instead raising homemade signs, placing hands over their hearts, saluting. *Goodbye Bobby. God Bless You, Ethel. We Loved You. The Gilbert Family is Sad. What Next?* On the faces of people, both black and white, tears and sweat mingled.

Her heart constricted when the first of twenty-two cars lumbered into view, a shape-shifting pool of heat leaping off the roofs. Some wept, quiet as spring rain, the rest, thunderclaps of emotion. Across the tracks, Melanie noticed two craggy-faced American Legionnaires raise flags, and a third saluted the oncoming train. A housewife in tears hugged her two wide-eyed children. Another woman, in sunglasses and pink curlers, cried softly into a handkerchief. A dozen or so nuns jostled in the back of a pick-up truck for a better view. A Boy Scout saluted.

Melanie looked into the train cars at the faces of the people, most of them watching the crowd as closely as the crowd watched them. Somewhere, her father was on the press train, but she didn't want to think about him just now. He didn't deserve her thoughts.

I wonder what car Bobby is on. Will I even know? The great and melancholy clanking of wheels filled her ears, and she peered to see better. She spoke sideways to Jack and mouthed "Where's the coffin?" knowing he wouldn't be able to hear her above the din.

He pointed toward the end of the train. "Last one."

"Please get a picture."

He nodded, patting the Nikon.

The train slowed, and then she saw beyond one window his casket, draped with an American flag, resting on a wooden bier. Her throat constricted. Her hand automatically went over her heart. *If only things had been different.* She needed something to cling to. Something more stable.

Several people tossed roses at the car, the flowers crushed immediately under the vast wheels, emitting a sad, sweet scent. A movement at the car's window caught her eye, a small, tow-headed girl pressing her face and a hand against the glass. *She has to be a Kennedy, probably one of his kids.* Then she realized this was the child who had interrupted her father's interview with the senator. Her pulse raced when the child looked straight into Melanie's eyes and waved three fingers. Melanie blew her a kiss. *What must she be going through? I can only imagine. I lost a parent, too, but not like she did.* Her eyes drifted back to the casket until the car lumbered out of sight.

An unexpected sense of peace seeped through the cracks of Melanie's emotions. She had seen Bobby. What might this mean for her life—that God could answer other prayers, other needs? She stepped onto one of the rails and picked up an intact yellow rose, hugging the flower to her breast. Just as she turned to find Jack, she was struck stock still when a soprano voice punctured the air.

"Mine eyes have seen the glory of the coming of the Lord …"

The quality of the woman's plaintive singing reached all the way to Melanie's toes, people of both colors joining hands and taking up the song as they faced the retreating train. Jack squeezed next to her, took her hand. An old black woman seized the other one as she sang from her heart.

"He hath trampled out the vineyard where the grapes of wrath are stored. He hath loosed the awful lightening of his terrible, swift sword. His truth is marching on. Glory, glory, hallelujah!"

Melanie and Jack joined the chorus as she watched the train slip into the late afternoon sun. Her clothes had become one with her body in the dense heat, covered by a garment of sadness. She was, like the flowers on the tracks, crushed … but she was not in despair.

CHAPTER FIFTEEN

AUGUST 1969

She unlocked the car door wishing she had the ability to drop the top on a convertible on such a day. Sliding onto the seat, already feeling like a heating pad underneath her, she gave a small laugh at the memory of buying her first vehicle. Cliff McKnight hadn't minded her desire for a cherry red Mustang, but he most certainly did object to his daughter driving a convertible, refused to even discuss such a possibility. Melanie slipped the key into the ignition and checked one last time to make sure she had her purse and her beach bag before heading toward the shore.

There were so few happy memories of her father in recent years she clung to this one with its sweet aroma of protectiveness. He might not be in her life very much, but he did care enough to ensure his daughter wasn't driving a death trap.

Once she reached the highway, traffic hadn't yet begun to bog down, and she let her mind consider the day ahead, as well as those recently gone by. She was looking forward to seeing Jack Clyde again, happy he had called and invited her to spend the day with him on Long Beach Island where he was working for the summer. She hadn't seen him since Christmas, when he and his family had come to New York to see the Rockettes, and he had pledged to take her to her senior prom in the spring. His appendix had other ideas. At the last minute, Melanie had ended up going to her dance with Trip Brody, Ralph Brody's son. She'd been in her father's office at the ABC studios having a meltdown about returning her dress to Bonwit's when Brody's secretary happened to come by. Upon hearing Melanie's distress, she acted with the efficiency and cunningness of a *yenta*. Trip had proven to be an entertaining and attentive date, but the evening had been largely forgettable. She grew warm recalling the memory of Jack's kiss after her junior prom—thankfully Trip had shaken her hand.

During the summer, she and Jack had exchanged approximately five letters, and when he invited her to see him, she jumped at the opportunity. His job puzzled her, though, and she wasn't sure what to make of his surroundings. Jack's initial correspondence in June was on the back of a post card featuring a weathered nineteenth-century hotel with seagulls perched on top of a cupola.

Hi, Melanie! I'm working this summer at Harvey Cedars Bible Conference. I do a lot of waiting on tables and odd jobs, not very exciting, but the fellowship is wonderful. I'm learning so much. Then there's the beach … See you soon, I hope! Jack.

His phone call had come the day before. "Hey, Melanie, it's Jack. Sorry I haven't called. There isn't a pay phone in our dorm, so writing has been better for me."

Her skin tingled at the sound of his voice. "That's okay. What's up?"

"Are you busy tomorrow?"

"Not particularly. I usually don't work on Saturdays, and the news cycle has been a bit slow since the moon landing last month."

"How is Miss Harper?"

"Doing well. I'll tell her hello from you."

"Is she giving you good assignments?"

Melanie smiled. "Nothing like interviewing Richard Nixon. I'm doing mostly local news, a little boring, truth be told, but I'm getting a lot of experience. I've actually learned a lot just living in her apartment, getting a feel for the life of a journalist." She'd only seen her grandmother once since her summer internship had started in June.

"Well, then, if you can, how about spending tomorrow with me at the beach? I'll be leaving for college in a few days, and I'd love if we could catch up with each other before I head out. Saturdays are more relaxed around here than weekdays."

She tried not to sound as eager as she felt. "I'd love to come."

"Great! Breakfast is at eight, and chapel's at nine-thirty—this week's speaker has been dynamic. Actually, they've all been good, but this guy's incredible. A word of warning—I'll still be waiting tables, but in between I can spend the day as I like."

Motoring east, she felt something like a twelve-year-old at a pool party in which everyone would be comparing their bodies in swimsuit mode. Her gentle curves and petite stature were out of step with the modishly cool, blond hair and skinniness of Twiggy, Michelle Phillips, and Peggy Lipton. *I wonder what type Jack prefers, long and leggy or short and curvy?* She wasn't even sure if the Bible conference had a dress code, so just to be on the safe side, she'd bought two bathing suits, a one piece and a baby doll style with a bottom covering her naval, sort of like "I Dream of Jeannie." She planned to survey what other girls wore at Harvey Cedars, then go with the prevailing winds. Either way, the salesclerk at Lily Pulitzer had assured her, "You look wonderful in both suits, my dear," which imparted a modicum of confidence.

She frowned as she slipped on her sunglasses against the sun's suddenly aggressive rays. She really had no idea what a Bible conference was or even how Jack had discovered this place. She just hoped she didn't find herself in the midst of a religious hippie commune. Melanie laughed at the image of Jack in a tie-dyed tee shirt wearing his hair long, sporting love beads and Birkenstocks. *Not in a million years.* She figured whatever happened at this place would likely mirror the Clydes' religiously thoughtful and sedate beliefs. *Ah, his family.* She had hoped to see Jack's parents and sister during the summer, especially during the Apollo 11 moon landing in July, given how Meg was such a space enthusiast. Instead, she'd spent those days interviewing people on the street about their reactions to the first man on the moon, as well as those with local connections who'd been involved with the mission. Her dad, who'd returned to the ABC anchorman's chair alongside Ralph Brody, was on TV providing continual updates throughout the historic voyage.

After Neil Armstrong's instantly iconic quote about "one giant leap for mankind" as he first stepped on the moon, Melanie had gone outside and stared up at the glowing orb, marveling to think there were human beings walking there. Had Jack been watching, too, she'd wondered? Her thoughts frequently wandered in his direction, and she'd always had in the back of her mind the hope he'd call and invite her to that Harvey Pinecones place—she could never quite get the odd name straight. And now the time had come. Their relationship, and its future, remained a study in ambiguity for Melanie. While they definitely had "chemistry," with college on the near horizon—she couldn't wait to find out where he would be going— the prospect of them ever being more than friends seemed as likely as her walking on the moon.

The trip across central New Jersey took her away from population centers to the scrubby Pine Barrens, supposedly home to the legendary Jersey Devil. In the dewy morning, she could almost imagine the creature bursting out of the forested shadows, feeling much safer than she would have in a convertible. The landscape gentled when the terrain became sandier and flatter, then the horizon exploded as she neared Manahawkin Bay, sea gulls whirling and screeching overhead. The soothing breeze stirred her hair as she drove onto the causeway, the sun asserting itself against great puffs of layered clouds. Just to the left they separated, and a rectangle of a rainbow splashed its signature. Her eyes gleamed, she shivered.

As if on cue, the Beach Boys came over the radio when she merged onto Long Beach Boulevard with other day trippers, the lure of the Atlantic just beyond the dunes. She followed Jack's directions, heading north up the narrow island past shops and businesses, hotels, motels, and restaurants wearing morning-after expressions. At seven-fifteen on a Saturday, only a few people were out, riding bikes, heading to the beach or a waffle house. No matter how hard she craned her head, she couldn't catch a glimpse of the ocean. Knowing the expanse of water was out there, yet not being able to see and experience its majesty struck her as a metaphor for something, perhaps her feelings about God. She'd been going to the Presbyterian Church of her childhood since returning to Manhattan, but the services left her hungrier than when she'd entered the majestic sanctuary. The sermons focused on social justice, using Bible texts to support the minister's views, and yet Melanie didn't really understand the Bible at all. Whenever she opened the book, whether for Sunday School when she was younger, or since Jack had given her a modern translation of the New Testament, the words didn't make much sense, aside from the stories about the life of Jesus. God had continued to seem so remote. *I just can't figure out how Jack and his family feel so close to him. Maybe some people just do, and some people don't.* In her heart, she hoped this was not the case.

At the "Harvey Cedars Bible Conference" sign, she turned left onto a side street dissected by a little bridge over an inlet. Houses with private docks clustered along the water, their sailboats and motorboats bobbing on the rippling current. She followed the road to the left where she recognized the old clapboard hotel from a postcard. Melanie found a parking spot in a graveled lot beside the building, turned off the engine and took a deep breath, hoping to slow the march of her thumping heart. Eight-fifteen. The temperature was already in the high seventies, but a crisp breeze had vacuumed humidity from the air.

Several adults were sitting on wooden park benches, and some young people tossed a volley ball back and forth on a sandy quad connecting the bay and the sprawling hotel. The place reminded Melanie of her Manhattan neighbor, Mrs. Edleston, an unmistakably elderly, yet still elegant woman. Like the lady, this establishment exuded grace despite fine lines and wrinkles.

Jack had instructed her to register as a day guest at the front desk and said someone would bring her to the dining hall where he would meet her. Inside, windows opened to the sea breeze, their lacy curtains fluttering like angels' wings. People sat talking to one another, reading newspapers, or watching the world go by in the old-fashioned lobby. At the desk, two young women greeted her, both wearing name tags and matching polo shirts bearing the Harvey Cedars Bible Conference emblem.

"Good morning," the older one said.

"Hi. I'm Melanie McKnight, and I'm here to see—"

"I know, you're Jack Clyde's friend."

She gave a laugh. "Why, yes."

"He told us you were coming. I'm Monica Allen. Let's get you signed in, then I'll take you over to the dining hall." The plump girl pushed a sheet of paper across the counter and handed her a Bic pen.

After registering her car and filling out a visitor's information form, Melanie followed Monica, whose shirt tail was hanging out, through a busy hallway and across a rambling wooden porch. A boardwalk across the sandy courtyard led to another building where, Monica explained, the dining hall and gym were located. "It also has dorm rooms for the guys on summer staff."

She opened the door for Melanie while a guy rang a ship's-type bell to signal breakfast, a Pavlovian herald resulting in a pouring forth of couples with children of all ages toward the building. Inside, she inhaled the coffee and cinnamon-scented air while taking in a series of round tables set with melamine plates, cups and saucers, plastic drinking cups, and well-worn stainless utensils. Pitchers of maple syrup and orange juice, along with pots of coffee, awaited the inhabitants of each table. People streamed in from two entrances and went to their places, standing as if they were waiting for something. She scanned the room for Jack but didn't see him as Monica squeezed through a wall of people to a table facing the bay.

"This is one of Jack's tables."

Lucky him. He had a great view of the water. Melanie stood behind a chair while her new friend introduced her to the others.

"Hey, everyone, this is Melanie. She's a friend of Jack's, and she's visiting today." Monica turned to her. "I have to get back to the front desk, but I hope you have a good stay. Just let me know if you need anything."

"Hi, I'm Helen Anderson," said a smallish blonde standing next to Melanie. "This is my husband, Carl, and our kids, Susie, Jeff, and Bob."

Carl held out his hand, which Melanie shook. "Nice to meet you." She smiled at the children, who looked to be about eight all the way down to two.

A big man to her left also introduced himself. "I'm Rich Webster, this is my wife, Cindy, and these are our kids, Sue and Mike." When he shook her hand, Melanie winced at his gorilla grip. She knew she'd never remember all these names. Before she could say anything, a man started speaking into a microphone at the top of the stairs leading into the dining hall.

"That's Al Oldham," Rich said. "He's the conference director."

After making a few announcements about the weather, chapel, and the day's activities, the man prayed over the meal and when he finished, everyone sat down to the tune of scraping chairs against the floor. The wait staff flowed through the room, whose decibel level rivaled Yankee Stadium when the Red Sox came to town, dispensing huge platters of scrambled eggs and French toast. Jack broke into a grin when he came to her table and squeezed Melanie's shoulder with his free hand. The awkward greeting couldn't belie the joy on his face or her sudden quivering. Neither one noticed the looks being exchanged at the table.

"It's great to see you! I'm so glad you came."

"Me, too." His deep tan and service apron looked good on him.

"I'm sure these guys will take good care of you." He cupped his right hand around his mouth and whispered loudly, "Although you have to watch out for those two." He pointed to Carl and Rich.

The former shot back. "Don't pay any attention to him. We're harmless."

"We'll be nice, Jack, don't worry," Rich said, and he winked at Melanie.

Someone called from a neighboring table. "Jack, we need some milk, please."

"Gotta go! I'll be back."

"So, Melanie, where are you from?" Rich glanced at her as he heaped his plate with eggs.

"New York."

"City or state?"

"City."

"Mets or Yankees?"

She laughed. "I like the Mets, but I haven't watched any games lately." She tucked into the scrambled eggs, which needed salt and pepper.

Carl moaned. "Not another one."

"Mr. Boston Latin School here is a Red Sox fan," Rich said.

Melanie bantered right back. "Well, it's a good thing I'm not a Yankees fan." She liked these people. She'd been afraid they might require her to name the Ten Commandments, in order.

"Is this your first time at Harvey Cedars, Melanie?" one of the teenagers asked.

She swallowed some French toast. "Yes."

"I've been coming since I was a baby," Sue said.

Her dad explained. "When I was a teenager, Jack Murray bought this place. It was an abandoned hotel."

Melanie didn't know who Jack Murray was and, as if in answer to her thoughts, Rich explained. "He was a pastor who also led summer Bible conferences at state parks, but he wanted to settle in a permanent location. This place was available, and the year after he bought it, my parents came for a summer program. You should've seen the place then—rough to say the least."

Melanie thought, but didn't say, "It's not exactly the Waldorf-Astoria now."

"This place has been a real beacon of hope to people for a long time."

His wife spoke up. "Seven years ago, a horrible hurricane devastated the island, and a lot of people died. God spared this hotel, though, and many people fled here, the only place around here where they could be safe."

Melanie was feeling safe here, too.

Finally, the bell clanged to signal the end of breakfast.

"Time for chapel!" Rich said.

Sue leaned over. "If you need a place to change your clothes or just hang out, you can use our room. It's one-o-three."

"Thanks. That's really nice of you."

Jack came over, minus the apron. "Ready for chapel?"

Rich leaned back. "So, the gallant young knight has come to rescue the fair Melanie from our clutches."

Jack laughed. "Were they nice?"

"Very." She smiled, relieved she hadn't come to a hippie commune after all.

CHAPTER SIXTEEN

Following chapel, Melanie took Sue up on her earlier offer to use her family's room in the old hotel to change into beach clothes, then she rendezvoused with Jack in front of the building. Jack, that is, and a cast of five other summer staff and not a few conferees, to her disappointment. They covered the distance to the beach in under five minutes where Melanie surveyed the expanse of ocean and inhaled the briny air while the wind flirted with her hair. Apparently in a hurry to stake their spots on the beach, the group trudged across the sand, leaving Melanie to bring up the rear, wishing she could linger at the crest of the dunes with Jack. The Harvey Cedars contingent homesteaded at a spot to the right of the lifeguard, rolling out beach blankets, opening chairs and umbrellas, removing cover-ups. Melanie glanced at the other females from the corners of her eyes, thankful Sue had advised her to don the one piece suit.

Some of the kids ploughed straight into the waves, others stretched out, soaking in the rays. She and Jack sat on his Hudson's Bay blanket perusing the peaceful view, a position she would've been happy to remain in for hours, basking in the sun's warmth and his lithe presence.

"So, what would you like to do?" he asked some ten minutes later, "swim or lie in the sun?"

"I'd like to put my feet in the water. I'm, uh … I'm not really used to the waves."

He tilted his head. "Can you swim?"

"Oh, sure, but mostly in pools, not the ocean."

"Let's go then. There's no need to fear—Jack Clyde is here!" He held out his hand, and he helped her to her feet. They removed their flip flops and stole across the hot sand to the edge of the beach where the low-tide's waves tickled their feet.

Melanie hopped back, stumbling, grateful Jack steadied her. "Wow, the water's cold!"

"This is warm compared to June when I first got here."

"Brr!"

A small plane buzzed overhead, trailing a banner for a local restaurant. The sound of waves and gulls absorbed the shouts and laughter of beach-goers, along with an occasional blast from the lifeguard's whistle for the benefit of someone who'd ventured beyond the prescribed bathing area. She took one step toward an incoming wave, shivered when the water poured up to her ankles, and stood firm, digging her toes into the wet sand.

"How do you like Harvey Cedars?"

"The beach or the conference?"

"Both!"

"I can see why you wanted to spend the summer here."

He grinned, nodding his head.

"This is the most peaceful place I've ever been, and the people couldn't be nicer."

"What did you think of chapel?"

She looked into his green eyes, glad he wasn't wearing sunglasses. She, on the other hand, enjoyed how he couldn't tell exactly what she was thinking behind her Foster Grants.

"I actually enjoyed the service. My church is, well, kind of boring. I've never been to a service where people sang with such feeling. By the way, there was a beautiful song I heard for the first time, something about a sweet spirit."

"I like that song too. It's called 'Sweet, Sweet Spirit.'"

She nodded her head. "And then the speaker was so, well ..." She grappled for the right words as she bobbed in the waves, suddenly aware she was further out than she'd intended. Fortunately, Jack and the lifeguards were nearby. "He was really energetic."

"All the kids have raved about Angus this week."

Melanie had never referred to a minister by his first name before, but then she'd never seen such a young pastor, or one who preached in a polo shirt. Her grandmother would have fainted.

"I liked the way he made the Bible so understandable."

"Like how?"

"He talked about sad people getting closer to God, and then, well, how people who are thirsty for God will be satisfied. I always thought of the

Bible as a book of stories and rules, but the way, uh, Angus spoke—well, I liked his style." She grinned. "I liked his Scottish accent, too."

Jack plunged under an incoming wave, then popped back up, shaking his head free of excess seawater. "Ah, that felt good!" He paused, tilting his head to the right, apparently to get water out of his ear. Then he picked up the conversation. "Some people might not think of going to church as a fun thing to do, but I've looked forward to every service this summer, especially Angus's, and I love the singing, from people's hearts, especially some people who can't carry a tune."

They laughed at the memory of the man two rows in front of them whose voice could have peeled paint.

Jack looked out to the horizon, then back to the beach. "You're pretty far out, there, Melanie. Can I convince you to go further?"

She almost laughed at what could've sounded like a double entendre, but she caught herself in time realizing Jack's remark had been completely innocent. "No, thank you. I'm fine right where I am. So, how are your parents, and Meg?"

"They're good. They were here a week ago."

"I thought of them in late July, during the moon landing. Meg must've been ecstatic."

Jack smiled. "My parents took her to Cape Kennedy for the launch."

"You're kidding!"

"She hasn't stopped talking about the trip ever since." Again the smile, except this time, sheepish. "Actually, I missed the event."

Her mouth fell open. "What?"

"Yup. When you're at Harvey Cedars, you get so caught up in the conference and the rhythms of the beach, everything else seems, I don't know, less important somehow—not that Apollo 11 wasn't important, but well ..." He seemed to be searching for the right words, "... *God* is here, you know?"

She didn't know, but she had a small awareness of the venue's set-apart-from-the-world persona. She considered some other things he'd missed during the summer, brutal things like the Manson murders and that weird accident Ted Kennedy had been involved in on Martha's Vineyard. She wouldn't have minded avoiding those headlines.

They returned to their beach blanket and lay in the sun discussing less weighty things, the weather, the configuration of Long Beach Island, the inherent greed of seagulls. Around noon, one of the older teens stood up. "Let's have lunch!" One of the girls produced a huge bag of sandwiches and chips, leaving Melanie wondering where the stash had come from. "What'll you have, Melanie, baloney or baloney?"

"I think I'll have baloney."

The girl slapped her palm to her forehead. "Uh-oh, I forgot drinks!"

"My mom took care of that," Sue Webster said. She reached for one of the totes she'd brought, and Melanie spotted a multitude of Coke bottles wrapped with beach towels, presumably to prevent them from breaking in transit.

Although the drinks were tepid, they washed down the sandwiches and chips. Melanie allowed herself to enjoy chatting with the other staff members about their hometowns, mostly in New York, New Jersey, and Pennsylvania, and their experiences at the conference. Then some of the kids started playing Frisbee, while others worked on their tans. At two o'clock Jack granted Melanie's unspoken wish to hang out with him apart from everyone else when some of the guys announced they were heading back to the hotel to get ready for a miniature golf tournament.

"Are you coming?" one of them asked Jack and Melanie. "We could use some fresh blood."

Jack waved his hand. "I think we've had enough sun for a while. Do you agree, Melanie?"

"Oh, yes. I certainly have."

After the group dispersed, he asked if she'd like to ride around the island. "You'll have to drive, though. I left Sam at home this summer."

She smiled. "Good old Sam."

"Yes, he's good, and he's old. Let me just say I look forward to getting in your Mustang."

Once again they caught up with each other in front of the Victorian hotel after showering and changing their clothes. She handed Jack the keys, and he got behind the wheel, rolling down the window. "I'll bet you've named this baby."

"'Mustang Sally.'"

He smiled. "Of course!"

"Speaking of music, what stations do you get down here?" She turned on the radio and listened for his instructions.

"I'll find one. I don't know them by name or number." He began playing with the dial, then stopped at the light on Long Beach Island Boulevard. "There's something I want to show you."

The light changed, and they headed north. "This is a sweet ride. I'll bet the cops keep an eye out for you, though." A station was playing "San Francisco," and he settled back, drumming his fingers on the dash with his right hand.

"I don't have a lead foot, unlike some people." Melanie winked at him, glad to be falling back into their accustomed bantering. She burst out laughing at a sign for one of the communities north of Harvey Cedars. "Loveladies! What kind of name is Loveladies?"

He grinned. "I know. There are some, well, creatively named places around here. I've gotten so used to them, though, I don't notice until someone else sees them for the first time. You've never been to LBI, have you?"

"Not that I can remember. We used to go to the beach when I was little, but we usually went to Cape Cod. I only recall one trip to the Jersey shore, and there was an amusement park along the boardwalk."

Jack scratched his chin. "Could've been Ocean City or Wildwood, maybe Asbury Park or Seaside Heights. The island doesn't have any boardwalks."

"That's unusual."

"I guess so, but this place is more peaceful. I do like a good boardwalk sometimes though—my favorite one is Ocean City."

"Where are we headed?" She checked her gas gauge, which was on half full.

"One of my favorite places here, Barnegat Lighthouse, or 'Old Barney.'"

"I love lighthouses."

"I'm glad."

"Eve of Destruction" came on.

"Ugh." Melanie scrunched up her nose.

"What's 'ugh'?"

She pointed to the radio. "That song has always given me the creeps."

"The message is certainly strong."

"And bleak. I don't like thinking about how there could be a nuclear war to destroy everything." She shivered as her mind conjured images of mushroom clouds she'd grown up seeing in her worst nightmares. He was quiet for a while, and Melanie wondered whether he wasn't afraid of the terrible possibility of the world being fried to a crisp.

"I guess I'm not bothered too much by the song because I know how it's all going to turn out."

They stopped for yet another light, and she turned to him. "How what's going to turn out?"

"The world. History."

"You do? How can anyone know such a thing?"

"When Jesus returns, he's going to make everything right, the way life was supposed to be all along."

She wanted to consider the bold statement, but an irate driver honked because the light had turned green, and Jack hadn't moved along fast enough to suit the woman. "Maybe you don't know about what I just said."

"I remember something about Jesus returning from a confirmation class when I was a kid, but I can't say I understood any of it."

"His return is the greatest hope we have. We both know what a mess the world is in and how confused and afraid a lot of people are. Just think of how bad things were last year."

So much death. So much rebellion and destruction. An image of Bobby Kennedy lying on the floor bleeding thrust itself onto her mind's eye.

"God is in control, and history is heading in the right direction, to a time when he'll make all things new."

Melanie liked the sound of those words better than being on an eve of destruction, but she wondered whether they could be more than wishful thinking.

CHAPTER SEVENTEEN

When they left the car, Melanie leaned so far back she looked like she was doing the Limbo, attempting to take in the soaring height of the white-on-the-bottom, red-on-the-top "Old Barney." She understood how such a dominant lighthouse deserved a nickname. "Can we go up?"

Jack beamed, seemingly quite pleased with himself. "You sound a lot like my little sister. Of course we can go up."

A uniformed guard welcomed them at the entrance and waved them inside after Jack paid the admission fee. "Just watch your step. All two hundred and seventeen of them."

Jack motioned for Melanie to go first, and as they began to climb nineteenth century stairs in the dimly lit, almost chilly, interior, their quickened steps gradually slowed as they ascended. Ahead of them a father and his tow-haired son forged ever upward, the boy's relentless chatter about the lighthouse echoing off the brick walls.

Melanie smiled to herself. *That kid would make a great news commentator.* She called over her shoulder. "How long has this been here?"

"Since the 1850s. There was a different one before Old Barney, but it was built too close to the water and eventually collapsed."

She pondered how this colossus had stood many tests of time and tides, a witness to the eras as they unfolded amidst wars and the rumors thereof. As they stood on the observation deck at the top, the wind intensified, whipping through their hair, the view from forty feet up rendering the intrepid party speechless, even the little chatter box. Melanie saw the dad put his arm around his son, wishing Jack would do the same with her.

"Wave to Mommy!" the man said, and the two looked over the protective barrier to the ground where a woman waved back, shielding her eyes from the sun. Melanie peeked over the side and drew back.

She gulped. "That is a very long way down."

The world was quieter here, and everything below appeared so small, so fragile. She wondered if that's how God considered the human situation from his vantage point in heaven, far removed from the flotsam and jetsam of humanity. Jack sidled closer, their sides touching.

"I love coming up here, although I've been so busy this summer I've only made the climb two other times."

Once they reached the bottom, they walked around the grounds and along the beach, where they finally settled on a blanket with two sodas they'd purchased at a corner store.

She took a deep breath, gathering her courage. "Let's talk about college. I've been dying to talk to you about where we're both going." *Oh brother! Could I sound any more eager?*

Jack was staring into the undulating azure distance. "Being at Harvey Cedars this summer has been a game changer for me."

"How do you mean?" She smoothed back a strand of hair from her face.

"I've been thinking about majoring in journalism, as you well know, but here, well, I received a different calling."

Melanie frowned. "I'm not sure I understand."

He gazed into her eyes with such tenderness she choked up. "I'm going to become a minister."

The ocean roared in her ears. *A minister?* "Why a minister?"

"I always wanted to broadcast the news, and I still do, except now the news I'm going to proclaim is the gospel of Jesus Christ. Instead of sitting in front of a camera, I'll be standing behind a pulpit."

"Where will you go? A seminary maybe?" Hope rose in her spirit. *Princeton Seminary?*

"I'll have four years of college, then seminary." His eyes held her gaze. "I'm going to Asbury College in Wilmore, Kentucky."

"Asbury? I never heard of it." She instantly regretted the impulsive and ungracious remark.

"The school is near Lexington. Horse country."

"I, uh, I'm not sure why you chose this school."

"Before I was born, my parents went to an evangelistic crusade led by a man called Ford Philpot, who'd graduated from Asbury. They were so impressed they've supported his ministry over the years, and they came to know more about the college through him. We all loved the campus and the people when we went for a tour and my interview." He smiled. "My parents are over the moon."

She nodded, swallowing around a knob in her throat. "I guess so. The school just seems so, well, far away."

"Asbury is a bit of a hike, but so worth the effort."

Attempting to lighten her own mood she asked, "Have there been other ministers in your family?"

"Not that I know of."

A sudden recollection dawned on Melanie of something she'd learned while living with Edith Markley. "There was one in my family, but a long time ago."

He lurched back his head and upper body. "No kidding! What do you know about him?"

"I'm pretty sure his name was Sharp, and he lived in the early seventeen hundreds, in Bucks County I believe." She reached back into her memory bank to make a withdrawal, surprised at her clarity. "He went to a log school or something …"

Jack's expression popped. "The Log College?"

"Yes! The Log College. You know of the place?"

"I sure do. The school was a hub of the First Great Awakening, a revival affecting the colonies in the decades before the Revolutionary War. The person behind the college was the Reverend William Tennent, who was friendly with George Whitefield."

"I've heard his name before. Wasn't he a leader in the Awakening?"

"Yes. There'd been isolated cases of revival before he came to America from England in 1737, but after he arrived, all heaven broken loose."

She smiled. "I like how you put that."

"If your ancestor or relative was educated by Tennent, chances are he was caught up in the spirit of revival as well."

Melanie wasn't sure what Jack meant, but she liked his enthusiasm. "I do know from a little booklet my grandmother has that Sharp served churches around Bucks County."

Her friend whistled. "That's quite a godly heritage you have there. Who knows? Your Pastor Sharp might've even known George Whitefield."

Now she wished she'd read more about the man.

Jack leaned closer. "Now then, young lady, where will you be going to college?"

"Actually, I wanted to go to Columbia for journalism, but my dad wasn't too happy with my choice. He insisted I go somewhere less volatile. As you know, the school is experiencing a lot of unrest."

"I've seen the news reports, and I think your dad is right, although it's a shame those riots kept you from your first choice of schools."

She shrugged her shoulders, having worked through the disappointment. "Also I applied to Vassar because my mother and both aunts went there, but I wasn't crazy about the school." She felt a blush rise to her cheeks. "You might find this hard to believe, Jack, but I'm going to Princeton." She didn't add, "And planning to stay as far away from my grandmother as I possibly can."

He squeezed her hand. "Your grandfather went there and taught there. Your father went there. Your going to Princeton makes sense."

She couldn't bring herself to look into his eyes, wishing he'd say how much he'd miss her, a tiny rivulet between them becoming a gulf.

⚜

She let him drive back to Harvey Cedars. "As soon as we get there, I'll need to get dressed for dinner. You are staying for dinner, right? Tonight's our banquet, and the chapel speaker will give a brief message after we eat. Everything will be in the dining room."

"Thanks for inviting me, Jack, but I only brought beach-type clothes."

"Not everyone dresses up."

"Okay, I'd like to come then. Thank you."

"My pleasure."

Melanie nearly jumped out of her seat when "Abraham, Martin, and John" came over the airwaves.

Jack pursed his lips. "Of all the songs we'd hear together."

"The words are so beautiful yet so heartbreaking. They take me back to spring a year ago."

He tapped his head with a finger. "Those memories will always stay here."

Did he mean the assassinations, or being with her?

When the dinner bell resounded, Melanie flowed with the tide into the dining hall, which had been transformed from a boisterous eatery filled with noisy families to an adults-only, candle-lit room. The conference director's wife was playing "Blessed Assurance" on the piano, followed by the song Melanie had heard earlier in chapel, "Sweet, Sweet Spirit." After everyone had found their seats and Al Oldham prayed, the eating commenced. Melanie smiled when Jack appeared in his apron and hovered near her chair, wishing this wonderful day wouldn't have to end, aching with the uncertainty of what would happen between them when they said goodbye.

Angus Marshall went to the top of the stairs when desserts had been eaten, dishes pushed to the side. Gripping a wooden lectern, he said, "I hope I can keep everyone awake after such a fabulous meal. Aye, I hope I can keep myself awake!" The laughter subsiding, he invited them to pray with him, then he tucked into his message.

Melanie positioned her chair so she could see him better, without obstructing the view of the person sitting behind her.

"There is a universal longing for peace these days, from the ubiquitous peace signs of the young, who yearn for an end to war, to the hallowed halls of government where VIPs deliberate about how to accomplish such a goal. You see the yearning in people, whose hearts ache from loss and loneliness. 'Peace, peace!' they cry! But there is no peace."

Melanie balked inside to think there was no peace to be had. Surely Angus wasn't going to lead them down a path of despair.

"There is but one path to peace, though it is not the way of Buddha or Confucius, the Maharishi Mahesh Yogi or Ghandi, or even Martin Luther King Jr., although he knew something of it." Angus leaned against the lectern. "Before he went to the cross, the Lord Jesus told his disciples, 'Peace I leave with you, my peace I give unto you, not as the world giveth.' Jesus, the Prince of Peace, invites you to put your trust in him, not in the prevailing winds of politics or politicians, or of culture, which changes like shifting sand. Do you have his peace in your heart, peace that passes all human understanding, and effort?"

Melanie's mouth fell open when Angus looked straight at her for a moment before continuing.

"Maybe you've followed him for years, but his peace still isn't there, obstructed by neglect or fear or sin. Perhaps you've never asked him into your life, to forgive your sins and set you on the straight and narrow way that leads to life, and peace. He now invites you into his peace."

Her hands shook, her pulse raced. Jesus was someone she looked up to, and she had positioned her life according to the Golden Rule her mother had taught her long ago. As for knowing Jesus, Melanie had no doubt she did not. She took a deep breath, inhaling the remains of their meal, the scent of coffee, the fragrance of hope.

"What do you have to lose by putting your life into his hands?" Angus asked. "Only your fear and hopeless condition."

When he bowed his head to pray, Melanie took a leap of faith, holding her breath in case God didn't catch her.

Angus invited the people to pray with him if they wanted to receive Jesus Christ. "Lord, I need you. There is an emptiness in my heart only you can fill. There are sins only you can forgive. I have tried to go my own way, but I am lost and cannot find salvation apart from you.

"Cleanse me from my sins, and renew a right spirit within me. I give you myself, my life, my here and now, as well as my future. I praise you for calling me to yourself. I trust you and love you. I thank you that now I belong to you. Amen."

❊

She stood in the parking lot with Jack saying the goodbye she'd been dreading, buoyed by her brand-new relationship with Christ.

He spoke with uncharacteristic tenderness, his right foot tracing an abstract picture in the gravel. "I'm so glad you came, Melanie." A group of adults passed by while the sun slipped behind the horizon over the bay.

"Thank you for inviting me, Jack. This is a really special place. I … I'm glad I came." Jack tilted his head, scrutinizing her. She rubbed the back of her neck. "I really liked Angus's talk tonight."

Jack's eyes were a freshly-lit match. "What did he say that you liked?"

She blurted, "I prayed with him—at the end. I prayed I would know God's peace and follow Jesus."

He grasped her shoulders and pulled her to himself. "How wonderful, Melanie! The very angels in heaven are rejoicing."

She could've stayed in his embrace, but he let go. "I haven't really trusted God since my mom died because, well, because she died. He didn't heal her." Tears stung her eyes.

"There are mysteries we'll never completely understand this side of Heaven, but I am learning to trust God with them in my life, to give him the benefit of my doubts." He smiled. "When I was a kid, I loved *The Chronicles of Narnia* by C.S. Lewis. In the first book, some children travel to another world, and they hear about a lion named Aslan. A character called Mr. Beaver tells them Aslan is the Great Lion, and he's going to set Narnia free from a witch's terrible curse. One of the kids asks if Aslan is safe. 'Safe!' Mr. Beaver says, 'Of course he's not safe … But he's good.'" Jack leaned closer and looked into her eyes. "He is good. I promise."

They embraced for a long moment, then he set upon her lips a light kiss. "I'm going to miss you, Melanie McKnight. You know we need to stay in touch."

Her hands shook as she reached into a pocket for a piece of paper. "This is my contact information at Princeton."

He didn't remove his eyes from her face as he took the note. "I'll write first since I don't know my new address yet. I'll pray for you, Melanie. I hope your dreams come true at Princeton, but maybe not all of them."

CHAPTER EIGHTEEN

Late October 1969

At times that fall, Melanie wondered whether she'd gone to a university in the Pacific Northwest rather than Princeton. The golden glow of first days, however soggy, lingered during the honeymoon phase of new classes, new friends, and continuing her work with the *Packet*. The syllabus for her Intro to English Lit course became a sort of key to unlocking great and wonderful things she'd not yet known, which would elevate her own writing. Her professors smoked pipes and wore Harris Tweed jackets. She walked quite literally in the steps of her father and grandfather.

Eight weeks later, Melanie slouched at a table in Firestone Library while rain and wind pummeled the windows, reminiscing about being at that very spot a year and a half ago with Bill, Cindy, and Jack. She wondered how her old friends were doing. According to Jack, Bill had gone to Cornell, Cindy had ended up at Douglass. Were any relationships supposed to be permanent? Could anyone be counted upon to stay the course of one's life? She and Jack were already running in far different circles, hundreds of miles apart, the odds of their staying in touch running low. She sat up a little taller, however, when she called to mind a letter he'd sent from Asbury College a few weeks ago, a chatty missive which ended, "This school is everything I hoped, and more." If only she could say the same about Princeton.

She rested her head on her hand, staring at the Bible she was supposed to be reading for comparative religion class, wondering how the freshness of college life could've gone so sour after just six weeks. Decay had begun when three weeks after school began, Ellen Harper tossed a bombshell—"I got an offer from a paper in Chicago, and since I'm from Michigan and want to be closer to home, I'll be leaving in ten days."

Melanie had managed little more than a gasp and an "Oh."

"Don't worry about your position. I've told the new editor all about you, and he's assured me you can stay on board." She had paused, smiled. "Working with you and your Jack has been a highlight of my time here. I'm so glad you decided to stay in Princeton and will still be writing for us. I have high hopes for you."

Jay Traynor, on the contrary, had no time for mentoring. To him Melanie was the perfect stringer—young, energetic, hungry, someone who had to work her way up just like everyone else—not some wunderkind-daughter-of-Cliff McKnight writing feature stories. He assigned her to police coverage, peewee football games, and meetings of the Independent Order of Odd Fellows. "If you're going to stay here," Traynor also said, "you're going to need to put in at least twenty hours a week. Otherwise, I'll need to hire someone else." Ellen Harper had been content with a weekly quality piece so as not to interfere with school.

Lacking sleep, Melanie dragged her heavy-lidded self to an eight o'clock English Literature class, struggling to stay awake for what had turned out to be a waking nightmare. Her professor, a bearded, black turtleneck-wearing Beatnik, surely had patented the sleeping pill. His doctoral dissertation had been on Joseph Conrad's *Heart of Darkness*, one of Melanie's least favorite novels, and he conducted every lecture with a surgeon's precision, parsing one or two sentences from the book. The only way Melanie stayed sane as well as awake was to concoct an elaborate daydream about David Soul.

She sighed, slumping further into the library chair, deciding to throw herself a pity party.

Her classes constantly disappointed and confused her. Two instructors openly denigrated her new Christian faith: "Christianity is responsible for most of the wars in the last two thousand years," said one. The other extolled the virtues of every other world religion, including Buddhism, to which he personally subscribed. "White Europeans slaughtered thousands during the Crusades," he said, "and when they came to the Americas, they ravaged the native populations." Meanwhile her religion professor dug away at the foundations of orthodoxy with complex redaction theories and form criticism, constantly comparing Bible "myths" to those of other cultures and religions. Judaism and Christianity weren't special, he intimated, but other people's faiths were to be highly exalted.

Hoping to find balance and strength in a good church, Melanie had instead left each service more parched than when she'd arrived. The ones she visited were either too emotional, too political, too country-clubbish, or just plain as dead. When she decided to go back to Jack's church, she discovered his pastor had gone elsewhere. The Clydes had been thrilled to see her and invited her to sit with them, but their welcome proximity had been the only balm in Gilead. The new minister read a Scripture passage, but rather than explain and apply the text to everyday life the way Mr. Bennely or Angus Marshall had done, he used the passage as a launching pad for social activism, women's lib in particular. Melanie hauled herself to the parking lot with a leaden spirit and spoke briefly with the Clydes before returning to campus.

"I really enjoyed seeing you, Melanie," Ann said. "I so wish we didn't already have a commitment, or we'd ask you to join us for lunch."

Rain started falling, again.

Michael Clyde spoke with apology in his tone. "Our new minister sure is different from the last one."

"I, uh, noticed."

Meg wasn't quite so diplomatic. "That man is dry as dust."

Ann mentioned the name of a congregation in Princeton Junction, but Melanie never got there, or to any other church after that Sunday because her editor had assigned her to the Saturday night graveyard shift.

I could use a good strong cup of coffee. She turned the page of the Bible she hadn't really been focusing on for her assignment when a voice startled her.

"I see you're reading my book."

"Excuse me?" She snapped to mental attention to discover Tall Dark and Handsome pointing to her Bible, opened to the book of Joshua.

"I said, I see you're reading my book."

"Uh, okay."

"You're Melanie, right?" He sat next to her.

For the life of her, she couldn't remember his name but knew he was in her religion class.

"Josh Nalley." He stuck out his hand, which she found oh, so warm.

I've heard that name before. She took a stab at recovering a measure of poise. "I'm Melanie McKnight."

"So, you're working on our assignment." He grinned.

She bantered back. "I make a good show of it."

Josh laughed and leaned back as if he owned the place. "My kind of girl. So, how do you like the class?"

She shrugged her shoulders. "Not so much."

"I know what you mean. Bosch is a bore, but some of the reading is interesting—all those old myths and legends. What's your major?"

"English."

"Mine's economics, but then with a father like mine, how could I study anything else?" He shrugged his shoulders, his crewneck sweater, which had been tied around his neck, coming loose. He pulled off the garment.

Who is his father, and why should I know about him? Melanie frowned.

He winked at her and rose from the chair. "I'll let you get back to your, uh, studies. See you in class."

He left a trail of stardust behind him.

In spite of her exhaustion, Melanie gave in to her roommate's ceaseless invitation to attend the Princeton-Dartmouth football game.

"You know the old saying about all work and no play," Tish Johnson said.

"How can I not? You've emblazoned it in my mind the last few days."

"Seriously, though, you need to get some fresh air. You're starting to show signs of prison pallor."

"Epic rainfall will do that."

"Oh, I know! I hate this weather." Tish clapped her hands and gestured toward their window. "But just look outside! This is a day meant for football."

She had to admit sun-sprayed Palmer Stadium offered much more to be desired than being crouched next to a scratchy police scanner.

At half-time, Melanie did a double take when she saw Josh a few rows ahead stand and stretch puma-like. She blushed when he caught her staring and with a wave, smiled in her direction.

Tish elbowed her. "Who is that?"

"His name's Josh. He's in my religion class."

"Well, here he comes."

He covered the distance between them in an instant. "Hi, Melanie!"

"Hi, Josh."

"What a game, huh? If not for that field goal, we'd be in big trouble."

When he glanced at Tish, Melanie introduced them. "This is my roommate, Tish Johnson. Tish, Josh … uh …"

"Nalley."

Josh's buddies came over and swept him away, and she and Tish headed for the women's restroom.

"What a hunk!"

Melanie giggled. "He certainly is."

Coach Jake McCandless's Tigers employed his single-wing, T-formation offense in the second half and, giddy with the thrill of victory, Melanie and Tish hugged each other, jumping up and down when their team won in the final seconds.

Tish was beaming. "I am so happy to see you so happy."

"Happy feels good."

Just then Josh intercepted her. "What a game!"

"I know! I think I screamed myself hoarse."

"A group of us are going out for pizza. Would you care to join us? Our treat." He looked first at Melanie, then Tish.

"Sure, thanks."

"I'm game," Tish said, and they broke into laughter.

Josh and five freshmen guys accompanied the girls to the shop on Nassau Street, Melanie warming up from the brisk walk and stimulating conversation. For the next two hours, they worked their way through three large pizzas, then Josh accompanied Melanie back to Pyne Hall with his friend Bob walking side-by-side with Tish.

At the entrance to the dorm, Melanie thanked them. "What a fun time I had! Thank you for inviting me, uh, us."

"My pleasure. And speaking of my pleasure, I have tickets to see *Man of La Mancha* at McCarter next Wednesday night. Would you like to go?"

She could not contain a smile rising to her lips while her recent, constant companion, Loneliness, took a step backward. Jack's letters were becoming less frequent, probably because Melanie was so exhausted from classes and her job at the paper she couldn't add another thing to her to-do list, including writing to him. Maybe life wouldn't always be so busy. Maybe Jack would come home for Thanksgiving, and they could see each other again, but for now, there were no formal ties of any kind to bind them. Even God seemed distant. Each day was a race against time, with no time for Bible reading or prayer.

She looked into Josh's keen and handsome face. She would go out with him. She needed a diversion.

CHAPTER NINETEEN

She tottered under a stack of books, notebooks, and the parcel she'd retrieved for Tish in the mailroom. *No doubt another care package from home.* Her friend hopped off the chair where she'd been studying at her carefully organized desk.

"I found this box for you." Melanie accepted Tish's help in releasing the package, roughly the size of a dorm refrigerator, onto her roommate's bed.

"Oh, thank you Mel!" She reached for a pair of scissors from a desk drawer. "I wonder what they could've sent this time, and so close to Thanksgiving. I mean, I'll be there in less than a week."

Such a burden. Melanie hung up her coat and sank onto her unmade bed, fatigued beyond exhaustion. She wrapped a blanket around her shoulders, although the room was a comfortable seventy degrees, while Tish opened the package with the anticipation of a three-year-old on her birthday.

Tish squealed at the sight of a cashmere sweater in Princeton orange, followed by a new pair of Bass Weejuns, in addition to an assortment of European cookies and pricy teas. "Can you believe my parents?"

"They're amazing all right." She wanted to express happiness for Tish, which wasn't easy while absorbing her own slings and arrows. The one time she'd heard from her father since starting college was when she'd called to remind him he'd forgotten to send her allowance. Rather than apologize, he'd dug in. "You know I can't be remembering such a small detail, Melanie. I'll open a checking account for you so you don't have to keep asking." He'd deposited a substantial sum, enough to keep her going for a year, enough to keep her from bothering him.

Tish opened a red plaid box of Scottish shortbread and offered one to Melanie, who normally would have accepted. The sight of the biscuits almost made her hurl, and she telescoped further into her blanket. "No thanks."

Tish drew closer, peering into Melanie's face. "Are you okay? You don't look well. Come to think of it, you haven't for a few days."

Since the incident with Josh a week earlier, she hadn't been able to get a good night's sleep either. Weary to the bone, she nevertheless found falling asleep as difficult as a final exam in physics, and when she did slumber, her body shifted into restlessness. Her clothes were beginning to hang on her since food had begun tasting of burnt ashes. She would've liked to tell someone what had happened, but she didn't want to burst Tish's utterly happy Princeton bubble. "I don't feel well." Relieved by the admission, Melanie allowed herself to experience the full effects of her pounding head and sore throat. "Would you mind turning off that light?" She pointed to the overhead boring into her eyes.

"I'm going to get Claire."

Their dorm assistant came to the room moments later, placing her hand on Melanie's forehead, frowning. "You're burning up."

She could've fooled Melanie, shivering almost uncontrollably.

"I'll get my car, Tish. We need to take her to a doctor right away."

In her feverish state, Melanie's trip to McCosh Infirmary on the other side of campus played out like a movie in which she was a viewer. At the clinic, Tish shared Melanie's information with the registration person, answering questions about her birthday, class year, campus address, and phone number, the voices pulsing through Melanie's brain. Three students were ahead of them, and Tish and Claire guided Melanie to a chair in the waiting room. Ten minutes later, she leaped from the seat. "I'm going to be sick."

Claire dashed to get a nurse, who escorted Melanie to an examination room and unceremoniously shoved a bed pan under her face, just in the nick of time. The nurse took her temperature—one hundred and two—then drew a vial of blood. Woozy, Melanie found herself hustled to a hospital-type room where a different nurse helped get Melanie out of her street clothes and into hospital pajamas big enough to accommodate all three Stooges.

"I apologize about the PJs. Since we just went coed, we only have them for the male students—our shipment of female gowns hasn't arrived yet."

Tish spoke from the doorway. "I'll bring some of your things, Melanie."

She muttered a thanks, which came out sounding more like *phlanksbeesom.*

Where am I? A soft light burned on a night table and outside, the light could have belonged to either dusk or dawn. Starched white sheets caressed her skin, and she pulled a thin blanket tighter in an attempt to get warm while swallowing to dampen her Sahara-like throat. The door was open a crack, and she could hear people walking around. *I am so desperately thirsty.* She couldn't form words, and some time passed before she discovered a call button lying next to her head on the pillow. A nurse in a white uniform and cap came right away.

"Well, hello, Melanie. I thought you might be waking up soon."

She liked the woman's voice, soothing as sweet tea. "So thirsty."

"Of course you are. Let's start with some ice chips."

When she returned with a large cup, she introduced herself. "I'm Mrs. Gordon. How are you feeling?" She reached for Melanie's wrist to take her pulse.

"Throat is awful. Head pounds. So tired."

"You're a very sick young lady. You have mononucleosis."

Her eyelids flew open. "Mono? Isn't that the … the kissing disease?" She cringed when Josh came to mind.

"So I've heard, but mono is more commonly caused by being run down. Like most college students, you've no doubt been dashing about and not getting enough sleep." She let go of Melanie's wrist.

"How long?"

"How long will you be here?" When Melanie nodded, the woman continued. "That depends on how well you mend. Hopefully, we can get you back on your feet in a week or two, but it's often a month before you start feeling like your old self again."

"But Thanksgiving."

"Let's not worry about that now."

She noticed her suitcase in a corner and guessed Tish must have brought her things. This was going to be a long stay.

She slept most of the weekend, waking up long enough to take a little soup and tea, admiring a bouquet of roses sent by the girls on her floor. When a chaplain came from the seminary, she sat at the edge of the bed, ready for spiritual consolation and prayer. The bearded pastor offered neither. Instead, he talked about how nice the weather was after all that rain, mentioned a recent movie he'd seen, and left without saying a prayer.

Following breakfast on Monday morning, Mrs. Gordon entered the room, or at least Melanie thought this was the nurse, as her face was obscured by a large evergreen sporting crisp red bows.

She sat up. "What on earth?"

She placed the plant on a chair and handed a small card to Melanie. "I hope you feel better soon. Love, Dad." She stared at the woman. "My dad sent me a tree?"

Mrs. Gordon scowled as she left the room, muttering about men who didn't visit their sick daughters. After a nap, Melanie called him at the office.

"How are you feeling?"

"A little better." She wanted to ask when he would visit but didn't want to set herself up for disappointment. "I ... uh, wanted to thank you for the tree."

"The what?"

"Tree—a big evergreen with red bows."

Cliff sighed. "I told my secretary to ask for the biggest plant the florist had. I didn't suppose they'd send a *tree*."

"That's okay, Dad. It's growing on me."

There was an awkward silence, then both of them burst out laughing. Though the conversation proved succinct, Melanie 's spirit had shed a load.

She fell asleep after lunch and began dreaming in her unguarded mind about recent events. Josh was kissing her goodnight after their first date as if she should have expected him to, although she hadn't. She pulled back and said, "Thanks, Jack. I had a nice time."

Josh chortled. "Jack? I've been called lots of things before, but never Jack."

Flushed with embarrassment, Melanie fled to her room. Still, Josh invited her to a dance on Charter Day, helping himself to her neck, then her lips as if he had some right to them. Tingling at her core, she went on red alert. Something was not right.

The same weekend, Cliff McKnight had come to campus to give an address on media and politics, and Melanie introduced him to Josh at a reception.

"You must be Hal's son." He clapped Josh on the shoulder. "I know him well."

Why is he never this amiable with me?

The two of them launched into a conversation about Josh's dad, a US Representative from out West. Each time Melanie opened her mouth, they looked at her as if they were wondering where she'd come from, then jumped back into their discussion.

Her dreams shifted gears from Charter Day to a letter she received from Jack, a vivid reminder this current flame couldn't hold a candle to her dear friend. Josh came to see her in the afternoon, and she begged off going out for ice cream. "I have a big deadline coming up for the paper."

"Oh, yes, we mustn't disappoint the Rotary Club."

She went through the next week, not seeing Josh except for religion class. Melanie thought their relationship had pretty much ended. Then he stopped by her room, glassy-eyed like her cousin Sandy after she'd been smoking dope or shooting heroin.

"Can I come in?"

She wanted the dream to end there, but the tape continued playing. Why had she let him in when Tish was at the library? *Stupid, stupid girl!* Once the door closed, Josh was all over her, tearing at her clothes. She prayed silently for help and, summoning strength beyond her own, shoved him. "Leave. Now!"

He looked as if she'd employed a cattle prod, standing stock still for a long moment when she wondered what he would do next, her throat dry and temples throbbing. Josh abruptly spit on the floor and left. Melanie shook in her sleep as she had for several hours after the incident. Tears flowed, wide open. She desperately missed Jack.

She awakened, drenched, newly traumatized. She inhaled sharply, then dispelled the horrible images. When would she stop having the dream? Wasn't this the third time now? She had an urge to flee, get away from this place, far away, but where, she didn't know. Melanie did in that moment know with complete clarity, however, Princeton and her current course of studies weren't right for her. She spoke aloud, wiping tears with the back of her trembling hand. "Please, Lord, show me what to do. I can't go on like this."

❧

The infirmary closed for Thanksgiving, and Melanie reluctantly went to her Grandmother Markley's, rather than make the trip home to Manhattan. Bea and Joe would take good care of her, and Melanie would do her best to stay far away from Edith. After dinner, she went to her room to doze and read, roused a half hour later when her door opened after a soft knock. She flew awake and sat up. "Aunt Jane!"

Jane Markley Fletcher covered the room in two strides, taking her niece into her arms. "Oh, my precious girl! Just look at you!"

"I know, I'm a mess." Melanie attempted to smooth her rumpled nightgown.

"No, not at all! My favorite niece is a beautiful woman."

She grinned. "Now I know why you've always been my favorite aunt." She stared at the woman, a slightly older, slightly bigger version of her mother, and before she could utter another word, the dam broke.

Jane's arms encircled her niece, and she crooned. "It's okay, honey, you just go ahead. You've been so sick." Jane's years in Virginia had softened her voice to a soothing, slight drawl. After emptying her reservoir of tears, Melanie leaned against the headboard, spent. Her aunt pulled the wing chair closer. "Tell me everything."

Melanie poured out the contents of her story—the horrible spring of 1968, writing for the paper, her estrangement from her father, her fondness for Jack and desperation for God, the debacle at Princeton. "Oh, Aunt Jane, I'm a screw-up. What a mess I'm in!" She wiped her eyes and blew her nose.

Her aunt's eyes pierced. "Darling, let me tell you something, everyone is a screw up. Every last one of us." Her sudden laughter lifted the curtains of Melanie's dark mood. "I've had a train wreck or two in my life."

"You? You're so pulled together."

"Wisdom comes by learning, my dear, and all too often comes the hard way."

She looked at her hands, noticing she needed to file her nails. "What do I do now?"

Jane sprang from the chair. "Come back with me to Richmond."

"Richmond!" The idea, both absurd and wonderful, beckoned with an outstretched arm of welcome.

"Yes, Richmond, Yankee girl. You come stay with me, and you can take your time sorting everything out."

She wanted to. Desperately. Still, she hesitated. "But what about school? What about Dad?" She couldn't imagine his wrath if he found out she'd left Princeton University.

Jane's lips pinched together, then she broke into an "aha" expression. "Why not take a leave of absence? That way you won't be burning any bridges should you decide to return. As for your dad—well, young lady, you can leave him to me!"

CHAPTER TWENTY

Melanie stood in the doorway of her dorm room, scanning each alcove to ensure she hadn't left anything behind. Tish's parents had come for her earlier, the coeds parting in tears.

"I wish you all the luck in the world, Melanie. I hope we can be roommates again when you come back."

"I'll miss you, Tish. Stay in touch."

Melanie appreciated the one bright spot Tish's friendship had been in a cheerless season. She picked up her last box and locked the door, knowing in her heart she wouldn't be passing this way again. Her only regret about leaving Princeton was missing Jack, who had decided to spend his college's long holiday break ringing bells for the Salvation Army in western Pennsylvania. She went outside to her car and loaded the last box, then took an envelope out of her tote bag and walked a few feet to a mailbox. Inside a letter to Jack, painted in broad strokes, was her decision to live with her Aunt Jane and Uncle Dean for the near future. She slipped into her Mustang, stuffed to the ceiling with her belongings, and began the long trek to Richmond, laughing at the first song she heard on the radio. Melanie belted the current hit about kissing a bad experience goodbye as the Princeton campus dwindled in the rearview mirror.

The snow weather forecasters predicted would not be arriving along her three-hundred-mile route until the following day, so she stretched what would normally be a five-and-a half-hour trip to seven-and-a-half, taking frequent breaks. She still tended to tire easily, especially after the last week's push to complete all her coursework before the Christmas holiday. By the time she reached her journey's end, she yearned to be still and have her aunt prepare a meal for her.

She pulled into the driveway of their sprawling brick house near the James River, adorned from foundation to rooftop with glittering white lights. A sizable Nativity scene illuminated by a spotlight graced the lawn, spreading peace to her heart. She was home. Melanie opened the driver's side door and grabbed her purse as her Aunt Jane appeared at the entrance wearing a bright red apron and a huge smile. Melanie rushed to her embrace, then hugged her uncle, a quiet man who was just as she remembered from her childhood, mellow and kind. Although his hair had gone mostly the color of stainless steel, his trim boyishness remained. The soft accents of his native Richmond bore a warm welcome.

"Thanks for having me, Uncle Dean."

"It's our pleasure. Do you want me to bring your things in now or after you've rested?"

"I can help."

He raised his right hand. "This is my job."

"Well then, now, if you don't mind." She couldn't wait to make this place home.

"Melanie?"

"Come in, Aunt Jane." She finished smoothing the comforter on her just-made bed. At her feet lay a full laundry basket. She turned toward the door. "Do I have time to put a load of wash in before we leave?"

"Honestly, Melanie, you're a lot neater than either of my two kids when they were your age. Of course you do." She waved an envelope, then handed the letter to her. "You got mail."

She glanced at the return address. *It's from Dad.* "Do I have time to read this?"

Jane nodded. "Sure. There's no particular hurry. I just want to get to the stores before they get too crowded."

"I'll be quick." Her aunt closed the door behind her, and Melanie sat on the side of the double bed, slipping her right index finger under the sealed flap. Inside, she found a red and gold card with the inscription, "To a Wonderful Daughter at Christmas." A check fell out, but she read the verse first. "I may not always say it, but a daughter like you is a rare and precious gift. Merry Christmas." The card was signed, "Love, Dad." Warmed to within an inch of her soul, she lifted the check and blinked several times—five hundred dollars. Much more than his financial generosity, the card imparted her father's tacit acceptance of her decision to move to Richmond, even if he didn't altogether understand her reasons. When she'd told him right after Thanksgiving, Cliff had tried talking her into staying at the university, but he'd relented upon realizing how determined—and dispirited—she was.

She pressed the card to her chest. *I'm going to buy two things today—a piece of jewelry to remind myself of Dad, and something special for his Christmas gift.*

❊

She and Jane spent most of the day downtown, first at Thalhimers, then across the street at Miller and Rhoads where dozens of children waited in Santaland to see the right jolly old elf. Jane bought her own last-minute gifts, helped Melanie shop her list, and purchased items for the upcoming holiday feast she'd be throwing. Melanie's two cousins and their small children, all living in Florida, would be passing through Christmas Day on their way to skiing and visiting other relatives. Since Melanie had only been with the cousins a few times in her life when she was little, she didn't know what to get them.

"You don't need to buy them presents," Jane said, but Melanie was hoping small tokens might help her connect with them. Jane helped her select candy everyone would enjoy, as well as books for the kids, then going off by herself, Melanie purchased a scarf for Jane, a polo shirt for her uncle, and a striped silk tie for her dad, one she thought would look especially good on the air. The department store kindly arranged to ship her father's gift for an additional fee, promising he'd get the tie by Christmas.

"I'm pooped." Jane slumped against a cosmetic counter. "Let's stop in the Tea Room for a piece of chocolate silk pie."

"Yum. I could go for that."

They waited a few minutes to be seated, then set their packages down and sat across from each other at a corner table. After placing their orders, they leaned back in the cushy chairs, pleased with the outcome of their labors.

"This is the nicest Christmas I've had in a long time."

"I'm so glad, sweetheart. You've had a hard time since Jackie died."

"You and Uncle Dean are very kind to let me stay with you for a while."

Jane leaned back in the chair, gazing at her niece. "I always wanted to look after you. I really thought Cliff would give in, too, especially when he was traveling with the presidential campaign and your housekeeper got sick or whatever. When Mother told me you were going to stay with her, I got right on the phone and called Cliff, figuring it wouldn't hurt to try again."

Melanie closed her eyes and tilted her head. "I don't understand."

"Oh, I badgered him over the years to let Dean and me raise you. My kids had left by then, and I had plenty of room." She smiled. "I always loved your mother, Melanie, and you were the sweetest little girl, a mirror of her personality. When I see you, she doesn't seem so far away."

Melanie's jaw dropped. "Why didn't Dad let me come? Grandmother was awful!"

A waiter brought cups of coffee, and Jane took a sip. "He didn't want you to be this far away. Anyway, the Lord had other plans."

Dad wanted me close to him? She shook her head, processing the unexpected news. Then she spoke again. "I would never have guessed."

"Guessed what?"

"Well, first of all, my dad wasn't trying to avoid me like I thought he was, and second, you wanted to raise me. I never knew any of that." She chuffed a truncated laugh. "My dad drives me crazy! All this time, I thought I was in his way. He isn't a warm person, not like you and Uncle Dean. His work has been everything."

Jane nodded. "He's the sort of person whose feelings run so deep others rarely know or are aware of them. I always liked Cliff, but I could tell he was more comfortable around work than people. The exception, of course, was Jackie. She was really good for him."

Melanie bit her lower lip. "He must've been devastated when she died."

"He was, and although he may be awkward with you, and doesn't always do or say the right thing, he loves you, Melanie, more than he is able to express."

⁂

When they reentered the fray of last-minute shoppers, Melanie sought Jane's advice at the jewelry department, explaining she wanted to buy something special with her dad's Christmas money. "I already have a lot of nice pieces that belonged to Mom, including this one." She reached into her coat and showed Jane the locket she constantly wore with her mother's picture inside.

"I've noticed you wearing that. Our dad gave us each one when we turned thirteen. I still have mine somewhere."

Melanie swallowed this latest piece of family history, savoring it as she would a piece of dark chocolate.

"How about some earrings?"

"That's what I'm thinking of."

The saleslady took them to a glass enclosed case gleaming with gold earrings, and Melanie tried a few on before deciding she liked a medium pair of hoops best. As the woman carried the small box to the register, Melanie held up her hand. "Excuse me, I'd like to see the cross over there before I buy these earrings." When she held the delicate necklace in her hands, she examined the deep etching around each corner, lending both elegance and meaning. Wearing the cross would signify this new season in which she hoped to recover her faith as well as discover what God had for her next.

⁂

"Are you sure you don't want another one of my famous chocolate chip pancakes?" Dean held one out on a rubber turner. The aromas of pancakes, sausage, and warm maple syrup mingled in the harvest gold kitchen.

"Oh, Uncle Dean, I've already had two big ones. I'm getting downright fat." Melanie laughed. "Fat and happy."

"Happy you are, but fat is not a word I would use to describe you."

"I've gained at least five pounds since I've been here."

"Then they were five pounds you needed to put on after being sick." He coaxed his wife. "How about you, Jane—another pancake?"

She shook her head. "I've had my fill, but they were especially good this morning."

Dean observed a standing tradition of making pancakes on Sunday mornings, a day he tried hard to take off, although the babies he delivered didn't always cooperate. Afterward, they'd pile into the Jeep Wagoneer and head for St. Luke's Church. Melanie wasn't used to the Episcopal worship style when she first started attending with them, but the age-old rhythms of the faith quenched her parched spirit. Despite the congregation's "high" style, Melanie found the people warm and appearing to be deeply committed to their faith. Jane and Dean took their beliefs seriously as well, not only praying over meals, but also before they left each other for the day and when anything significant occurred. Melanie found in their paneled library a decent collection of inspirational books, which Jane invited Melanie to borrow at her pleasure. She was especially drawn to biography. *A Man Called Peter*, about the late Senate Chaplain Peter Marshall, whose closeness to God captivated those whose lives he touched, was a special favorite. Melanie sensed God using this time to prepare her for something as well, although what remained inscrutable. Whenever she tried to figure out her future, she encountered a mental roadblock, something she mentioned to her aunt after church that morning.

Jane nodded her head. "I've found sometimes you just have to wait quietly for God to show you what's next."

"I just feel like I should be *doing* something. Idleness isn't my strong suit."

"No, it isn't, but you'll know what to do when the time is right."

"I feel so strange, though, not going to school or working or helping you very much."

"First of all, it's 'y'all' down here."

Melanie couldn't help but laugh and loosened up.

"Second, just having you here is wonderful. We want you to take all the time you need to find your way."

At ten o'clock on Tuesday night, February third, the phone rang. Dean was in the family room looking at the paper. Melanie was seated across from him reading another book from the family's library, *Great Lion of God*.

Jane turned down the volume on *Marcus Welby*. "Do you want me to get that?"

Dean stood and went to the phone. "I'll answer. Mrs. Cryor might be calling. She was about ready to deliver around suppertime." He picked up the receiver. "Hello, this is Dr. Fletcher." He glanced at Melanie. "Yes, she's here." He held the phone to her, winking. "It's a man."

"Dad?"

"Definitely not your dad."

"I won't stay on long. I know you're expecting a call."

He smiled as if she had all the time in the world.

Puzzled, she took the receiver. "Hello?"

"Hi, Melanie."

She recognized his voice in a heartbeat, her pulse racing. "Jack! How are you?"

"Never better, and you?"

"I'm doing really well here in Richmond with my aunt and uncle. You sound excited."

"You wouldn't believe what's happening at Asbury."

She sat on one of the chairs, wondering where her aunt and uncle had gone. "Tell me."

"This morning we had our usual chapel service at ten o'clock."

Part of her thought, "So? What's the big deal?" The other rejoiced to hear anything he might have to say.

He paused. "Melanie, chapel is still going on."

The hair at the back of her neck stood up. "I don't understand."

"The dean was scheduled to speak, but instead he invited students to give their testimonies—you know, to say what God was doing in their lives. The first guy got up, and he started talking about how he was sorry for certain sins he'd committed, then others followed, and ... well, people were confessing some pretty heavy things, but the air in the auditorium was so pure, so clean." He sighed. "This isn't an easy experience to describe, Melanie, but as more people started confessing their sins and finding forgiveness ... *God* came. I mean, he just showed up."

She lowered herself onto the chair her uncle had vacated, trembling.

"He's doing amazing work in people's lives right in front of us. We have no idea how long this is going to last—no one wants to leave the chapel!"

"How incredible, Jack!"

"I've been here all day and, well … God has been speaking to my heart, too, about a lot of different things. When I was praying about an hour ago, you came to my mind, and the thought I had just wouldn't let go." He cleared his throat.

"Wh-what was it?"

"'Tell Melanie to come. I want my daughter here.'"

CHAPTER TWENTY-ONE

At any other time in her life, she would surely have questioned Jack's sanity, but his message had strangely warmed her heart. In the depths of her soul, she intuited whatever God had planned for her waited at Asbury. After a long moment she found her voice. "How far is Asbury from Richmond?"

"I checked. Roughly five hundred miles. Don't worry about where you'll stay. Do you remember Monica Allen from Harvey Cedars? She was at the front desk when you came." He was moving forward as if she'd already agreed to come.

She smiled at a mental image of the sweet girl with a shirt tag hanging out. "Sure."

"She's a student here and says you could stay in her room."

Apparently, he'd shared his experience with Monica, who also agreed Melanie should be part of this strange movement on campus.

"Can you stay on the line for a few minutes, Jack? I'd like to tell my aunt and uncle about this. I know this is a long distance call, so I'll be quick."

"Of course I can wait."

She went to the kitchen where they were preparing tea, obviously trying not to be nosy, and told them about the call. She wondered how in the world they would react to such a narrative and Jack's urgent summons.

Melanie took a deep breath and spread her hands as she told the story about what had happened during the morning chapel service at Asbury College. She concluded with Jack's appeal for her to come. "I know this may sound strange, but Jack said while he was praying, he sensed God was telling him I needed to be there too." She jittered her foot against the floor as she waited for their response.

Her aunt and uncle gazed at each other, and she tried to interpret the personal signals they'd developed over the length of their marriage and were sending each other.

At last, Jane spoke. "This could be the thing you've been waiting for, sweetheart."

She blew out a puff of air. "I feel the same way."

Dean went into all-out fix-it mode. "Flying might take half the time of driving, but I'm not sure if our airport services Lexington, Kentucky."

She pursed her lips. "I could drive. If Asbury is five hundred miles away, like Jack thinks, wouldn't that take eight or nine hours?"

Jane nodded her head, pursing her lips. "Do you feel physically up to such a trip?"

Melanie smiled. "I do, Aunt Jane. I feel better than I have in a very long time."

"Very well, then. Driving does seems a more direct way to get there."

"I'll help you plan the route," Dean said.

"Thanks. I would rather drive—I'll also have more mobility once I get there." She hugged her relatives, then dashed back to the phone. "Everything's clear for me to come, Jack. I'll start out right after breakfast tomorrow."

"Super!" He gave her a number where he could be reached, as well as Monica's. "When you get here, park anywhere you can and come straight to Hughes Auditorium. I'll meet you there."

She repeated "Hughes Auditorium," writing the name down. "Um, Jack, I thought you said you were meeting in the chapel."

"We are. The chapel is called an auditorium. Anyway, freshmen sit in the balcony, and you'll find me there. I'll be looking for you some time in mid-afternoon."

"You won't be in class then?"

"They've been cancelled for the time being. No one, including the administration, wants to get in God's way. I have to say, what's happening in Hughes is the greatest learning experience I've ever had."

She'd never heard of such a thing or such a school. Certainly nothing like Jack was describing could've happened at Princeton or Columbia. She couldn't wait to see for herself.

They spoke just a few more minutes, then she returned to the kitchen where Dean had spread a map across the table. "This isn't a complicated drive, Melanie, but the Blue Ridge Parkway can get pretty snowy this time of year. Jane and I decided we'd like you to take the Jeep. Your Mustang isn't made for mountains or harsh weather."

If possible, she would have picked up her aunt and swung her around. "Oh, thank you so much!"

He removed his glasses, waving them as if their decision were simply the right thing to do for someone you loved. "We'll just switch cars." His eyes twinkled. "Maybe your Mustang would be tough to drive in snow, but I have to be honest with you, I've been wanting to get behind the wheel ever since you got here."

She burst out laughing, then hugged her uncle, and her aunt. Out of the blue, she stood still, focusing on the ceiling fan. "Do you think I should tell my dad what I'm going to do?" Unsolicited thoughts jabbed her mood. *What if he doesn't want me to go? What if he thinks the whole Asbury happening is ridiculous, or worse? What would I do if he told me not to do this? Would I go anyway?*

"Let me do the telling," Jane said. "I think I'll call him tomorrow after you leave."

Melanie pressed her palm to her heart. All would be well.

Dean gave his niece a wink. "If I'm not mistaken, it's not only God you're hoping to get closer to at Asbury."

The miles rolled under the Jeep passing through Virginia, then West Virginia, and into eastern Kentucky. Though she moved according to the legal limit, she yearned for the speed of an Atlas rocket to propel her to Asbury before she missed out on anything else happening there. What if she missed the phenomenon? *What if I miss God?*

The radio provided a distraction along the mostly two lane highways, but at times she lost the signal. Nor was she particularly fond of the ubiquitous country/western music the stations played. Those tunes, however, were better than the static she often picked up. *Uncle Dean would feel right at home with this music*, she thought, perusing his stash of eight-track tapes featuring Johnny Cash, Hank Williams, and Patsy Cline. *At least he also has Ray Stevens and Andy Williams.* There were also a couple of collections by Pat Boone, Anita Bryant, and some artists she'd never heard of before, singing Christian songs she also didn't know, except for "Sweet, Sweet Spirit." She smiled, remembering the first time she'd heard the tune at

Harvey Cedars, thinking, *Couples have their special songs—maybe "Sweet, Sweet Spirit" is God's and my song.*

She stopped a few times for gas and rest room breaks, enjoying the friendly people she encountered in remote towns. Melanie knew little of the South, having visited Richmond only as a child—trips in which her parents had kept to main roads tenanted by restaurants and lodgings more generic than regional. Although she didn't always understand people's accents while venturing deeper into Dixie, she caught the connotation of their kindness.

Just after three o'clock, she noticed the first road sign for Wilmore, her body vibrating in tandem with the Jeep. She sang louder to a radio station she'd been able to pick up as she passed horse farms and beheld the peaceful beauty of the state's signature blue grass, showing signs of promise even in the bleak midwinter. Something far more beautiful than even this scenery seized her essence, something transcendent. Almost palpable, the actual presence of the Almighty drew her to the Asbury campus, intensifying as she got closer. Any tiredness from her all-day drive became as fleeting as time itself.

She smiled upon encountering Wilmore's tree-lined streets and small businesses, appearing as if they had come right off the set of "The Andy Griffith Show." *Maybe there is a Mayberry after all!* Then the two campuses came in quick succession, first that of Asbury Seminary to her left with Asbury College on the right. She craned to find a sign indicating where she could park but found the initial lot she came to full, so she circled around the red brick college buildings until she found a spot. Getting out of the Jeep, she stretched her arms and legs, grabbed her purse, and buttoned her coat against the bitterly cold afternoon air, a soft dusting of snow crunching underfoot. No one was rushing to get to classrooms or the dorms, not even milling around. The campus seemed utterly deserted yet full of life at the same time. Her eyes shone when a man in a suit and black rimmed glasses came into sight.

"Are you looking for Hughes Auditorium?"

She took a step back. "How did you know?"

"Because everyone is there."

He pointed the way, offering blessedly simple instructions. Then she sprinted across the charming campus, repenting over how she had initially looked down her Markley-esque nose at the thought of Jack's coming here instead of Princeton or some other elite school.

Every nerve tingled as she approached graceful Hughes Auditorium's red brick exterior, white columns, and limestone staircase bearing a striking resemblance to those at Washington's Lincoln Memorial. Had the man she'd just met not told her otherwise, she would have entered through the front doors, but he had directed her to go to the back where she came across a guy wearing a varsity jacket and long sideburns. He opened the door for her and two elderly women in fur coats who had just shown up, seeming out of context. The sound of music reached her ears—rich, melodious, poignant.

Inside, a sudden breeze broke over Melanie, who instinctively smoothed back her hair only to discover not one strand had been out of place. The flags on the platform stood perfectly still. The experience sent shivers down her spine. A power station seemed to have taken up residence in the auditorium, pulsing with some kind of electricity. She nearly swooned when she thought, *Jack was right—God really is here.*

She couldn't decide whether to laugh, cry, or fall to her knees, grateful to her marrow for not having missed out during the lengthy journey from Richmond. Asbury students, packed cheek to jowl with people both older and younger than themselves, were on their feet not only singing "Just a Closer Walk With Thee," but presenting an offering of their voices straight to God. Every word sparkled, a two-carat diamond in the glow of God's presence.

She longed to see Jack, yet stood rooted with several others near the entrance, getting her bearings, taking in the pale golden walls accented with dark wood, and the magnificent pipe organ with an inscription above, "Holiness Unto the Lord." She'd been to medieval cathedrals, five-star hotels and restaurants, but Hughes Auditorium was the most beautiful place she'd ever beheld. She had the sensation of being swaddled in a warm blanket against a season of violence, unrest, and fear in America with a dawning realization of the nativity of Jesus Christ being much more than a sweet little scene in a Christmas pageant. The Holy One had condescended to live among a motley crew of human beings who had soiled his perfect creation. She would have fallen to her knees and worshiped, but where she stood, there was no room.

Melanie heard one of the fur-coated women whisper when the music ended. "I feel like I should take off my shoes."

Her companion nodded. "This is holy ground."

Melanie's breathing stalled when the chic women removed their well-tooled pumps and plunged into the throng at a wooden rail across the front of the sanctuary. Dozens had gathered there, most of them kneeling, some with heads bowed. Throughout the auditorium hands lifted in praise, something she'd never seen before in church. She remembered to remove her wool mittens and hat and started singing the next hymn, although she'd never heard the words before. As she sang, she gazed up at the balcony forming a U shape along the back and sides of the auditorium. *Jack is up there with his freshman class. I need to see him.*

When the song ended, Melanie tapped a young woman on the shoulder. "Excuse me, but how do you get up to the balcony?"

She shrugged her shoulders. "I'm sorry, but I don't know. I don't go here, I just live in Wilmore and came to see what was happening."

"I can help," a young man said. "Come with me."

He guided Melanie through the crowd to a stairwell at the side and back of the sanctuary.

"Just take these steps up to the balcony."

"Thank you."

"Praise the Lord!"

She smiled at his retreating figure, and when she reached the upper story, Melanie scanned the multitude for her friend. Moments later, Jack saw her first and, climbing over some students who were still standing as a new song began, he came to her, his face glowing like Moses's after coming face-to-face with Yahweh. "Melanie!"

They stood in the back near a stained glass window, its colors alive in the afternoon light.

She wordlessly fell into his embrace, more intimate than the kiss they'd shared after the prom.

CHAPTER TWENTY-TWO

"Are you okay? How was the trip?"

Melanie glowed inside and out. "I'm doing great. I'm so happy to be here. This is fantastic." The wave of her hand took in the scope of the auditorium. "I was nearly falling asleep at Lexington, but once I neared Wilmore, I totally woke up. I'm not tired, or even hungry."

Jack was nodding his head. "Other people have been saying similar things. Since this broke yesterday morning, I know I've spent most of my time here. I can't remember the last time I ate or even slept." He made a hand motion toward the rows of seats. "If you're sure you don't want to rest or eat just yet, we can stay here a while."

"I can wait, believe me."

"Super. There's an empty spot next to mine. All students have assigned seats, but since yesterday, there's been a lot of moving about, and no one seems to mind if someone else ends up where you're supposed to be."

She was dying to ask him what had happened since they'd spoken the night before, but she decided her curiosity could stand to wait. She didn't want to miss a single thing happening here and now.

They shimmied down the aisle and stopped at the middle row toward the back of the balcony where Melanie caught the eye, and waving hand, of a familiar figure on the right side of the upper seats.

"There's Monica!"

The plump young woman beamed at Melanie, who waved back and grinned.

Instead of sitting when they reached Jack's seat, they stood and took up the melody, "Jesus, the Very Thought of Thee," which he found in a hymnbook without aid of program or signage at the front of the chapel.

Jesus, the very thought of Thee
With sweetness fills the breast;

But sweeter far Thy face to see,
And in Thy presence rest.

Singing the hymn, Melanie's eyes filled but without self-consciousness, caught up in something much bigger than herself. A glance at others revealed their own tear-filled faces, and she knew she was safe here to express whatever needed to emerge from deep inside. When the song ended, everyone sat down, although no one at the front of Hughes Auditorium had indicated they should. As if according to some unwritten script, a girl went to the lectern and opened her Bible. Suddenly, Melanie took note the young woman was wearing a skirt, just like every other coed in the chapel, except for her. A flush crept across her cheeks for having violated what certainly seemed to be an Asbury dress code. Jack hadn't seemed to notice her attire, and no one sitting near her had done anything but smiled in her direction. Her shoulders began to relax, but she laid her coat across her lower half when everyone started sitting down.

"My heart is steadfast, O God; my heart is steadfast!" The girl at the dais looked up from the Bible to the audience and smiled. "I can't think of anything I'd rather be doing right now than thinking about Jesus, my Savior. I had a million other things on my mind before yesterday morning, but now my heart is steadfast! I only want him."

She closed the Bible and walked down the side steps where she disappeared into the crowd kneeling at the wooden railing.

A young man in an Asbury jacket replaced her at the lectern, and Melanie whispered in Jack's ear, "Is there a bulletin or program we're supposed to be following?"

He shook his head, grinning. "Not at all. This is simply playing out."

"Everything is so orderly." She couldn't get over this.

"Amazing, huh?"

The young man adjusted the mic to accommodate his height. "A reporter asked me what this event means to me, and I told him I can't express it. I tell you, the Lord has been planning this for so long, and prayers have been going up in the girls' and the guys' dorms, and all over the world, and I tell you—it's finally happened. He let us know the day before it happened. He said during a prayer meeting in our dorm, 'It's gonna happen tomorrow,' and it did, and he just opened it up, just let it fly, that's all that I can say!"

He seemed to be in a great hurry to expel the words, to speak his heart.

"He told me he wanted me to get up and say something, and I said the only way you're gonna get me up there is to kick me out of my seat, and he did."

Melanie laughed, accompanied by a wave of mirth sweeping over the auditorium.

"I tell you it's just blessed everybody. I'm not kidding, it's the greatest outpouring of God's love and the Holy Spirit, and I can't express it. I tell you, I'm just amazed. I'm glorifying his name. I'm praising his name today, and that's all I can say."

Shaking his head as if he'd failed to communicate all he had hoped, the student stepped away from the lectern. He smiled when a few other guys slapped him on the back and embraced him.

A ruddy-faced guy spoke next, and Melanie noticed a long line of people trailing past the platform and down several aisles seeming to contain those waiting to take a turn to say something at the mic. Looking back in the speaker's direction, she caught her breath—the guy reminded her a great deal of her cousin Mac, who'd died during the Tet Offensive, lanky with reddish hair. She leaned forward in her seat.

"Hi, y'all. I'm not an Asbury student, but my neighbor in Lexington told me what was happening here, and I've tried everything else, so I thought I'd come and see for myself."

The man clenched and unclenched his hands. "I, uh, I just got back from Vietnam, so the last place I ever thought I'd find myself was a college campus. Soldiers aren't exactly welcome at most of them."

He looked up as if he wondered whether someone would start throwing something at him or heckle him. Melanie's heart pounded. A titter of laughter rippled across the auditorium.

"I went to 'Nam two years ago. I was nineteen. It was pretty bad, and I saw a lot of bad things … I *did* a lot of bad things." He was looking down now. "I thought booze would drown the pain, but I just started sinking in it. Drugs gave me temporary relief, but they left me worse off than before. Women let me down, too."

He scratched his nose, continued.

"When I came home, some protestors were in the airport, and they spit on me when they saw my uniform, like the war was my fault. It felt bad, man. I thought I'd be a hippy and not tell anyone about being in the war, but I knew."

He gazed out at the people, hesitating until several called out, "Tell it," then, "Go on, brother."

"Thank you for listening to me. Um, last night my neighbor brought me here, and I'm so glad he did. He's an old guy, meaning no disrespect." He looked at someone down front and smiled for the first time, his body slightly less rigid than when he'd first begun. "He was in the big war, so he knew some of what I felt. He told me he found God here, and I thought he was kidding, but I figured that was something I had to see, so I came."

His voice broke. "None of you spit on me when I told you who I was, what I was, but ..." he bit his lip and Melanie saw a tear glisten on his cheek "... but a lot of you *hugged* me. You told me to give it all to Jesus, and so I have. I met Jesus last night here ... and I'm never going to let go."

Melanie was surprised to find herself in tears when a clean-cut man from the crowd around the railing pushed onto the platform and embraced the young veteran. The audience applauded, many shouting "Praise the Lord!" "Glory to God!" She caught her breath when some people even began clapping—in a church! *Wouldn't Grandmother Markley have a cow!* Then again, she considered, these displays of emotion were spot-on, like a soloist hitting just the right note.

She'd been raised to hold her cards very close to her chest, never letting others see her weaknesses, but here were people revealing their flaws to the world, or as her cousin Sandy might have put it, "Letting it all hang out." They were naked, but not ashamed, in a display of the starkest form of honesty she'd ever witnessed.

Someone went over to the organ and began playing "To God Be the Glory."

She leaned over to Jack. "I can't believe how many people are down there at the kneeling rail."

"I know. It's been like that since yesterday morning. By the way, you might like to know we call it an altar, but you have the right idea." His smile reassured her.

"Oh, Melanie, I'm so glad to see you! How are you?" Monica had found her way over to them and hugged her.

"I'm glad to see you too and to be here. How are you doing?"

She clapped her hand against her breast. "I've never felt so blessed in my life. God is here, and there's no getting around him. People are getting delivered and saved." She bounced up and down. "Two days ago, there were roommates in my dorm who weren't even speaking to each other, and now they're as close as can be. I also got word the revival has spread across the street." She shook her head.

Melanie frowned. "I'm a bit confused."

"Oh, so sorry! I mean the revival has spread to Asbury Seminary, which is across the street."

"Is the seminary part of the college?"

"It's not officially connected to us, but there's a close relationship between the two," Jack said.

Melanie wondered in what way the revival had spread. Were they having lengthy chapel services as well? Or maybe some of their students had come across the street to participate in what was happening at Hughes Auditorium. A persistent question begged to be expressed.

"What I can't figure out is who's leading this, this, service." She'd expected to see a minister up front, or maybe the college president, directing the proceedings.

Jack and Monica looked at each other and grinned. Together they blurted, "God is!" She surprised herself by not being surprised at this. Still, she wondered, "How do you know what will happen from one minute to the next?"

Monica spread her hands. "We don't, but every time someone gives a testimony or gets up to pray or sing, everyone gets blessed."

"What if someone goes on too long?" She could think of times when someone had been given a microphone and seemed to hold on for dear life. Or her English professor at Princeton who rode his hobby horse every single class, a man she was amazed to discover she could now think about without despising him.

Jack shook his head. "It hasn't happened yet."

A deluge of humanity surged toward the lectern, no one speaking for more than a few minutes at a time, as if someone were watching the clock. No one was. Then, the multitude broke into more songs, followed by people asking for prayers for a boy who was losing his sight, for Christian schools to be true to their missions, for a grieving family to know God's comfort and hope for all eternity. Others praised and gave thanks to God for what he was accomplishing, their voices a fragrant incense heavenward. No one indulged in a spirit of gossip, or wrung their hands over suffering and injustice. These prayers flowed on a current of praise and certainty. God was there. He cared. He affected change. He could be counted upon.

Her old, familiar fear flickered for a brief, dark moment, accompanied by resentment—why hadn't God saved her mother's life or protected Mac or Bobby Kennedy? Even so, his very presence doused the spark, and for the first time, she found herself fully trusting him. No matter what. She perked up upon hearing the confident strains of a girl's voice as she quoted Romans 8:28: "And we know that in all things God works for the good of those who love him, who have been called according to his purpose."

This was *God* she was talking about, the One who brought order out of chaos at the birth of time, who promised a Savior after the first humans had royally screwed up, who defeated Satan at the cross. Melanie called to mind certain newsreel images of D-Day, when the Allied forces began to take back ravaged Europe from the Nazis a bit of beach at a time, sacrificing the lives of many brave soldiers. While victory was assured, the battle still raged. So it was, in this aftermath of God's storming the beaches at Calvary. People still suffered, got sick, died, but God was in his heaven, working out his eternal plans, even if all was not yet right with his world. Melanie couldn't have stopped the smile on her face or the radiance in her heart even if she wanted to. Tears streamed down her face as she lifted her hands. God was in control, and he cared. About her.

"Would you like to get some dinner, Melanie?"

She gave a slight hop when she checked her watch—seven o'clock. The hours had passed so quickly, without any sense of time's march.

"Yes, I think I would, although I hate to leave here. I should also call my aunt and uncle and let them know I got here okay."

He turned to Monica. "Would you like to join us?"

"Sure! Then I can get you settled in my room before we head back here, Melanie."

She smiled at the Tigger-like young woman. "Thanks for inviting me."

"My pleasure!"

❖

"Melanie? Melanie?" He waved his right hand in front of her face.

She came to, as if she'd been in a trance. "Huh? Oh, right, Jack."

"Are you all right?"

"Yes, never better." She shook her head. "It's just that I've never been in a more beautiful dining hall."

Jack and Monica exchanged glances.

"Wow! And you go to Princeton," the coed said.

Jack had been in that university's dining hall several times—Melanie's observation wasn't accurate, at least by human standards. Asbury's refectory exuded a genteel southern ambiance, but something far more compelling had led the young woman to make such a statement.

Melanie turned to him. "He's here, too, isn't he?"

Jack smiled, nodded his head. "His presence seems to be all over campus."

She shivered, though not with cold or fright. This was awesome.

"Come with me, and I'll show you where the payphones are."

"If you don't mind, I'm going to get some dinner now," Monica said, "unless you want me to wait with you."

"No, go right ahead. I'll stay with Melanie, then we'll join you."

Jack led Melanie to a phone and waited several steps away while she made the call.

"Hello, Aunt Jane, it's me!"

"Oh, good, dear. I was beginning to worry. How was the trip?"

"Just fine." She bounced from one foot to the next. "You just can't imagine what's happening here at Asbury—God really is here! People's lives are being changed. Actually we just came to the dining hall, and I can even sense his presence here. This is amazing."

"How absolutely wonderful!"

"Nothing else seems to matter when you're there. Jack says he's not even tired after being up all last night. No one wants to leave the audi—er, chapel."

They spoke for a few more minutes, then Melanie hung up, and Jack took her through a sparse line for their evening meal. Only a few students were in the dining hall, regular meal patterns having been cast to the four winds.

A man in a suit, whom Melanie judged to be in his thirties, walked over and introduced himself.

"Hi, there. I'm Steven Livesey from the *Louisville Times*. Mind if I ask some questions?"

Melanie and Jack looked at each other before bursting out laughing, leaving Monica and the reporter to shrug their shoulders.

Melanie touched her forefinger to her chin. "Sorry about that. Jack and I have long a history with the press. Of course we'll talk to you."

Livesey pulled out a chair, which he straddled, and opened his notepad, asking their names. Then, "How did this church service get started?"

Jack spoke up. "We have chapel three times a week, and one of those times was yesterday at ten o'clock. Dean Reynolds was supposed to preach, but instead of giving a message, he said he wanted to give his testimony instead."

Livesey grimaced. "I don't understand. What's a testimony?"

"You tell others what God is doing in your life," Monica said.

Jack nodded, then continued. "After he spoke, he invited students to give their own testimonies, and, well, that's when it happened."

"What happened?"

"I'll try to explain. I'm a freshman, and my class sits in the balcony. Each of the four classes has assigned seats in Hughes Auditorium."

"That's the church, right?"

"Well, sort of. Some other schools call them chapels, so they're not exactly churches."

The reporter scribbled on the pad. "Got it."

"I sit in the back, and there's a window behind me, which was open a little bit."

Melanie listened as intently as the reporter. She hadn't heard this story before now.

"Well, just as the first person finished his testimony, I heard a sound, something like wind whooshing in, but the sound was soft, not like when you hear wind whistling through a window. This was different. I ..." He cocked his head, bit his lower lip. "… I think the Holy Spirit was coming in."

The reporter dropped his pen on the table, and it rolled onto the floor. Melanie broke out in goose bumps.

He bent to retrieve the writing instrument. "My readers aren't going to believe this. What's the Holy Spirit? Some kind of God ghost?"

Jack smiled and shook his head. "The Holy Spirit is how God is present with Christians. You see, after Jesus died and was resurrected, he returned to heaven, but the Holy Spirit came to live in and empower believers, to be his presence on earth until Jesus comes again."

As he wrote in his notebook, Livesey said, "I certainly felt something in there. I've been covering sit-ins, love-ins and campus protests for a year, and I've never seen anything like this."

"Do you know Jesus?" Monica asked.

Melanie's eyes opened wide, never having heard anyone speak so bluntly of such an intimate spiritual matter.

Livesay grimaced. "I was raised in the church, but I never took to it. Religion isn't my cup of tea."

"This isn't about religion," Jack said. "This is about a relationship with God through Jesus Christ, something meant for everyone. You were created to know him, and until you do, you'll never find your real purpose in life."

Livesey jumped up as if scalded. "Well, thanks for the comments. I need to be shoving off."

When he hurried beyond their range of sight, Monica slapped her hand against her mouth. "I can't believe I did that! I've never witnessed to anyone in my life. I've always been too scared."

Jack grinned. "You didn't seem scared then."

"I wasn't! Not one bit. Oh, wow!"

"Maybe we should pray for him," Jack said, and they bowed their heads together.

CHAPTER TWENTY-THREE

After dinner they retrieved Melanie's suitcase from her car, then made their way back across campus to Monica's room in the Glide-Crawford dormitory. On the outside, the beautiful red brick building boasted white columns, inside Melanie sucked in her breath at the chandelier spilling light onto a parlor graced by a striking staircase and baby grand piano. *I think even Grandmother Markley would be impressed.*

Jack handed over her suitcase. "I'll wait here."

"Oh. Okay." She couldn't understand why he wasn't going to carry the bag upstairs for her.

Monica reached for the heavy piece. "I'll help you."

"No, thanks, I can carry this." Climbing the stairs she asked, "Why didn't Jack come with us?"

"He's not allowed."

Her eyes widened. "Not allowed?"

"This is a girls' dorm. Guys aren't permitted in the rooms, just the entry."

She smiled and sniffed. "Toto, I think we *are* in Kansas."

Monica laughed at the reference.

The girl's room, decorated in a cheerful pink floral theme with matching curtains and bedspreads, was much nicer than Melanie's quarters in Pyne Hall.

"I got a cot for you from housing." Monica pointed to the temporary bed along one wall.

"I could've slept on the floor."

"Well, now you don't have to!" She stood with her hands on her hips. "You drove a long way today, Melanie. Are you tired? Do you need to rest?"

"Not, a bit. I'm dying to get back to Hughes." For the first time since she'd come down with mono, she felt entirely healthy, entirely herself.

Melanie noticed dozens of people still cramming the altar area as she, Jack, and Monica entered Hughes and made their way up to the balcony. His seat was still open, as well as the adjoining one.

"I'll just go over to my row now," Monica said. "When you're ready to go to bed, Melanie, just let me know."

"Thanks." At this point, sleeping couldn't possibly be as compelling as watching God at work in people's lives. She settled into the wooden chair as two girls went to the lectern, and without any prompting, silence fell over the auditorium.

The shorter of the young women spoke first. "We just want to say that we went into town today to tell shopkeepers and people on the street about what's happening here. The people listened to us, and then a few of them asked if anyone was welcome here, so we invited them to come."

She moved aside to let her friend speak. "Some of them asked for prayer, so we just stopped what we were doing and prayed with them. I think they were surprised—I know we were! I just want to praise the Lord for what he did today."

An outbreak of "Amen! Praise the Lord!" erupted, the coeds' eyes and mouths opening wider when an older couple started walking toward them. Melanie slid further to the front of her seat for a better view, smiling when the girls embraced the man and woman. The petite student went back to the microphone.

"We witnessed to this couple today, and they want to tell us about what God has just done for them, and how he has given them victory." She waved the man to the dais.

He lumbered to the lectern, gripping the sides, shifting his weight, sighing. Then he pointed to the mic. "I don't like these things. But I just wanted to say I have found a new love for God and for my wife, and I just had to tell everyone." He backed away as if the microphone might detonate, and putting his arm around his obviously pregnant spouse, hastened from the platform.

Applause broke over the gathering, Melanie adding to the din, her eyes shining. The piano played again, and hundreds of voices filled Hughes with "Great is Thy Faithfulness," sending shivers down her spine. Initially she'd shifted in her seat when people started lifting their hands as they sang, but soon understood they weren't being overly emotional or garish. Rather, they seemed to be lifting their very sprits to the one who had come among them, and before realizing what was happening, she found herself joining them.

She leaned over to Jack when the song ended. "How many people do you think are here?"

"I think the capacity is fifteen hundred, and the auditorium is just about full."

The altar overflowed with people of all ages praying, some with arms draped around others. There was weeping, but no gnashing of teeth. These appeared to be healing streams of tears, leading to repentance and renewal.

Just one word came to Melanie to describe this phenomenon. "Wow."

Jack smiled. "Yeah. Wow! I am so glad you came."

"So am I."

A pageant of people came forward to pray at the altar and to give their testimonies, Melanie wondering whether Jack had done so before she'd arrived, curious about what he might have said, or would say, if he did speak. His life always seemed so together, especially when hers had been unraveling. She sighed upon recognizing most of their relationship had been all about her—her needs, her desires, her pain. When had she stopped to listen to his heart? She leaned against the chair in front of her, bowing her head. *Lord, I'm sorry I've been so selfish in general, but especially with Jack. I think you brought him into my life, and I'm so grateful you did. He's the best friend I've ever had. Through him, I found you at Harvey Cedars, and now I'm finding you again here. Somehow, Lord, let me be a blessing to him too.*

"Hey, Melanie." She felt the upward tug of her eyelids, someone's hand on her arm administering a tender shaking. "Maybe we should get you over to the dorm."

She awakened to the sound of soft singing, a kind of lullaby. "Umm." She sat up straighter, pulling a hand through her tousled hair. "I am sleepy, but I don't want to leave."

"I understand, but I really think we should get some sleep. Monica's ready to go, and I'll walk back with both of you. We can get back here first thing tomorrow morning."

"Promise?"

He grinned. "Promise."

"Do you think God will still be here?"

"Yes, Melanie, I think he will."

❦

Having completed her bedtime routine in the dorm's bathroom and slipped into her pajamas, Melanie discarded her immediate need for sleep. In fact, she was on her second wind when Monica's roommate arrived around midnight.

Monica stumbled through introductions. "Melanie, I'm sorry, I forget your last name."

"McKnight."

She slapped her forehead. "That's right! Melanie, this is Paula French."

"Nice to meet you." The young woman, slim and short-haired, didn't have what was becoming to Melanie a familiar southern accent.

Before Melanie could ask where Paula was from, however, Monica took the conversation on a different course. "I've been wondering how you know Jack."

She went over to the cot and sat cross-legged, ready for conversation. "I spent part of my junior year with my grandmother, who lives in Princeton, and I met Jack at Mercer Academy."

"Oh, here I thought you were from Princeton," Monica said. "I seemed to have heard something along those lines."

"I'm not, but my mother's family is."

"You do go to Princeton University, though, right?"

"Yes, well, no." Melanie looked down at her hands, as if she'd find information there. "My story is a little confusing. I started out there in the fall, but I got sick and took a leave of absence at the end of the semester." The cut hadn't fully healed. "I'm staying with my aunt and uncle in Richmond." She hoped the information would satisfy curious Monica so they could latch on to a different subject.

Paula finished taking her jewelry off and climbed into her bed. "Didn't Princeton just start admitting women?"

"Uh-huh. I was one of the first undergraduate women."

In this place of human transparency and the very real presence of almighty God, she realized there was no need for pretense, even if she disliked talking about her recent journey.

"Didn't you like the school?" Monica asked.

"Like I said, I got sick near the end of the fall semester."

Her new friend's eyes narrowed. "I hardly recognize myself right now. First, I asked that reporter if he knew Christ, and now I'm compelled to ask you something personal. If I'm being too snoopy, just say so."

She was, but Melanie detected more than human prying at work. She shook her head "no."

"The university wasn't as I had hoped, Monica."

"In what way?" Monica popped in a retainer from a plastic case on her nightstand and leaned forward.

Melanie briefly described her disillusionment with her professors, the unfortunate turn her job at the paper had taken, and how she had desperately needed spiritual direction but couldn't find any. She left out the story about Josh.

Monica and Paula patted the bottom of Melanie's legs. "What a difficult experience."

"How long have you been a Christian?" Paula asked.

"I grew up going to church, but I didn't go much after my mother died seven years ago. I never knew a person could actually know Jesus until I went to Harvey Cedars last summer to visit Jack." She paused and glanced first at Paula, then at Monica. "Does she know about Harvey Cedars?"

Paula smiled. "Monica has told me about her summer there and what a great place it is."

"They had a great speaker there and after hearing him, I decided I wanted to know God. I started college a couple weeks later and hoped I'd find a good church. I'd gone with Jack once, right after Bobby Kennedy died, and I went back there, but the minister was replaced by someone who sounded like a lot of other ones I'd heard, somehow not fully engaged with Christ." She lifted her hands. "Do you understand?"

"Absolutely," Monica said. "I've heard similar ministers. It's like they have religious beliefs, but they're not really connected to Jesus Christ personally."

Melanie bobbed her head. "Yes, exactly. After trying a handful of churches, I stopped going out of discouragement and because my part time job required me to work Sundays." She hung her head. "I wish I had just quit the job, but I didn't. I kept thinking my work was the only stable thing I had." *Here it comes. The part about Josh. I don't want to tell them, but I don't think I can hold back any longer. No one else knows what happened.*

"There's more, isn't there?" Monica asked.

"Yes." She took, then released, a deep breath, trembling. "I met this guy at school, and I was so dejected by then, and he made me laugh, so I started hanging out with him when I really shouldn't have." Tears stung her eyes and she snorted. "Let's just say he wasn't Jack." She kept quiet for a long moment, gathering the rest of her courage to continue.

"You seem really close to him. He talks about you a lot," Monica said.

"Really?"

"Really. I thought maybe you were, you know …"

Melanie smiled. "We're really good friends, but we weren't exclusive, which brings me back to this guy. I didn't think dating him would be an issue. The thing is, he got, uh, pushy, you know? What he did really shook me up." Judging from the looks on Monica and Paula's faces, she knew she didn't have to go into the gory details. "Then I came down with mono, as if my body was just too tired to go on, and the semester went the rest of the way downhill. My Aunt Jane convinced me to take the spring semester off, to recover and reevaluate."

"What did your father say?" Paula asked.

Melanie gulped. "My dad is super busy with his work." She skipped ahead, not wanting to go down that particular path, not tonight. "Since the Christmas break, I've been at my aunt and uncle's house in Richmond and going to their church, which is a lot like Jack's was before the new pastor took over. I've been praying about what's next." She smiled. "That's when Jack called and told me I needed to come to Asbury."

Paula reached over and squeezed her hand. "I, for one, am glad you're here. You know, my dad had some experiences with professors like you did when he was in college. They almost ruined his faith."

Monica broke in. "You should see her dad now—he's a physicist at Cornell and a Christian leader on the campus."

"Wow," Melanie said. "How was he able to keep his faith?"

"He just kept seeking God, no matter what, and I think because he did, the Lord led him to some devout people who helped him stay on track. When I needed to pick a college, he encouraged me to come here because we heard Asbury nurtures your faith while allowing you to ask important questions. This is such a great place. Don't get me wrong—no place is perfect, but Asbury is wonderful."

Monica laughed. "I would say, it's a little better than perfect!"

"Melanie, let's stop right now and pray for you," Paula said, "that God will use this time and place to bring healing after a hard season."

She nodded, unable to speak, bowing her head as Paula began.

"Lord, we just thank you for bringing Melanie to Asbury and for your hand on her life. She's been through some hard times, and we know you haven't let her go. We also know when we seek you, we will be found by you, and she is seeking you. We ask you to heal her spirit, even as we look forward to the wonderful plans you have for her life, plans to prosper her and not to harm her, plans to give her a future and hope."

The impact of the verse struck her like a snowball made of cotton, at once bracing and gentle. When they finished praying, she asked Paula where she came up with the words about the future and hope.

"They're from Jeremiah." She grabbed her Bible from the nightstand she shared with Monica and opened to the twenty-ninth chapter.

Melanie wiped away more tears after listening to the entire passage.

All at once, someone knocked on the door, then burst into the room. "Oh, I'm so glad you're still awake!" She pressed her hand against her chest.

"Hey, Susan! This is our friend, Melanie. She's visiting from, uh, Richmond," Monica said. "What's up?"

The blonde pushed up her glasses and plopped on the end of Paula's bed. "I just couldn't wait to tell you until tomorrow. You know Anne and Brenda?"

For Melanie's benefit, Monica explained, "They're roommates, down the hall. Unfortunately they dislike each other."

"No more! Brenda got saved tonight, and Anne confessed her bad attitude about her. God made their relationship brand new!"

Melanie thought Susan might just fall off the bed.

Paula shouted, "Praise the Lord! We've been praying for them for months."

"Oh, I'm so glad we're at Asbury to be part of this!" Monica said.

Melanie grinned. "So am I." She hesitated for a moment. "I'm a little confused about something. I thought everyone at Asbury was a Christian, but you say Brenda got saved tonight."

Monica nodded. "I'd say most people who come here have a relationship with Jesus, and almost everyone has been raised in church, but not all Asburians are necessarily saved. I know people who are here mainly because their parents made them come, and there are others who think they know Christ, but … they really don't."

Paula jumped in. "She's right. I think one thing happening with this revival is those who do know him are becoming more fully committed to Christ—maybe they were saved, but they hadn't given all of themselves over to him yet, or they're renewing their dedication to him. The other thing is, those who don't know him are coming to faith."

The girls talked, sometimes pausing for prayer as people and situations came to their minds, until two o'clock. Melanie awakened at six, surprised by how well she'd slumbered on the cot when normally she tossed and turned her first night in a strange place. As she lay in the semi-darkness, listening to her roommates' soft breathing, she considered how familiar Asbury felt, although she'd never been there before. Somewhere in her heart, she seemed to have always known this place. She nodded off again, waking a good hour later when Monica opened the curtains revealing a campus under a fresh coating of snow. They all dressed quickly in order to get breakfast and hurry back to Hughes after learning from a group of students in the lobby there were to be no classes that day either.

⚶

Melanie kept an eye out for Jack while standing in the dining hall line behind two guys, one who seemed barely able to contain his energy.

"Can you believe what's happening here?" He nudged the other guy, who shrugged.

170

Melanie tilted her head, curious about his apparent apathy. When she sat down, she asked Monica, "Who's the guy in the green shirt over by the window?"

Following her gaze, Monica puckered her brow. "That's Tim Philpot. His father is an evangelist, kind of like Billy Graham. He's really well known in the south."

Philpot. Philpot. She'd heard the name before, from Jack she'd thought.

"Too bad Tim doesn't seem to get what's happening."

"What do you mean?"

"No doubt he's heard the gospel hundreds of times, but instead of being a solid Christian, Tim is really … proud of being his father's son. I'm sorry. I sound like I'm gossiping, but I'm really just trying to explain how lost he is, and how we should be praying for God to open his eyes."

Melanie did pray for the student while she ate. She knew all about growing up in a famous father's shadow, trying to find your own way in life.

Before they finished, she asked the girls if she could still hang out near Jack's seat when they got to chapel.

"I don't see why not," Monica said. "You're his guest."

As they approached Hughes Auditorium, Melanie saw several news vans parked outside, including one from Cincinnati bearing the familiar ABC logo. She followed the girls into the auditorium, which was beginning to fill again, the crisp winter's daylight glistening through the windows. No one was speaking just yet, but a young woman played hymns at the piano, while off to the side, a reporter started to interview a dignified man in a suit. Melanie edged over to listen.

"I'm here in Hughes Auditorium at Asbury College where a continuous love-in has been going on since the start of chapel two days ago. With me is Custer Reynolds, dean of the school. What's been happening here at Asbury College?" He tipped the mic toward the administrator.

Melanie smiled at the immediate association she made between the dean and the photo of Peter Marshall on the back of *A Man Called Peter*.

"We've had a spontaneous revival that's broken out here," Reynolds said. "It's the greatest I've ever had the experience of being in."

"What do you mean by spontaneous? How did it get started?"

"Well, really, it's unique in that we had no preaching service. It was just a regular chapel. We decided to have testimonies—and all we had was singing and testimonies from the students. But toward the end of the chapel service, which lasts about fifty minutes, something broke, and the students started coming to the altar in droves, and we've been going ever since."

"Now, when did the chapel service start?"

"Tuesday morning at ten o'clock."

"And what would you guess is the maximum crowd at any one time in the auditorium?"

"You know, our auditorium seats around fifteen hundred people, and our student body is a little over a thousand. I think it's a conservative estimate that we've had around eight hundred people at the altar."

"How long do you think it might last?"

"I must say, I have no idea."

CHAPTER TWENTY-FOUR

A professor in a bow tie spoke in a voice seemingly too big for his small frame, his studious face ruddy. "I am happy to report, the revival has spread not only across the street to the seminary, and throughout the town of Wilmore, but now is reaching into nearby churches and even schools. Let's just praise the Lord!"

"Praise the Lord!"

Led by the pianist, the people took up the hymn "All Hail the Power of Jesus' Name."

Part of Melanie's spirit was being transported to the edge of heaven, praising God among the great congregation, the other part like old Jacob Marley, dragging chains along the cobblestones. Some burden she couldn't put her finger on encumbered her. When the last verse faded, she leaned over to Jack, but before she could say anything, he spoke. "I can't tell you just how happy I am you're here." He squeezed her hand, and she treasured the warmth as he lingered.

"I am too." She smiled then took a deep breath. "Can I tell you something?"

"Of course." He faced her while the next song began.

She spoke quietly enough not to disturb those around her, twisting an invisible tissue in her hands. "Last night, Paula and Monica prayed with me after I told them what a rough time I had last semester. I felt like a weight came off me."

"I'm so happy you feel better now, yet really sorry you had such a hard time at Princeton." He pursed his lips.

"I don't understand why, but this morning I feel so heavy again."

He tilted his head to the side. "Perhaps God's dealing with another hurt?"

Just how deep do I need to dig here? She didn't think she wanted to continue the excavation. "Has God been, well, dealing with you at all?"

"Funny you should ask." He smiled and leaned forward, gazing at her, provoking a different kind of quavering. "Mostly, I'm just basking in his presence, feeling closer to him than ever before." He scratched his left ear. "I've also felt a sense of conviction, though, about how I treat people sometimes."

"How do you mean?"

"I have a way of manipulating people to get what I want, and my friends at Mercer Academy just laughed about it—'There goes Jack, wrapping himself around so-and-so's finger.'" He paused. "I'm realizing using people isn't a God-honoring way to act."

She understood what he was saying, having seen him in action, especially during their interviews with people. At the time, she'd thought he was being charming. Now she could see why he wanted to change.

"Hey, you know what? We ought to pray together," he said.

"Sure."

Jack put his hand on her arm, and they bowed their heads. "Lord, I'm so glad you brought Melanie here and for all the things you're doing in her life, in this amazing place and time. We rejoice in this. You are so wonderful, and we praise you. You have already spoken to her spirit, but we sense there might be more you want to say to her, so please, give her eyes to see and ears to hear whatever she needs to receive from you. And, Lord, please show me anything else I need to repent about. In Jesus' name, amen."

"Amen."

Their spirits were somehow naked before each other, but Melanie felt no shame. She'd never been so intimate with anyone before yet had never felt so pure.

She turned her attention to the front of the auditorium while the last chorus of "Amazing Grace" ended, noticing a familiar figure at the altar. Monica was on her knees next to another coed, both in tears, their arms about each other's shoulders. She wondered what was on Monica's heart and said a prayer for her new sister in Christ. She liked talking to God, now knowing without hesitation he really was listening, and would answer.

Stragglers dotted the dining hall in the two o'clock hour, Melanie hearing snatches of conversations about "witness teams."

She sipped her Coke, listening for clues. Finally she asked, "What are they talking about, Jack?"

"Some of those students are from my dorm. I heard them talking last night about going to other campuses to talk about what's happening here."

"Do you think Asbury wants them to go?"

He nodded. "The administration is encouraging them, and helping however they can. I think a lot of people believe this revival isn't just meant for us here."

She wondered whether she'd have courage enough to speak to others about God's work in her life. Then her eyes fells upon another student, a slump-shouldered young man looking as if he wished he could disappear into himself.

She nudged Jack. "I'm curious about that fellow over there."

Jack dug back into his chef's salad, his eyes following the subtle pointing of her finger. "So, you're noticing another guy, eh?"

She gave a little snort and elbowed him.

"That's Tim Philpot."

"I was talking with Monica about him earlier, and something just doesn't seem quite right with him. I mean, everyone around us is so fired up about God, about their relationship with Christ and everything, and he looks like he'd rather be anywhere else."

Jack frowned, nodding. "I don't know if you remember a while back when I told you why I was going to Asbury, and I mentioned his father, Ford Philpot?"

"I sort of recalled that last night. I knew you had mentioned him."

"I know Tim from some classes, and I have to say, he's a really nice guy." He took a deep breath, put his fork down. "Sometimes, though, he does brag about his dad, and I know he's broken some of the rules." He was quick to add, "Nothing major, just little things like breaking curfew by ten or fifteen minutes."

Once again—maybe because of their both having famous fathers—she experienced a connection with Tim and wanted his life to turn around.

"I'm going to pray for him."

"Good idea, Melanie. I will too."

When they'd started eating their dessert brownies, an older student stood on a chair and waved to get everyone's attention. "Thanks, everyone. One of the witness teams needs to get to the Lexington bus station in two hours, and the driver's car isn't too good in the snow. Could anyone here give them a ride?"

She might not be able to speak in front of people like these students were about to do, but Melanie knew she could drive them to where they needed to go. She leaned over to Jack. "I have my uncle's Jeep. I could take them."

"Do you think he'd mind?"

"I don't."

"Great!" Jack stood and raised his voice. "We can take them, John!"

"Hey, thanks, man. I'll be right over with the details."

With a half hour before Jack and Melanie's rendezvous with their passengers, they returned to Hughes to catch a few more testimonies. A young man had just stepped forward, gripping the lectern as she'd seen so many do.

"Some friends asked me to come here, and I wasn't too excited about it, but I figured, 'What do I have to lose?' I felt like I'd lost everything else." He paused. "I grew up in the church, but my family wasn't Christian. My mom or dad, usually my mom, would drop me off at Sunday school, then they'd go to the club until it was time to pick me up. After I was confirmed, I stopped going. I figured religion was for kids." He sighed, gazing into the faces turned toward him.

"My parents gave me a lot of stuff, but none of it seemed to make any difference. I mean, my home wasn't peaceful. They didn't have anything to hold on to, except maybe the nice cars and house and clothes, but they don't last. They can't give you peace. I wanted something meaningful in my life. I sort of resented them for not giving me what I really needed, but then, they didn't have it to give."

He reached into a pocket and produced a handkerchief, proceeding to wipe his nose.

"I became a social activist, got into causes—the Civil Rights movement, helping the poor, politics, anti-war demonstrations. I can't tell you how upset I was when Martin Luther King and Bobby Kennedy were killed."

Melanie's skin prickled at the mention of RFK. She felt Jack take her hand.

"I felt like there was no hope left, nothing to live for, so I bummed around for a while, aimless. Had a couple dead-end jobs. I came here thinking, 'Why not?'" His voice broke. "Well, last night I met the living God."

Clusters of people called out "Praise God" throughout the auditorium.

Something inside nudged her in the direction of the altar, and her heart pounded. She resisted. *There's not enough time. We need to meet those kids on the witness team.* The prospect of kneeling there in front of God and everybody both terrified and exhilarated her.

The young man continued. "Jesus came into my heart, and now I know why I'm here. I have something to live for, what I've been looking for all my life."

Melanie noticed the bobbing of his Adam's apple while he paused.

"I no longer resent my parents. I called them last night and told them what happened. They had a little trouble believing it, but they listened, and I'm praying for them—that they'll know Jesus, too."

The audience stood and broke into "To God Be the Glory" when the guy stepped aside but Melanie stayed seated in her chair, wrestling, her voice breaking on the words. On the second verse, she made up her mind. "I'm going down there."

Jack stopped singing and raised his eyebrows. "To testify?"

She shook her head. She wasn't *that* brave. "To pray at the altar."

"Want me to go with you?"

"No, thanks. There's something I need to do on my own, between me and God."

He got up to let her pass.

Down on the first level, she located a spot on the far left side and knelt, leaning her head on her arms, trembling as a steady parade of suffering passed before her mind's eye—her father leading the procession. Her shoulders shook as she wept, wrapped up in a package of pain until she became aware of someone kneeling beside her, a woman, her face wrinkled but radiant. Melanie gave a little start when the stranger put her arm around Melanie's shoulders, the singing above and around her, a blanket of praise.

The woman pressed her cheek to Melanie's as if she were her own granddaughter, but Melanie didn't flinch this time.

"Is there anything you'd like to tell me, sweetheart?"

She had never been one to talk about herself to someone she didn't know, but she trusted this woman. "I, I, well, I feel like God is healing some hurt and resentment." Dared she say what was on her heart? She gulped. "Especially toward my father."

"These resentments and hurts happen, even in the best of families. Would you like to tell me more?"

She sighed, then unloaded. "I had a wonderful mother, but she died several years ago, and I haven't been close to my dad since then. He doesn't seem interested in me most of the time, and he's rarely available." She choked on the ache, looking into the woman's brown, moistening eyes. She wasn't especially pretty, but Melanie found her beautiful. As the sobs subsided she said, "I feel, like I'm giving this to God now—the pain. Even my own sin. I've had harsh thoughts about my father. At times, I've come close to hating him."

There was no condemnation as the woman sat-knelt on the floor. "Let me tell you a little story of my own. My parents were missionaries in China, and when I was six, I had to leave them to go to school. My heart was so very broken. From then on, throughout my school years, I saw them only twice a year, and just for a few days at a time."

Melanie couldn't imagine such a life.

"Although I loved the Lord, I clung to bitterness about my separation from them, which affected every part of my life. In an attempt to have a need for intimacy met, I made friends with some people who betrayed my trust."

She nodded her head, hanging on each word.

"I came to Asbury Seminary for graduate studies, and while I was there, a revival broke out here at the college."

Melanie jerked backward. "There was another revival here?"

"Oh, yes, my dear. This is not the first. I suspect it will not be the last either."

She processed this news while the woman unwrapped her story. "At the time of the revival, I surrendered my lifelong pain to Jesus, including resentment I had toward him for making my parents missionaries in the first place. He cleansed me, right here on this spot. He made the broken places whole."

"And now you're here with me, dealing with an issue with my parent."

"Yes, I am convinced ours was a divine appointment."

"What happened with you and your mom and dad?"

"Shortly after the revival, we came to terms with how we had disappointed each other. You see, after I graduated from that missionary school, I withdrew my presence from them, didn't often go to visit, mostly out of spite. I wanted them to know how they'd made me suffer." She shook her head. "Thanks be to God, we got to know each other very well before they died." She held Melanie's chin with her right hand and gazed at her. "He restores the years the locusts eat. I believe he'll do the same in your relationship with your father."

Melanie had no idea why she was talking about locusts, but the strange words rang of some untold truth.

As the woman held Melanie's hands while praying, a feeling of chains being cut from her body and falling away occurred. The words Jack had spoken to her Tuesday night over the phone floated back to her—"I want my daughter here." Startled, she realized there was more than one meaning in the words. She was God's child, and *he* was her Father—her perfect Father. The realization poured over and through her—a sweet fragrance. Here was a Father who would never leave her or forsake her. There was another part of Jack's message though—"I want my daughter *here*." At Asbury. Not just for the revival, however long the movement of the Holy Spirit would last, but throughout her college career.

She felt another hand on her shoulder and looked up to see Jack, smiling—a look of "What happened here?" on his face. "I hate to interrupt, but we need to take those students to the bus station."

Looking into his face, she loved him. *Might God have yet another reason for me to stay here?*

CHAPTER TWENTY-FIVE

Jack rode shotgun as Melanie pulled the Jeep onto North Lexington Avenue. He inclined his head to the back where two juniors sat with their duffle bags. "So, where are you off to?"

"Milikin University in Illinois." Mike, the fairer of the two answered. "A lot of other schools and churches have been asking Asbury students to come and share what's happening."

"So I've heard," Melanie said.

The other guy, Dennis, spoke up. "It's incredible what's going on out there. Did you hear about the Asbury student who went to Azusa Pacific?"

Melanie and Jack shook their heads. "Somehow we missed hearing about that," he said.

"The Asburian went there, and after telling them what's happening here, that campus broke out in a revival."

Melanie had a sudden case of goose flesh. She suddenly hated leaving Hughes, not wanting to miss a single thing, but helping a couple students take news of the revival someplace else more than compensated. "How far could this spread?" she asked while Jack pointed her to the main road.

Mike shrugged. "I guess only the Lord knows, but I have a feeling this is going to get really big. I mean, we're living in tough times. People are divided over the Vietnam War, and many campuses are breaking out in riots, but God is still in control, doing his own redemptive work wherever he pleases. I'm just thrilled to be a small part of what he's doing."

After a few moments, Melanie posed another question. "I've been wondering about something ... maybe you guys can help me."

"What's that?" Dennis asked.

"There've been college administrators and professors apologizing to one another about things, and I've seen a couple of people from Wilmore talking about being proud and needing to forgive others from Asbury. Do you know what happened between them?"

"Actually, I do," Mike said. "My dad teaches at the seminary, and I've lived in Wilmore for ten years. When Dr. Kinlaw, Asbury College's president, came a few years ago, there was a lot of divisiveness among the board members. Some factions had developed during the time of the president who came before him. Wilmore's a small community, and a lot of the drama spilled over into area churches. The people who are getting up and apologizing include my dad, who told me the Lord compelled him to confess his resentments and pride to the people he'd hurt."

"What courage he exhibited!"

"Only God could do something like that," Dennis said. "My dad is so different these days. Even the atmosphere at home is better, like God's spilling his light into all the dark places."

Mike directed Melanie to tune to a certain radio station providing regular weather and traffic information. While they waited for a report, a new song came over the airwaves, one beginning with a catchy guitar riff.

Jack turned up the volume. "Have you guys heard this yet?"

"No," they both said.

"The song is called 'Spirit in the Sky,' and the words discuss where you go when you die."

They listened closely to the lyrics, and after the song ended, Melanie said, "What a strange song. Part of the words seem Christian, but not all of them."

Dennis leaned against the back of the driver's seat. "When he talks about never being a sinner because his friend is Jesus, well, salvation doesn't work like that. Everyone's a sinner in need of Christ's forgiveness, and then he helps us not to sin, even though we all still will mess up sometimes."

"Do you think the singer's making fun of Christianity?" Mike asked.

Jack shook his head. "I asked myself the same thing, but there's a real sense of peace about the song, as if the guy is hoping what he's saying is true. There's another one out that is more tongue in cheek about our beliefs. Oh, what's its name?" He thought for a moment. "Something like 'When I Die,' by Blood, Sweat and Tears."

Melanie surprised herself by singing some of the hit song for her small audience, emphasizing lines about swearing there's no heaven, praying there's no hell. "That one doesn't really offer any hope at all."

"At least 'Spirit in the Sky' does," Jack said.

Dennis propped his arms on the back of Melanie's seat. "A lot of people are also talking about a musical they're calling a rock opera, *Jesus Christ Superstar*."

"I've heard some of those songs, too," she said. While she was participating in the conversation, she remained careful about avoiding slick spots.

"This is new to me," Jack said. "Tell me more."

"The play is about the last days of Jesus' life, and there's controversy because the text isn't straight out of the Gospels, but mixes the Bible with the composer's imagination. The story also strongly implies Mary Magdalene was in love with Jesus."

Jack's brows furrowed. "How do they have Jesus respond?"

"Um, I don't think he reciprocates or anything."

"All of this makes me think, though, about the student unrest we mentioned earlier. Young people like us are wondering just who Jesus really is," Mike said. "They don't seem content to accept what their parents taught them."

Dennis nodded his head. "There's a spirit of rebellion out there. I hope this revival continues to spread, and lots of them will find out personally!"

❧

People cast sideways glances at the Asbury students huddled in prayer while others embarked on the Greyhound bus.

"Lord, we just ask for you to use Dennis and me to reach Millikin's students and administrators, for your Spirit to move there as you are moving here. As we open our mouths to speak, may you put words in them, especially your holy word of truth and redemption."

A brusque voice broke into their conclave. "Are you getting on this bus or not?"

Mike hastened to the end of his prayer. "We have to go, Lord, but bless these friends and bless our travels to the praise of your glory. Amen." He looked into the face of the grimacing driver. "We're coming, sir. Sorry to keep you waiting." Turning to Melanie and Jack, he thanked them. "God bless you for bringing us here, for sacrificing your time in Hughes."

Jack shook his hand, then Dennis's. "No problem. Glad to do it. God bless you both!"

Melanie hugged the two students and waited with Jack for the bus to pull out of its bay, waving, wondering what God might be up to in their lives.

❧

Melanie and Jack were retracing the miles back to Wilmore when he asked, "I was wondering, do you need to do any shopping?" He grinned across the seat. "I know when my family travels, my mom and my sister always seem to forget to pack some things."

She smiled, warmed by his sensitivity. "I hate to miss a single minute of what's happening at Hughes, but I could use a few things." She didn't want to elaborate on her very personal needs.

"Do you want a chain store, or will Sim's in Wilmore do?"

"What is Sim's?"

"It's a totally old-fashioned drug store, even has a soda fountain."

"Wow! I didn't know those still existed."

"And next door's the barber shop." He chuckled. "The whole downtown, which is about a block long, reminds me of the old Andy Griffith Show."

She gave a laugh. "When I first got here, I kept thinking how much the town reminded me of Mayberry."

"Great minds think alike!"

Melanie let the radio fill an easy silence between them, wondering how to bring up the subject of what had happened to her before they took Dennis and Mike to the bus station. She was still working through the experience herself, unsure how to describe what had taken place, especially the part about baring her soul to someone whose name she still didn't know. When a Carpenters' song ended, she took the plunge.

"Jack, do you mind if I tell you what happened to me this morning in Hughes?"

He turned to face her. "You can tell me anything you like."

She took a deep breath, gathering courage, then related her encounter with the older woman. Several minutes later, she concluded, "God just reached in and touched all the pain, and the sin. I started forgiving people who hurt me, especially my dad. It was like chains were shackling me, but they're gone now. I feel so free, as if I could just lift off the ground and start flying over the tree tops." She raised and fluttered her right hand.

When she lowered her hand, Jack caught and held it. Even through her wool mitten she could feel his warm strength. "That is so wonderful, Melanie!"

"I definitely want to call home today and talk to our housekeeper Mrs. Lemunyon about the revival, but I especially want to tell my dad, too, if he's around." She gave a laugh. "I can only imagine how he'll take the news of what I'm saying, but I think God will help me know how to respond."

"He will. Promise. As a matter of fact, let's talk to him now."

As she drove, Jack prayed. "Lord, thank you for bringing healing to Melanie's spirit, for helping her forgive and be forgiven. We ask you now to open her father's heart to Jesus so he may also know you and follow you."

"Amen." Grinning, Melanie added, "This spontaneous prayer thing is becoming increasingly more natural for me."

"I'm glad. You know how we're talking now?" When she nodded her head he said, "This kind of prayer is like acknowledging God's presence with us, talking as if he's right here, which of course, he is."

She wasn't sure how he would receive the rest of her story. "Um, Jack, there's actually something else I need to tell you."

Jack grinned. "Tell away"

"Yeah, well ... Do you remember when you called me the other night and said God impressed on you how he wanted me here?"

"Sure do. Oh, excuse me, but here's the street. You can park anywhere on the right side where Sim's is."

Melanie followed his directions, found a spot, turned off the engine. "Do you mind if I finish before we go in?"

He faced her. "I was hoping you would."

"Well, while I was praying at the altar, I knew ..." She paused, working her hands together. "I knew he wanted me to come not just to the revival but to leave Princeton. I, uh, I want to transfer here."

She dared look up, releasing her tension at the look of pure joy on Jack's face. He enfolded her in a vast hug before pulling back, inches from her face. "I also have something to tell you."

He started rubbing his jaw. Her heart pummeled her chest. "I have loved you since I first met you at Mercer Academy. I can't thank God enough for the way you've stayed in my life since then, how he's brought you here now."

Melanie broke into a huge smile, and they laughed, and kissed.

❧

Cliff wasn't home when she called, but there was no mistaking the housekeeper's enthusiasm. "I'm thrilled you want to stay there, Melanie, but I will miss you so much." She paused. "I can't promise your father will be as enthusiastic, not by a long shot."

"Do whatever you can to soften him up, Mrs. Lemunyon, and I'll keep praying for God to work in his heart."

"I will, too. Softening up Cliff McKnight surely will take an act of God. Oh, and before we hang up, how's that young fellow you're always mentioning?"

Melanie smiled and glanced over at Jack through the pay phone window to where he waited for her in the Jeep. "He's doing fine. In fact … *we're* doing fine."

Mrs. Lemunyon seemed to get the hint and chuckled. "God bless you, Melanie."

"You too, Mrs. Lemunyon."

❧

She sat by herself while Jack finished running some of his own errands, eyes half-closed, hands lifted, singing from her heart what was becoming her favorite song, "Sweet, Sweet Spirit." When the hymn ended, she noticed her roommate get up and go downstairs where she waited in line to speak at the lectern. By the time Jack returned, Monica was stepping to the microphone, having exchanged her characteristically upbeat expression for one far more somber.

"I just had to tell everyone what happened today, how God worked in my family's life," she said. "This morning, I felt a burden to come to the altar and pray about something that's been bothering me since last summer. My eleven-year-old brother got hit in the head with a baseball during a

Little League game, and since then he's had double vision. Doctors were doing all they could to help him, but Kevin wasn't getting any better. I let a root of bitterness grow because he loves being active, and he's really smart, and the vision problem bothered him so much." She stopped, swallowed, continued. "Early this morning I came to the altar and confessed my anger and bitterness. I told God how sorry I was for demanding he heal my brother, and this supernatural peace just came over me."

Melanie couldn't imagine her ever being bitter about anything. *You just never know what people are carrying around inside of them.*

"Just after lunch, I had a call from my mother back home in Maryland, and ..." Monica bit her lip, her voice trembled. "She told me at school this afternoon, Kevin suddenly realized he could see normally!"

An excited murmur and shouts of "Praise God!" intermingled. Melanie embraced Jack, beaming.

Monica broke into tears. "My mom took him to the doctor, and Kevin's vision is completely normal. I just want to thank God so much for doing this."

Jack turned to Melanie. They spoke just one word. "Wow."

Midnight Thursday found Melanie once again oblivious to the hour, unable to move for the indescribable nearness of God. Her attention turned to movement throughout the auditorium, a kind of rush to the altar, people actually running. At the piano, a young woman began playing "Blessed Assurance."

Jack leaned into her. "Do you want to go to the lectern and say what happened to you?"

She shifted in her seat. "I don't think I'm quite ready."

"No worries. You'll know when, and if, you need to."

He briefly put his arm around her shoulders, and she rested there until her ears perked up, overhearing a conversation between Tim, the guy she'd asked Jack about, and the girl sitting next to him. She wasn't trying to eavesdrop, but their voices carried.

"I know you're going to find this hard to believe," he was saying, "but ... I'm not a Christian."

Melanie nudged Jack, who nodded, eyes closed. Guessing he was praying, she also talked to God about what they were hearing.

Gentleness mixed with firmness in the girl's voice. "Tim, everybody already knows that, but you needed to know for yourself. There are five guys in the basement who are praying for you right now."

Tim was silent, his eyes narrowed, head nodding. "Well, then, I need to nail it down."

Melanie opened her eyes when he sprang up from his seat and headed downstairs. "Do you think he's going to make a commitment to God?" she asked.

Jack smiled. "I would say so!"

When Tim's turn to speak came, he waited a moment. Melanie imagined this might be one of the most difficult things he'd even done. Finally, he began.

"I was out of town Monday night, and I had a test scheduled for Tuesday after chapel, so I skipped chapel to get ready for the test. In my room, I thought things were awfully quiet when the chapel hour ended, and I didn't hear anyone leaving the building." He grinned. "I had this moment when I thought maybe the rapture had happened, and I was the only one left."

Laughter rippled through the auditorium, but Melanie frowned, not knowing what Tim was talking about. *I'll ask Jack or Monica later.*

The once-proud young man continued, his shoulders slumping. "I was curious, and I wondered what happened, so I left the dorm and slipped into chapel where I discovered no one had bothered to leave. I sat down and took my usual place, like I had so many times before this year. Over the next two or three days of this revival, I pretended I was excited, pretended to be a good boy Christian, but a little while ago, I had this strong compulsion. I felt I needed to do something." He paused, took a deep breath. "My parents would've said I was a Christian, but in reality I've had a secretive life that involved some … un-Christian behavior. I feel like the worst sinner in the world, but this is my moment. I feel so flooded with God's love. I just love him, truly, and I love all of you so much. I know this is real because of all this love."

"Praise God!" "Praise the Lord!" people cried out, including Melanie.

I don't think anything will surprise me after this.

At three o'clock, Melanie went back to Monica's room where she slept until six and, careful not to awaken her roommates, took a two-minute shower and dressed, grabbed a muffin and coffee in the dining hall, and ate on the way back to Hughes, a homing pigeon returning to her roost. There was nowhere else she wanted to be, although by then God's presence was all over the campus with prayer meetings spontaneously erupting in dorms and other buildings.

Melanie planned to visit the admissions office after a few hours in the chapel, where she hoped to become an official Asbury student. *The sooner the better.*

If the night before had electrified, Melanie encountered a far different mood this morning—calmer, sweeter—among the five hundred or so people there. Singing, praying, and testifying continued, the Spirit moving like a warming sun on a tranquil beach.

Jack arrived at nine o'clock, and they embraced as a couple, having crossed a relational line the previous day. He sank into the wooden seat. "The chapel is so peaceful this morning."

She savored the atmosphere for three hours, taking in the music and testimonies until she saw from her watch the time had come for her mission to commence. She touched his right shoulder. "I have to go now, but I'll be back soon."

His eyebrows raised. "Go? Where?"

"The admissions office."

He broke into an expansive smile. "Do you know where it is? Want me to go with you?"

"Yes, and no. Don't miss this. Monica showed me the building yesterday."

"I'm so glad you're doing this, Melanie."

"Me too."

An hour later, she walked back to the auditorium, radiant, a human flashlight. She would be an official Asbury student in a few weeks at the start of the next quarter, pending her father's consent. Not even her apprehension about his reaction could douse her joy.

CHAPTER TWENTY-SIX

Melanie and Jack spent time at the altar, praying not only her father would agree to her transfer to Asbury, but more importantly, for his relationship with the Savior. Instead of being worried, goodness and mercy followed her, resting as she was in God's promises to guide and direct her life. As for being openly in love? Icing on her cake.

Close to two-thirty, they walked through the snowy campus to the dining hall and were half way through lunch when Monica burst in, red-faced, her jacket buttoned in the wrong holes. She caught Melanie's eye, breaking into an "aha" expression. "I'm so glad I found you! I went to Hughes, and you weren't there." She stood across the table, panting.

Melanie put down her soup spoon. "Is everything okay?"

"Your Aunt Jane's trying to reach you."

She nearly knocked the chair over in her haste, concerned there might be bad news, yet shielded by peace. *This place is so much better than Tiffany's. Even if something bad does happen here, God is with me.*

"I'll go with you to the pay phone," Jack said.

"Don't worry about your trays. I'll put them away."

"Thanks, Monica." Melanie grabbed her purse and followed Jack, who stood close by while she made the call. After two rings, her aunt's voice came on the line. "Hello, Aunt Jane. I just got a message to call you right away. Is everything all right?"

"Yes, dear, everything's fine. I'm sorry for getting you worried."

She released her breath, standing at ease, and catching Jack's eye, gave him a thumbs up.

"Our priest, Father Decker, called me this morning. He's been following news reports about the Asbury revival, and he said he'd heard you might be there. When I told him you were, he asked a favor."

Melanie leaned against the wall, facing Jack. "What favor did he mention?"

"Since students have been traveling to other schools and churches telling the story of the revival, he wondered if you'd speak this Sunday at both services."

Her mouth fell open, thoughts marching into and out of her mind— news from the lectern of witness teams like Dennis's and Mike's speaking in other venues, followed by an outbreak of revival in those places—requests from colleges and churches for students to come and testify there. She hesitated, not wanting to leave Asbury in what might be just the middle of God's movement on campus, as well as a strong reluctance to be apart from Jack. The idea of testifying unnerved her.

"I'd like to talk to Jack first … you know, run the idea by him."

"I thought he might be with you." Melanie could hear the smile in her relative's voice. "Go ahead. See what he says."

"Um, Aunt Jane, this story isn't really mine, you know. I mean, God has touched me here, but Asbury's not my school." *Yet.*

"Sweetheart, go talk to your Jack, and then let me know your decision."

Your Jack. A shiver ran up her spine. "I'll call you right back." He came closer when she motioned for him. "My aunt's pastor asked me to speak about the revival at both services this Sunday." He was looking closely at her leaving her to wonder what was going through his mind. "I said I wanted to discuss it with you."

He reached over and touched her cheek. "What do you want to do?"

She bit her lip, thinking aloud. "Well, I'm honored he asked. I keep thinking about those witness teams from Asbury going to other places and how God is bringing revival there too. I'd love to be part of something so amazing." She seemed to be talking herself into going. Jack loosely folded his arms in a listening mode. "Then again, I hate to leave and miss what's going on here." She looked into his eyes. "I also don't want to leave you. Am I being selfish?"

"Not if God wants you to stay."

She continued, "I'm not an Asbury student. I mean I have a story to tell, but this isn't my school." She let out a sigh. "Am I making any sense?"

"Melanie, what's happening here isn't really Asbury's story either—it's God's." He looked into her eyes.

All at once she knew what she must do. "I need to go. Jack, will you go with me?"

He broke into a smile. "You bet!"

❋

They discussed how the trip might unfold as they returned to where Monica waited for them.

She asked, wide-eyed, "Is everything okay at home?"

"Everything's fine. My aunt's pastor wants me to speak at his church this Sunday, to tell the people about the revival. Jack is going with me."

Monica was all exclamation marks. "Oh, Melanie, I want to go, too! God's been laying on my heart I should be part of a witness team, and here's a great opportunity! Can I go with you? I can tell your aunt's church how God healed my brother!"

Melanie looked over at Jack, who was laughing. The coeds hugged, jumping up and down, not drawing much attention to themselves, because by then, the Asbury community had come to expect outbreaks of random joy.

Moments later, Melanie returned to the pay phone. "I'll come, Aunt Jane, but there's one little catch. Actually, two littles catches."

She heard amusement in the woman's voice. "And what might those be?"

"Jack and Monica want to come, too. Is that okay?"

"Of course. They can stay here as long as they like. Father Decker will be so pleased. So, I'll get to meet your Jack, eh?"

"Yes, Aunt Jane, you'll get to meet my Jack."

❋

She awakened at six o'clock after less than four hours of sleep, noticing Monica was already getting ready. Melanie showered, packed her suitcase, and went with her roommate to the dining hall where they ate breakfast and discussed their trip with Jack. A strong cup of coffee and a warm bowl of grits took the edge off the cold winter morning.

Jack paused at one point, a forkful of scrambled eggs suspended in midair. "What would you think about going back to Hughes and kneeling at the altar before we leave, to commit our mission to the Lord?"

Melanie liked the sound of the word "mission" to describe their journey. "I'd love to, Jack. First of all, praying for God's blessing is important, and second, I welcome any excuse to be back in the auditorium."

Monica nodded. "I agree."

They hastened to finish the meal and walked back to the chapel, packed to the rafters with worshipers.

Jack gave a low whistle. "I'll bet there are a thousand people here this morning."

Melanie was growing accustomed to God's dear presence, though not indifferent—she still kept breaking into gooseflesh. During the half hour they sat and listened, speakers brought fresh reports of the revival's spread to Christian campuses across the country, including Millikin University where Dan and Mike had gone.

A coed beamed as she spoke. "I am filled with wonder over God's choice of Asbury to manifest his presence and to use our witness in a nation darkened by conflict."

Melanie, Jack, and Monica also went to the altar, praying to shine the Lord's light wherever and however he chose to lead them.

❦

They stopped for a late lunch at a dining spot along the main highway rather than a similar establishment across the street because one had more cars with West Virginia plates in the parking lot than the other.

"When you see local plates, that's always a good sign," Jack said. "People who live here always know the best places to eat."

Melanie was so hungry she decided not to point out there were more pick-up trucks than cars in this lot. Inside, the paneled restaurant reeked of smoke and grease, and she shrank from the stares of a trucker on a counter stool. A waitress with a drooping corsage grabbed three dog-eared menus and led them to a table. They ordered soup, sandwiches, and Cokes, and Melanie debated whether or not to try to find the rest room.

After the waitress quickly delivered their drinks, Melanie put her head down as she asked her friends, "Is it my imagination, or are we drawing stares?" She noticed she didn't have nearly enough ice in her drink to suit her but decided against pushing the issue. She'd never been in such a seedy place in her life. Neither the gum-chewing waitress nor the ogling patrons struck her as the friendliest sort.

Monica whispered, "I have the same feeling."

Jack took a deep breath, coughed, probably from the curtain of smoke, then put his hands on the table, along with his cards. "We could just get the food to go."

Before they could decide, a man at the next table called out, "Are you kids from Asbury College?"

Melanie was struck dumb until she remembered Jack was wearing a varsity jacket.

He smiled at the man. "Yes, sir, we are."

"What would you be doin' in these parts?" he drawled.

The woman with him gazed at their party. She was about forty-five going on sixty, her wrinkles and droopy hair bearing witness to a hard life.

"We're just traveling through."

Melanie was glad he hadn't been more specific, disliking the idea of someone following them. Their present situation already reminded her too much of an Alfred Hitchcock movie. The waitress brought their soup— Melanie's bowl was chipped—and the three of them tried as quietly as possible to pray without drawing more attention to themselves. As they began eating, their questioner intruded, a gnat at a picnic. "I hear curious things about Asbury these days, on the news you know."

Jack put down his spoon. "Yes, we've had an amazing week."

He crossed his arms over his copious chest. "I reckon I'd like to hear what you have to say."

Melanie's eyes darted from the man's to Jack's. *He might just be sincere, not trying to create trouble for us.* She noticed the trucker at the counter wasn't looking her up and down anymore, but his gaze was fixed upon Jack. She nudged Monica, made a praying hands gesture. Her friend nodded, and the two of them silently interceded while Jack spoke. The old comfortable style he'd always had as a journalist seemed to fall upon him.

"Maybe you'll think this sounds strange, but God came to our campus a few days ago, sir, and he's still there."

An elderly man in a John Deere cap made no pretense of hiding his eavesdropping. "I cain't hear ye, son! Speak up!"

"Sorry, sir." Jack raised his voice, which carried throughout the restaurant, where other conversations wound down. "At Asbury College in Wilmore, Kentucky, our Tuesday chapel service is still going on. We're having an all-out revival, and people's lives are being changed."

The grizzled man nodded, working something in his mouth. By now, the rest of the diner's patrons were also listening. Someone cried out, "Stand up so all of us can hear you!"

Melanie caught her breath. *The Holy Spirit is here with us. Here of all places!* Quite suddenly the impact of something she'd heard since childhood slammed into her consciousness. God sent his Son to earth as an infant, born in a smelly stable among animals, not a pristine palace surrounded by courtiers. There was no corner of this fallen world he wouldn't visit to redeem one of his wayward children. Too excited to eat, Melanie listened closely as Jack spoke about being a Christian studying for the ministry at Asbury where God was touching lives. She lifted her chin, proud of him for the easy way he engaged people, the winsomeness of his faith-sharing.

A tattooed man with a trucker's wallet hanging from his back pocket spoke up. "How did the thing start?"

"When some people started confessing their sins and a desire to get right with the Lord, we began sensing God's presence. I believe God honors our honesty. He'll change your lives, too, if you'll let him."

A few people applauded and Jack sat down, his face flushed, hands shaking. *Funny, he doesn't seem a bit nervous.* She realized she was trembling too. The run-down restaurant had become a sacred space.

The trucker, built like an industrial-capacity washing machine, rose from his stool and walked over to their table. "I heard what you said. How do I get what you're talking about?"

Jack motioned for him to sit with them, and the girls scooted their chairs closer to each other to make room. He proceeded to give a simple presentation about man's sinfulness before a holy God and how Jesus came to save and cleanse people. He concluded, "Do you want to ask him into your life?"

Smelling of diesel, the man nodded his grizzled head while Jack led him in a prayer. Three other people came and asked how they could be saved. Wonderstruck, Melanie's teeth chattered. The revival had followed them.

CHAPTER TWENTY-SEVEN

They reached Richmond in time for dinner, Melanie feeling her jaws would lock from smiling as she introduced Monica and Jack to her aunt and uncle, particularly Jack.

Jane hugged each of them. "Oh, I'm delighted to meet you. I can't wait to hear all about your adventures."

Dean shook hands with Jack, Melanie realizing her boyfriend was being thoroughly sized-up.

"Let's get you settled, then we'll eat. I'll bet you're starving. Monica, you'll be staying with Melanie, and Jack, you get the guest quarters at the other end of the hallway." Jane was pointing this way and that. "Melanie, be sure to show them where to find extra towels and blankets." She pursed her lips. "Oh, I do hope there's no snow tomorrow."

Once they stopped feeling the rolling of wheels underneath them and had freshened up, Melanie and her friends shared their experiences while they ate.

"I've never heard anything of this kind before," Dean said. "I might have been skeptical at first, but something of this magnitude has 'God' written all over it."

At seven-thirty, the priest came to discuss the next day's services over coffee and warm cherry pie. "You folks will have ten minutes to speak during concerns of the church, right before the sermon." Dr. Decker put down his plate, reached into his briefcase, and handed each of them a mimeographed bulletin. "You'll address the people at eight-thirty, then again at ten."

"Do you care who speaks when?" Melanie asked.

He tented his hands. "Although we want to hear from all three of you, we obviously want Melanie to speak at both services since she's been attending St. Luke's. I am so glad you could come. I find what God is doing at Asbury remarkable. If you aren't too tired, I'd love to hear some of the story now if you don't mind."

Melanie had forgotten what tired felt like. Apparently, so had her companions.

The priest didn't leave until three hours later, his step noticeably lighter. Dean removed Decker's hat and coat from the hall closet, and the minister smiled as he put them on. "I don't know if I'll be able to sleep tonight. I can't wait to see what God will do tomorrow."

Jane frowned. "I just hope we don't get any snow."

Melanie wondered why her aunt kept bringing up the subject of snow.

"I wouldn't be too concerned," Decker said. "God has this very much in hand."

Melanie showered after Monica and followed the smell of bacon downstairs to the kitchen, catching her breath as she entered. Her aunt, looking so much like Melanie's mother, stood at the counter pouring coffee for Monica, their laughter an audible fragrance. Dean flipped pancakes at the stove, pausing to smile at Melanie.

"Good morning!"

"Good morning, Uncle Dean." She swallowed hard. *Life used to be like this before Mom died. We were happy. A family. My father was happy.* Somewhere inside rose an assurance—life would once again offer a generous serving of joy. *A future and a hope.*

Jack, on the phone in the family room, smiled at her as he spoke to someone else. *I wonder who he's talking to?*

Melanie made an exaggerated move toward the kitchen window. "So, Aunt Janet, did you get your snow?"

Janet administered a playful swat to her niece's bottom. "For your information, Miss Smarty Pants, we did get a little dusting, but nothing to keep anyone from coming to church this morning."

Jack got off the phone and walked into the kitchen. "Thanks for letting me use your phone, Dr. Fletcher." He turned to Melanie. "I called my roommate Ted for an update on the revival. I want us to be able to mention in this morning's service what's happening now at Asbury."

"Good idea. What did he say?" She stepped aside as Dean moved toward the table with a platter of pancakes.

Jack's eyes sparkled. "The revival's as strong as ever and spreading to other places like crazy."

Could God possibly come to St. Luke's this morning when we tell the story?

"I'm utterly amazed," Jane said. "Words fail."

Jack nodded. "Ted told me something else I think you'd be particularly interested in, Melanie. The revival's been especially strong at Azusa Pacific, and one of the students actually went to the home of Sirhan Sirhan's mother. He spent a long time with her and her other son, talking about Jesus."

Melanie gaped, her eyes misting. "That staggers my imagination. I never really thought about Bobby Kennedy's assassin having a mother or brother. To me, he was just a monster." She shook her head. "I wonder if Sirhan himself might someday come to the Lord."

"Stranger things have happened," Monica said.

They met with Father Decker in his book-dominated study to ask God to bless the service, especially their testimonies. As he concluded his prayer, Jane turned to Melanie, her eyes shining. "I am so proud of you, my dear. What a beautiful young woman you've become. Your mother would be so pleased."

Melanie hugged her, inhaling her aunt's powdery perfume. *I wonder if Dad would also be pleased, or if he'd think my faith is kooky, or even when I'll get to see him again.*

She pushed the intrusive thoughts aside, following Father Decker and her friends into the sanctuary dominated by stained glass, gleaming pews, and the lingering smell of incense. St. Luke's presented itself in a far more elaborate manner than Hughes Auditorium, but Melanie discerned a spiritual continuity when the congregation began singing "Holy, Holy, Holy." There was one Lord. One faith. One baptism. One God and Father of all.

She and her friends stood to the right of the priest, sharing a hymnbook, the soaring lyrics leaving her on the verge of giddiness. *Lord, when my time comes to speak, please don't let my teeth chatter. I don't want to do or say anything distracting. Let them only see You in me.*

Following the opening liturgy, Father Decker made the usual sort of announcements—a clothing drive, next weekend's potluck supper, Ash Wednesday services. He finished then, laying the bulletin on the side of the lectern.

"This morning I have the distinct pleasure of welcoming to St. Luke's three young students from Asbury College in Lexington, Kentucky."

Melanie glanced at Jack, smiling at the priest's mistake. She didn't mind so much—her heart's desire was, after all, to matriculate at Asbury.

"Many of you have heard of the amazing revival that broke out last week at the college, and these students drove all the way to Richmond to tell us what they've seen and heard. They are Melanie McKnight, Jack Clyde, and Monica Allen."

He nodded toward Melanie, who swallowed what felt like a camel's hump as she rose and walked to the lectern, careful not to trip on its one step up. The priest helped her adjust the microphone to her height, and she looked out over the congregation, never realizing before just how big the sanctuary was. She cleared her throat, but no one could've heard the sound she made for the loud honking of a congregant blowing his nose. She held her three-by-five cards in hands she noticed had surprisingly stopped trembling. Even her heart had slowed into a more relaxed rhythm. She jammed the cards in her jacket pocket, feeling no need for them.

"Good morning."

"Good morning."

"Like Father Decker said, my name is Melanie. My aunt and uncle, Jane and Dean Fletcher, are members here at St. Luke's, and I've been coming here since I started staying with them at Christmas. My, uh … friend, Jack Clyde"—she turned in his direction, then faced the people again—"called me last Tuesday evening to tell me about a revival at his college and how he sensed God telling him I needed to be there too. His call came at an important time for me. I was taking a leave of absence from Princeton University after well, a rough semester, and I really didn't know what to do next."

Without warning, she froze, her mouth open, no words pouring forth. *I am standing here baring my soul to a group of strangers. Why in the world am I doing this?* Panicked, she glanced at Jack, who smiled and nodded. She discerned him mouth, "You're doing great."

She continued as if on autopilot, words coming before she realized what she was even saying. "Well, when I got to Asbury last Wednesday, I couldn't believe what was happening there. As soon as I walked into the chapel, which is called Hughes Auditorium, I felt God's presence, as real as my standing here in front of you. I knew he was there and more real to me than anything else I'd ever known.

"When I listened to the people singing, the sound was angelic, so beautiful, both piercing and soothing at the same time. People were constantly praying at the altar, and then they would testify to what God was doing in their lives."

She knew she needed to stop now, not wanting to encroach on Jack and Monica's testimonies. "I'd like to invite my friends, Jack Clyde and Monica Allen, to tell you what they saw, and what happened in their lives."

Jack got up and briefly squeezed Melanie's hand as he passed her on the way to the podium. "Nice job," he whispered. He adjusted the microphone and began to speak. "Hi, I'm Jack, and I'm a freshman at Asbury. Melanie and I went to prep school together in Princeton, where I'm originally from. I was in Hughes Auditorium last Tuesday morning when what began as a typical weekday chapel service became anything but."

He went into detail about the outbreak of the revival, how classes were cancelled when the service continued after a few days, about the transformation of people's lives at school and in the community, and the spreading of the revival to other places. He concluded with the story about their experience in the West Virginia restaurant the previous day and how several people had been converted.

"When I called my roommate early this morning, he said the movement of the Holy Spirit is still going strong, and people are still at Hughes twenty-four hours a day." He paused to wipe a tear from his left eye. "I've never ever experienced anything like this before, but to be in God's presence—well, I know nothing else in my life will ever compare to this."

He abruptly turned away and sat down next to Melanie, who began fishing through her purse for a tissue. A low rumble of murmuring filled the congregation. She eyed Jack, his head now bent in prayer, then caught Monica's eye and nodded to reassure her as the girl visibly steeled herself on her way to the podium. As soon as Monica opened her mouth, silence ensued.

"Hi, I'm Monica Allen. I'm from Maryland, and I'm also a freshman at Asbury, like Jack. He gave a great description of what's been happening at school, so I'll talk about what God has done for my family since the revival started." She told them about her brother's accident and how angry, resentful, and demanding she'd become. "Last Thursday morning, I felt the Holy Spirit nudging me to go to the altar and confess my sinful attitudes. I just knelt there crying and praying, telling God how sorry I was, and afterward, I had such peace come over me. In the afternoon, my mother called and told me Kevin had just realized he could see normally again. I couldn't believe what she was telling me! The doctor said my little brother's vision is actually a little better than before the accident! I've just been praising God ever since!"

She blushed when applause rippled across the sanctuary, and she returned to her seat, hugging Melanie and Jack. Father Decker moved to the podium, lifting his hands for silence.

"Dear brothers and sisters in Christ, I have a feeling, like the dean of Asbury last Tuesday, I shouldn't preach this morning. Instead, I'd like to have a prayer and testimony service, inviting anyone who has a need or something they want to praise God for to come to the kneeling rail. Perhaps our Asbury friends would even pray with some of you." He looked over at them, and they nodded, although Melanie froze. She'd never prayed aloud with people before this past week, fearing she wouldn't know what to say. Just as quickly as the fear sprang up, however, she "heard" a still, small voice inside whispering, "I will be with you."

Not one, not two, or even a half dozen people came forward, but a great movement of congregants pulsed toward the altar resulting in a line up and down the outer aisles. Several people simply knelt right where they were, in the pews.

Melanie reached for her friends' hands. "I think God is here!"

"I think you're right," Jack said.

"Incredible!"

Normally a one-hour event, the eight-thirty service drifted into, then past the coffee hour, its volunteers joining others in the sanctuary for testimonies, prayer, and singing. By ten, those arriving for the next service streamed into the church rubbing their foreheads, seeking an answer to "What's going on?" Following the singing of "Amazing Grace," Father Decker strode into the pulpit.

"For those of you who are arriving for the ten o'clock, you have just entered a place where God's Spirit has chosen to visit us." He briefly shared the Asbury students' testimonies and how he'd decided not to preach that morning. "For the next hour, I invite all of you who remain from the early service to make room for the next group of worshipers. We will once again hear from the Asbury students, then we'll continue with testimonies." He lifted his hands and smiled. "Whatever way God chooses to lead!"

The organist played "Holy, Holy, Holy"—the very rafters seeming to shake with the singing. Melanie shook as if fevered, but she'd never felt better. *I cannot believe God used me and my friends to usher in his presence here. I never knew how much he cared for me, for all of us, how very close he is.* Once again, the small voice "spoke" to her. "Tell them what I've done for you." *Yes, Lord. This time I won't hold back.*

Jack and Monica went to the pulpit first, then Melanie followed without her earlier hesitancy or nervousness. She was a woman on a mission.

"Hi, I'm Melanie McKnight. I've already met some of you, and rather than recap what I said in the first service, I'd like to go in a little different direction."

She spoke succinctly about her mother's death and how Jackie Markley's passing had left an open wound for Melanie and her father.

"We muddled along for a few years, and then my dad got a new assignment for his work, and I needed to spend the spring term with my maternal grandmother in Princeton. That's where I met Jack." She smiled at him over her shoulder, emboldened by his look of encouragement. "That was a spring many of us found difficult. For me personally, my dad and I drifted even further apart. I don't know—we were just never the same after my mom died. Then Martin Luther King Jr. was assassinated. I was pretty involved with the Bobby Kennedy campaign. To me, he was the only one who could heal our country, who could turn around the problems overwhelming us. All my hopes were in him." She swallowed. "We all know what happened on June 5, 1968. Needless to say, I was devastated. I didn't know where to turn, how to go on with my life. Everything important seemed lost to me."

Melanie talked about the service Jack had taken her to where she sensed a glimmer of promise. "I understood on a basic level we can't put our hope in princes, as the Bible says. They are human, which makes them fallible and mortal. Only God is perfect. Only he never leaves or forsakes us. The following summer I came fully into the faith when I visited Jack at a Bible conference where he was working. I gave my life to Christ there, but my first semester in college was brutal. My faith came under assault, and I was weak. I lost sight of God, forgot how much he cared for me and was involved in my life."

She took a deep breath, empowered by the Spirit, unafraid despite having hundreds of eyes and ears on her.

"From the moment I stepped foot in Hughes Auditorium last Wednesday at Asbury College, I felt God's presence. The experience was exactly as Jack just described—time was no longer important. I didn't seem to have any physical needs to be met. I just savored being with God and his people, watching him at work. When I went to the altar to pray on Thursday morning, a lovely woman let me pour out my heart, and she prayed with me. The peace and freedom I experienced just seemed to fall over me and fill me, and I just want to tell you how much I love Jesus, how much I'm looking forward to living for him."

"Amen!"

"Hallelujah!"

"Praise the Lord!"

Father Decker hugged Melanie before he broke into the joyful noise. "I don't know, dear people, but I wonder if I might have erroneously stepped into a Baptist church." He had the appearance of a young boy who'd just scored the winning touchdown.

Laughter exploded. Applause. Melanie hugged her friends and upon seeing people lunge toward the kneeling rail at the front, they stepped off the platform to pray with some of them. Making her way down the short set of side stairs, Melanie was drawn to a man in a suit a few feet away, his head bowed and leaning against his right forearm.

She whispered, "Excuse me, sir. Would you like me to pray with you?" He looked up. Her hand flew to her mouth. "Dad."

He held out his arms to her, seeming unmindful of tears tracking down his face. She rushed to him, resting against his chest as if she were five years old. She pulled away after some moments. "How did you know to come here today?"

He reached for a handkerchief and wiped his face. "Your Aunt Jane called me. I kept reading about the revival on the newswires, and when Mrs. Lemunyon told me you had gone to Kentucky, I followed the events more closely. At first, I thought there were just some hysterical kids getting religion, but somehow the story wouldn't let go of me." He closed his eyes and pursed his lips.

"What I've been through the past several days is unlike anything I've ever experienced."

Melanie hoped he would tell her how he'd been affected spiritually, wondering if he now had a desire to follow Christ, but he didn't say anything. *Do I dare?* She dared. "What does the Lord mean to you, Dad?"

He chuffed a short laugh, lifting his chin. "God and I haven't exactly been on speaking terms since ..."

"... Mom died?"

He looked at the ceiling, nodding.

"I was like that too, Dad." She found more words she needed to say. "Then, I lost you." The brashness of her comment left her breathless.

He sighed, lifting his hands. "Oh, Melanie, dear Melanie, I'm so sorry. You're right—you did lose me. How I wish we could get those years back."

She was going for broke. "Why were you so distant, Dad?" She noticed Jack out of the corner of her eye looking eager to be near but holding back. He made the sign of praying hands. She closed her eyes in gratitude.

When her father spoke again, she strained to hear. "I was afraid."

My father—afraid? She touched his arm, gazed into his eyes. "Afraid of what?"

His voice was husky. "Losing you too. Melanie, I lost so many close friends during the war, and then your mother ... Any time I got close to someone, they died. Even your poor cousin Mac." He met her eyes. "I couldn't bear losing you."

"Oh, Dad ..." Melanie wrapped her arms around him, his body shaking, or maybe she was feeling her own trembling. Was she dreaming? The situation was surreal.

When their tears receded, her father held her at arm's length and fixed his eyes on her. "Can you forgive me, Mel?"

"I already have, Dad. God will, too, if you ask."

He nodded. "Yes, I believe I will. Let's start all over again."

AFTERWORD

The Asbury College Revival of 1970 began on Tuesday morning, February 3rd, and lasted through the chapel on February 10th. At the end of the regular chapel period a week later, the administration resumed classes while pledging to continue holding nightly meetings. Services had lasted unbroken for some one hundred eighty-five hours. Most students at the college and seminary at one time during that week knelt at the altar, and thousands poured into Hughes Auditorium. Lives were completely changed. For the rest of that spring semester, people continued to gather for prayer and praising, often late into the night. Witness teams went about their work for many months to come, taking the story to over a hundred thirty other colleges, seminaries, and universities, as well as scores of churches. Wherever they spoke, revival broke out there as well. The outpouring in one Indiana church lasted some fifty days, with twenty-five hundred people in attendance each night.

A reporter asked Asbury College President Dennis Kinlaw to assess what was happening. "Well, you may not understand this," he said, "but the only way I know how to account for this is that last Tuesday morning, about twenty-of-eleven, the Lord Jesus walked into Hughes Auditorium, and He's been there ever since, and you've got the whole community paying tribute to His presence." The president chuckled when he remembered the journalist's reaction years later: "It got real quiet." (http://www.forerunner. com/forerunner/X0585_Asbury_Revival_1970.html)

Robert Coleman concluded, "Those of us who were there can never look upon the things of this world quite the same." (Ibid. p. 25)

I first heard of the Asbury Revival in the summer of 1995, twenty-five years after its occurrence, and the story has never left me. My husband and I were attending his reunion at Asbury, and there was a special video presentation about the revival in Hughes Auditorium. Many who had been present there a quarter century earlier spoke. As I listened, I experienced

God's presence in my life, so real, so transcendent. I went to the altar and prayed, assured about his lordship over a particularly vexing situation I was wrestling with. He impressed upon me how I never needed to be afraid of the thing again. Nor have I.

I've written short accounts of the revival in a couple of my previous books, but the tug to write a full narrative also never left me. I give this book as a thank offering to the Lord in hopes that each person who reads the story of Melanie McKnight and her participation in the Asbury Revival will also be touched by the same sweet Spirit who changed so many lives fifty years ago.

I also wish to thank the many people who have shared their experiences of the revival with me over the years including Stan and Katy Key, Carolyn Ridley, Homer Pointer, and Tim Philpot, who generously allowed me to use his story. The staff at the Asbury University Library have provided wonderful and timely assistance. Many others have helped and encouraged me over the course of writing this novel: Richard Dreyfuss, Hillary Cosell, Ross Slaughter, Mary Beth Veres Duddy, Julie Cloutier Hamilton, Rick Steele, Marlo Schalesky, Robin Jones Gunn, and Tamela Hancock Murray. I am deeply grateful to my publisher and editor, Deb Ogle Haggerty, and my agent and brother in Christ, David E. Fessenden.

Finally, to those who never stopped believing—my mother of blessed memory and my beloved Scott.

Rebecca Price Janney
January 2020

REBECCA PRICE JANNEY

At fifteen, Rebecca Price Janney faced-off with the editor of her local newspaper. He nearly laughed her out of the office. Then she displayed her ace—a portfolio of celebrity interviews she'd written for a bigger publication's teen supplement. By the next month, she was covering the Philadelphia Phillies. She's now the author of twenty-three published books, as well as hundreds of magazine and newspaper articles. Rebecca is the author of the beloved Easton Series, including Golden Scroll Historical Novel of the Year, *Easton at the Crossraods. Sweet, Sweet Spirit* is Book Two in the Morning in America Series. Golden Scroll winning *Morning Glory* is Book One. She, her husband, son, and their sweet and somewhat rascally dog, live in Pennsylvania's Lehigh Valley just outside Philadelphia.

OTHER BOOKS BY REBECCA PRICE JANNEY

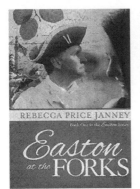

Great Events in American History (AMG)
Great Women in American History (Moody)
Great Stories in American History (Horizon)
Great Letters in American History (Heart of Dakota)

Harriet Tubman (Bethany House)
Who Goes There? (Moody)
Then Comes Marriage? (Moody)

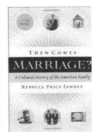

The Heather Reed Mystery Series (Word)
The Impossible Dreamers Series (Multnomah)

Morning In America Series (Elk Lake Publishing, Inc.)

Made in the USA
Monee, IL
23 February 2023

28565404R00129